FOOL ME twice

Lilliana ANDERSON

INTERNATIONALLY BESTSELLING AUSTRALIAN AUTHOR

FOOL ME TWICE

A CARTWRIGHT BROTHER ROMANCE

LILLIANA ANDERSON

LILLIANA ANDERSON ROMANCE

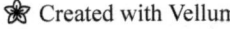

For the fools who dare

This book was a dream. I woke up one night, laughing from the silliness of it, and the first thing I did was grab my phone and put everything I could remember into notes. I just *had* to write it. So it went on my list along with everything else I wished I had time for.

This story had been itching the back of my mind, and I talked about it frequently, eager to work it into my schedule. I couldn't really find time for it, then I thought *fuck it,* and shuffled everything to fit it in. And wow, did I have *fun* writing this book!

It's supposed to be funny. It's supposed to be silly. It's supposed to be a little out of the realm of possible. The whole point of this story is to have a little fun and get lost in the crazy for a while and swoon a little while an expert lover behaves like the man every woman dreams off.

If you finish this book smiling, then I've done my job.

I'll stop talking now. Enjoy!

"I CAN'T BELIEVE your cousin themed her hens night pink and black. We look like we're extras in a shitty stage production of *Grease*. Or worse, stewardesses on the Barbie Glamour Jet."

"Oh, Holland, it's really not *that* bad." Alesha sighed, leaning close to the worn-looking mirror of the club's bathroom while she carefully touched up her bow-shaped pout. The colour she used was a shade of pink a little darker than the Barbie pink of our outfits. Pink looked great on her. It made me look like I fell in a vat of fairy floss while I got my snack on. Not pretty.

With my mouth tight, I positioned my bleached-blonde locks over my shoulder and studied my reflection. My most striking feature peered back at me: two very big, round, honey-coloured eyes. In the warmth of the evening, my kohl eyeliner had smudged, giving them a slightly smoky look that I was unable to create on purpose. But I liked this happy accident, and decided to wear pencil eyeliner on hot nights more often. I sucked in my cheeks and turned my head side to side. The rest of my face was super-basic—round with a functional nose and some very average lips—nothing to write home about. I considered applying a fresh coat of lip gloss for something else to do while I waited for Alesha but chose not to. I was just going to drink it all off again, anyway.

"I don't know why we let her have outfit approval as well. We could've worn all black with pink earrings or something tiny like that to buck the trend."

Alesha laughed, moving on to powdering her nose. "Because we're pushovers. And because it's her wedding. We'll get to boss everyone around and force them to wear unflattering colours too one day."

I scoffed. "Unlikely. We're already in our thirties and haven't even come close to a long-term relationship, let alone a marriage proposal."

Alesha and I had been best friends since primary school, when I moved in with my aunt who lived next door to her. She was practically my sister. In all that time, I could count our collective boyfriends on one hand—and that wasn't even using all my fingers. We were perpetually single, a fact I'd grown accustomed to since my big three-oh. That was two years ago.

She tucked her make-up into her purse, shrugging. "I still have hope."

She would. Out of the two of us, Alesha was by far the prettiest. She was tall and Olive Oyl thin, with light brown hair, chocolate doe eyes, and a heart-shaped face that she accentuated with a carefully crafted layer of make-up. Guys often approached her, but she was painfully shy and socially awkward. The last time a hot guy spoke to her, he asked if he could buy her a drink and she just looked at him, then blurted, "I put make-up on dead people." Yes, Alesha was a beautician at a funeral parlour—a fact I kept advising her to save for at least the second date, but her awkwardness always beat out her common sense.

I, on the other hand, was short and a little on the round side. Growing up, my aunt used to assure me that I was like a caterpillar, eating my way through all the leaves until I spun my cocoon and emerged a beautiful butterfly. She lied. I'm still a chubby caterpillar. But as I've gotten older, I've learned to embrace my curves and be unapologetic over my love of food—life's too damn short to apologise for enjoying anything. I knew that better than anyone, especially since I was currently the exact age my mother was when she and my father died in a car accident. I was thirty-two and had hardly done a thing with my life. It was hard to imagine having it over already.

The fact that my parents were gone wasn't the reason I was still requesting a table for one. I wasn't damaged in any way because of their passing; I'd been raised by an awesome woman who loved me so fiercely that I never once felt alone. Sure, I missed my parents, and I often wondered what my life would've been like if they'd stayed home that night, but I wasn't defined by my orphan status. No, the only thing that defined me was a single word—big. Big booty, big personality, big boobs. I was larger than life in every way, and that wasn't easy for a lot of men to take.

I wasn't always without male company, however. Every now and then, I managed to hook up with a chubby chaser. You know, those guys who just *love* the sight and feel of *all that flesh*. They were a riot for a short period of time. It just rarely went anywhere because I couldn't handle that fetish long-term. I mean, what if I got sick and dropped all the weight? Would they leave because I didn't fit their ideal anymore? At the end of the day, I just wanted someone who liked me for me. But at my age while attending the hens night for Alesha's twenty-four-year-old cousin, I was pretty sure that *particular someone* didn't exist for me. And I loved myself too much to settle for anything less than what a big beautiful woman like me deserved. I wanted a man who worshipped every part of me, inside and out.

The bathroom door burst open, causing the previously muffled noise of the club to invade the room at full blast. Two giggling twenty-somethings rolled through the door and rushed for the stalls.

"We should probably get back out there," I said, dreading rejoining the black-and-pink, penis-straw-wielding gaggle of women. Hens nights typically stuck out like sore thumbs, but with us all dressed the same, it was even more obvious. Honestly, it was embarrassing.

"One sec." Alesha ran her fingers through her super-straight hair, neatening it even more than it already was. For someone who struggled to speak to the opposite sex, she sure spent a lot of time on her looks.

Still waiting, I looked in the mirror and studied my face a moment longer. Maybe I should put a little more effort in too. Maybe wear a little more make-up, figure out what the hell all that contouring business was about. I was often told that I had 'such a lovely face'. I didn't know exactly what a 'lovely face' was supposed to be, but I did always hear the unsaid part of the sentence: 'If only you'd lose the weight.' Not like I hadn't tried. I didn't get why people needed to be so freaking judge-y; it wasn't like they could catch my fatness from me.

"OK. I'm done." Alesha smiled, then tucked her purse under her arm. "Ready to sing some karaoke?"

I laughed, following her out of the bathroom. "It's literally the only reason I came."

MOST CLUBS HAVE dark walls and a colourful light show to create the ambience. This particular one was all white: white walls, white floors, white tables and seating. The lighting glowed soft and blue, and the stage was a round platform directly across from the bar, big enough for a DJ, a microphone and the TV prompter. At full capacity, there was no shortage of warblers to take the stage. Some of them were OK, but others were nails-on-a-chalkboard terrible. I sat and listened, made conversation, sipped my margarita, clapped, and even whistled in all the right places. Then my patience was rewarded—it was my turn.

"Holland, whooooo!" The hens girls cheered when my name was called, hooting and hollering while I made my way up to the stage. Once there, I waited for my song to start with a smile on my face as I adjusted the height of the mic. I could hear the murmurs in the audience, see people whispering to each other. I knew I harped on a lot about my size, but that was the world for a big girl—it was the sole focus of everyone who looked at you. Every time you stood up and tried to shine, everyone was judging and thinking the F-word—*Fat*. That's why, whenever I got up to sing, I chose the most empowering song I could think of. My current favourite was Meghan Trainor's "No".

When the DJ nodded my way and the words loaded on the screen, I took a breath and began. This was when the magic happened. It didn't take long. The moment my voice floated from my throat, I could feel the shift in the room, see their expressions change as their scowls turned into smiles and their head started bobbing along with the tune. Suddenly, I was OK—*untouchable*. They may not have liked looking at me, but my voice was killer, and as I sang and danced along, animatedly performing with the words, they clapped and cheered. Suddenly, I wasn't just the big girl anymore. I was the *big girl with the voice*. And I was fine with that.

"Encore! Encore!"

I stepped down amid the applause, a grin plastered on my face. There was nothing like pleasantly surprising people to make a girl feel good about herself. It was fucking awesome.

"That's some voice you've got trapped in there," a male voice said next to me when I reached the bar.

My smile shifted and my lips pressed together. "Didn't you hear the song, buddy? The answer is n—" The word caught in my throat as I turned my head and looked at him. The hottest fucking guy I'd ever seen. Tall? Check. He was the tallest man I'd ever met with shoulders so broad I was surprised he could find clothes to fit him. Dark? Check. He was tan with dark hair that looked like you could grab handfuls of it while he buried his face between your thighs. Handsome? Check, check and check. But handsome wasn't a strong enough word. This guy was an easy ten on the hot-o-meter. Actually, I think he'd break the needle. He had *muscles*—I could see that through the stretched cotton of his grey long-sleeve shirt.

He'd pushed those sleeves up to his elbows, exposing two very tan and ripped forearms. I had an urge to lean over and bite him. Was that weird? But on top of all that, he had a nice bit of scruff along his jaw, framing two very smooth and kissable lips. *Yum, yum, yum.* I was a total sucker for that stylish unkempt look. I had to press my knees together to keep myself from falling in a heap of arousal at his feet. *Please be a chubby chaser.* One night with this guy and I'd be singing Salt-n-Pepa's "Push It" for weeks.

I smiled in his direction, taking in all that was in front of me with an obvious sweep of my eyes. "Actually, the answer is *yes*."

He grinned. *Beautiful.* His whole face smiled. "You don't even know the question." Was that an accent I detected?

"You were about to ask if you could buy me a drink."

He chuckled, a deep rich sound that rippled just below the surface of my skin. "I guess you've read this book before." He signalled for the bartender. "What's your poison?" He indicated the shelf of spirits behind the bar.

There was definitely an accent. American, perhaps? I couldn't pick from where.

"I'm drinking margaritas tonight."

He ordered that, and a rum and Coke for himself. Then he held out his hand. "I'm Ben."

His large hand felt like the promise of sex as it wrapped around mine. My insides tingled and tightened. It had been months since I'd taken a man home, and my panties didn't stand a chance against a big sexy man with lust in his eyes.

"Holland," I replied, not wanting the handshake or the

eye contact to end. His eyes were the colour of a tropical ocean, and if I wasn't careful, I could drown in them.

"It's a pleasure to meet you, Holland." The way he spoke my name sounded like melted chocolate poured from his tongue. *Delicious*.

"Likewise. Is that an accent I'm hearing?"

With a nod, he released my hand with a slow caress and my entire body shivered. "I'm from the good ole US of A."

"You been here long?"

"About twenty years." He smiled and picked up the coaster on the bar in front of him, spinning it around in his fingers. I was about to ask him where in the US he was from, but he met my eyes again and changed the subject. "You planning on giving your cheer squad the encore they deserve?" He looked towards the other pink and black-dressed women. They were huddled together and swaying with their arms in the air while one of them did a stepped-on-cat rendition of Celine Dion's "The Power of Love". It hurt my ears, but she was having fun.

"Oh, they're not my cheer squad. They're barely even my friends, to be honest." He quirked a magnificently shaped eyebrow in question. "Hens party," I explained.

"That explains the matching outfits. I was thinking you were like those *Pitch Perfect* girls or something. But then she started singing." He nodded towards the stage and winced a little.

I laughed. "Alcohol bolsters the confidence, but I'm impressed by your movie reference. Have you seen the trilogy?"

Our drinks were set in front of us and he slid mine in front of me. "Yes, ma'am."

Thanking him, I took a sip. "Fat Amy is my spirit animal."

He laughed. "You hiding from a criminal past too?"

I held a finger to my lips and winked. "Holland isn't even my real name."

He leaned in close. "I'll let you in on a secret. Ben isn't my real name either."

I opened my mouth in mock surprise. "Is it *Benjamin*?"

With his shoulders bouncing as he took a mouthful of his drink, I noticed the way his eyes became half-moons when he thought something was funny. "How did you know?"

"I'm *very* perceptive."

"I'll bet."

A comfortable pause took over while we both watched the next singer get up on stage. "Do you sing at all?" I asked.

"Only in the shower." His eyes travelled downwards and landed on my chest, staying there and heating my skin while I pictured him naked and singing in the shower. I wanted to rub my breasts against his soapy chest.

I was so focused on imagining that scene playing out that I didn't notice Alesha until she touched me on the elbow and startled me.

"Hey, Leesh!" I put my arm around her. "This is Ben. The only things I know about him are that he drinks rum and watches the *Pitch Perfect* movies."

Barely making eye contact, Alesha did a little wave. We were total opposites, she and I. Not just in body type but personality too—she was a mouse, and I was a lion.

Ben held out his hand but looked confused. "Nice to meet you... *Leech*? Is that what she called you?"

Alesha shook her head, then leaned close to my ear. "He's American," she whispered.

"Yes he is," I responded. "Maybe you should shake his hand and say hello." I tilted my head towards his upturned palm and opened my eyes wider.

Giving the action far too much thought, she timidly slipped her hand in his. "It's Alesha," she forced out, pulling her hand back as if burned. "We're friends." She pointed at me. "We're at my cousin's hens party. I actually work at a funeral home."

Oh no. Stop talking.

I laughed as if it was a joke and pulled her closer to me so he wouldn't be able to hear anything else she said over the music. I loved the girl, but she really needed to learn how to talk to men. She'd grown up in a strict religious family with an overprotective father, which meant no access to boys until she left school. The result was the quivering mess spouting random facts beside me.

"A *funeral home*, you say? Is that how you two know each other?" He was playing a good game, completely nonplussed. Very smooth. I liked him.

"Nooo," I responded, my eyes wide as I shook my head. "I work at an all-girls high school in the eastern suburbs. We grew up next door to each other."

He lifted his head in acknowledgement, taking a sip of his drink as his blue eyes assessed us. "A teacher?" I nodded. "Let me guess—you teach music or choir?"

"Physical education, actually." My lips pulled at the corner as I watched the smallest reaction cross his features and then fade away. This guy was amazing at keeping a straight face; I'd been expecting him to choke on his rum and Coke like most people did. PE was the last thing anyone expected me to be teaching.

"She teaches drama," Alesha put in, her voice surprisingly even, perhaps borrowing strength from having her arm looped in mine. Seemed I was her confidence conductor.

"Drama?"

Alesha nodded. "She wanted to be an actor growing up. She was always pretending to be someone else. Once, I was banned from going to her house because Holland told my dad she was possessed by a spirit called Anniki. She would go into weird trances and start rambling incoherently. My dad freaked out and called our priest for help. Then Holland started laughing and he got very upset."

Ben grinned that gorgeous grin of his and met my eyes. My stomach was tight from all the flip-flopping it was doing. "Is that true?"

"Guilty as charged," I said with a shrug. "It was one of my best performances."

Ben's eyes shone with mirth as he continued to study me, a smile lifting his cheeks. I desperately wanted to lean into him and run my nails over those cheeks, feel the scruff press against my fingertips. Then I wanted to pull on that full bottom lip with my teeth.

His tongue poked out just a touch, wetting the seam of his lips. I was fairly sure that I groaned out loud while watching the action and tightened my grip on Alesha's arm.

"She was a riot growing up. You know, sometimes she sings at weddings on the weekends. And she just tells that physical education joke to everyone to see how they react. She thinks everyone is always judging her size."

I let go of Alesha immediately, pushing her to arm's length and cutting off her confidence supply. Next she'd be telling him about the time I tried to see-saw with her nephew and shot him off the end of the damn thing. He only got a grazed knee, but still, the whole incident made it very clear that I was not to be trusted around children without supervision.

"No filter on this one," I joked, taking a large gulp of my margarita and draining the glass. "Maybe the bride-to-be would like her cousin back?" I smiled sweetly and she winked at me. Cheeky bugger.

"The bride-to-be is actually why I'm here. She'd like you to sing 'Total Eclipse of the Heart'. She says it's her jam." She laughed, then shrugged.

I pushed away from the bar, more than a little disappointed that I couldn't continue talking to beautiful Ben. "Guess I shouldn't keep the woman of the night waiting." I turned to him. "Thanks for the drink. Don't judge me on a couple of crazy stories from my best friend."

As I stepped away, he wrapped his hand around my upper arm, stopping me as he lowered his head to speak into my ear. "The only thing I'm judging you on is the size of those gorgeous-looking tits and those full, incredibly fuckable lips."

I gasped, a bolt of lust heading straight for my nether region. *Did I hear that right? Do I seriously have fuckable lips?* I turned to meet his eyes.

"Too forward?" He smiled unapologetically.

"Not at all." My lips curved in return. I liked a man who was direct about what he wanted. It saved any complications later.

"Then come back to me when you're done. I haven't finished talking my way into your bed yet."

Oh.

My.

God.

This was going to be the best night *ever*.

CHAPTER TWO
I DIDN'T COME HERE
TO TALK

"THIS IS IT." I opened the front door to my apartment and set my keys on the table with my purse. Nerves danced in my belly as Ben lowered his head slightly and stepped through the door, looking too big for my tiny Malvern apartment.

Moving in a slow circle, he took in his surroundings, hands on his hips. My décor was mostly shabby chic. I loved finding old pieces of furniture and doing them up, mismatching them to create a fun yet homey feel. Some things were antiques, others were bought new, but it all blended together nicely, mixing with technology in an unobtrusive manner. I was very proud of the home I'd created.

"Yours?" he asked when he finished his perusal, his eyes landing on mine. I felt like giggling. I couldn't believe I'd attracted a man so beautiful into my home.

"It's the bank's right now. Ask me again in twenty years."

His brow rose, and I realised I'd just made an incredible faux pas—talking about a time in the future when we'd only just met. The problem was I felt incredibly comfortable around Ben. We'd talked non-stop in the cab on the way here. He had an easy laugh and asked a lot of questions, seeming genuinely interested in me. I liked that he was forward, liked it even more that when my song was finished back at the club, I was able to walk right up to him and say, "Your place or mine?" He'd grinned, held out his hand for me to take and said, "Yours."

And now here we are.

"I didn't mean that this was anything more than it is. I mean, if by some random chance you run into me in twenty years' time on the street, ask me *then* and I'll be able to say, 'Wait, who are you again, and why are you asking me if I own my apartment?'"

He chuckled as he stepped towards me. "You think I'll be that forgettable?"

My chest tightened and my uterus started waving those little arm bits in the air like the kid in the *Home Alone* movies. *Oh God. He's about to kiss me.*

I looked up into his eyes, breathing in his scent as he crowded my space. I could smell the rum he'd had, sweet on his breath, but mostly I could smell the sea, and that wonderful manly scent that only the most attractive of men seemed to exude. If I was a dog, my nose would be permanently shoved in his neck and I'd lick him all over.

"Well, twenty years *is* a long way away, and there'll be *so* many men between then and now. I can't guarantee I'd recognise you." I tried to remain coy but was unable to stop my mouth from curving at the corners.

His grin broadened as he slid his hands over my hips

and down to my bottom, pulling me flush against him. "Then I guess I'd better bring my A game."

I could feel the size of his 'A game' pressing into my stomach. *Holy shit!*

"Um… please tell me that's a tube of tennis balls you're carrying in your pants."

His chest bounced with laughter. "That's all me. Think you can take it?" He grinned, pressing himself into me even harder. I almost passed out. *How on earth is that going to fit?*

I moved my head from side to side. "It seems—" I gulped. "—*big*."

He chuckled. "In case you haven't noticed, I'm *big* all over."

A nervous giggle burst from my lips. "So am I."

Shaking his head, he brought his face closer to mine, his breath washing over my face as he spoke. "Tiny compared to me." He was right—he dwarfed me. He was an easy six-six, broad-shouldered, with thighs that rivalled tree trunks. I wondered if he needed to have his clothes specially made. I liked big muscular men, loved the way their hulking frame made me feel. Still, I'd never been with a man who was quite as endowed as Ben was. Women's bodies were made to deliver babies, so we stretched, but I was worried about my ability to welcome such a… er… *mammoth* cock into my body.

"M-m-maybe we should have a drink first?"

"I don't want a drink."

"O-or maybe a sandwich? I make a mean ham and cheese toastie." I pressed my hands against his chest, pushing him away.

Tightening his hold on my arse, he shook his head

slowly, his eyes locked on mine, dancing with mirth. "Are you frightened it'll hurt?"

I gulped, then nodded.

He brushed his mouth across my cheek before speaking close to my ear. "I promise I'll make you nice and *wet* first. I have a feeling we'll fit together in all the right ways."

"Oh," I gasped, my knees shaking and my clit pulsing from the promise in his words.

He moved his mouth, lips brushing lightly over my skin, teasingly moving past my lips and to my other ear. "Still think you're going to forget me?" I shook my head and he chuckled, pulling back slightly to meet my eyes. "Good. Because I didn't come here to talk. My intention is to fuck you senseless, Holland." I loved hearing him say my name.

"Senseless?" I didn't know if I'd survive the night, but what a way to go.

Here lies Holland Williams, beloved teacher, awesome friend, plundered to death by a giant cock. At least she went out smiling.

He did this slow and sexy nod where his eyes held the assurance of a thousand orgasms. "Are you ready for me?"

"Yes." I swallowed and then parted my lips, waiting as I watched his handsome face inch closer, closer until our lips touched and ignited, need coiling tight in my body as his tongue sought entry and slid against mine. My heart pounded as I struggled to keep my knees locked to remain standing. I'd never been kissed so thoroughly, never felt the entire world still the moment a mouth was on mine. It was transcendent.

As the kiss intensified, he groaned, the sound vibrating

through my body, pebbling my nipples as he slid a hand into my hair, pulling my head back to force the exact angle he wanted to aggressively ravage my mouth. *Oh God.* Everything about him was over-the-top fantastic, and more than I could take.

"Bedroom?" His voice was a soft rumble against my lips as he undid the zip on my dress and pushed it to the floor.

Unable to speak, I just moved my head in the general direction, then let out a yelp when he lifted me off the floor as if I weighed nothing at all.

Wow. I could totally fall for a guy like this.

Careful, Holland. Men who look like Ben don't do long-term.

But he's so beautiful. I want to keep him.

You know he'll be gone in the morning. And if he isn't, it'll be an awkward goodbye.

Shut up and let me enjoy this.

I shut the argument I was having with myself off and focused on the here and now as he lowered me to my feet at the foot of my bed. His hands rested on my waist as he stepped back and drank me in, his eyes widening in amazement. "What even?" His fingers moved over the red silk and black lace that spanned my midsection and held up my stockings.

"A corset. It gives me a sexy shape." I bounced my hips from side to side to prove my point.

Sliding one hand lower, he hooked a finger into the elastic suspender, then flicked it against my thigh with a snap. "I like. A lot. We're going to keep this on. But this"—he placed both hands on my shoulders, then pushed at my bra straps— "is going to have to come off. I need to see these babies with my own eyes." My double Ds spilled out of the black lace that had been containing them as he dragged the cups down and undid the clasp. "Oh. Fuck. Yes." His eyes darkened as he palmed my flesh, thumbs and forefingers working my nipples, sending shots of electricity coursing through me.

"Ohhh." *Fuck yes, indeed.*

"These are beautiful." He fondled, pushed, pulled, and tested their weight in his palms. When it came to women's bodies, there were two types of men in this world: tit men and arse men. Fifty bucks said Ben was the former.

"Thank you." My voice was all breathy as I enjoyed his exploration. "I grew them myself."

Looking up from the flesh he played with, his eyes met mine and he smiled. "The rest of you is beautiful too," he said with all sincerity.

I just about melted where I stood and fell against him, sliding my arms up and over his massive shoulders as he captured my mouth with his. I was lost in a cloud of lust, wanting nothing more than for him to do dirty things to my body.

"Hmmm. Do you know what I want to do to you?"

Dirty things to my body? Was he reading my mind?

I shook my head, my eyes feasting when he reached one hand behind his head and dragged his shirt off, giving me my first look at that deliciously hard body. *Wow.* This guy was *ripped* and tanned a delicious toffee brown. I didn't think I'd ever seen that many abs in real life before. I salivated at the idea of covering them in chocolate sauce and licking them clean. I had to swallow before I drooled.

"I want you"—he pushed me back on the bed and pulled my black heels off my feet, flinging them to the side

—"to sit on my face and ride me until I almost drown in your juices."

"What?" I almost laughed. Who said stuff like that?

He undid the snap on my suspenders, pulling the stocking down my left leg. "I. Want. Your. Pussy. In my mouth, and you"—he did the same on the right side—"sitting on my face while I eat it."

That was a crazy idea. What if I squashed his head? I wasn't as feather-light as his biceps had indicated. I'd be up for manslaughter.

"I don't know," I hesitated. "What if you can't breathe?"

He hooked his fingers in either side of my panties and dragged them down my legs, pausing for a moment to run his fingers over my mound. "Then I'll lift you off."

I thought for a second. "I suppose that could work."

He grinned and then climbed over my almost-naked body, rubbing his smooth chest against mine. "Your skin is so soft," he murmured, pulling at my bottom lip with his teeth. "Like velvet. And you taste like vanilla ice cream."

My God, I was on fire.

"Is that a good thing?"

He gripped my hips and rolled so I was on top. "It's my favourite kind." His strong hands urged me to move up his body. "Now, give me what I want."

"Do you always get what you want?"

"I find a way."

I placed a finger against his forehead and ran it slowly down the centre of his face, smiling when he bit it after I touched his lips. "I'll bet you do." Positioning my knees on the pillow above his shoulders, I held myself above him, gripping my headboard. "Like this?" As confident as I was, I'd honestly never done this position before, so I could use some pointers.

"Exactly like that."

With his hands at my hips, he guided me towards his mouth. The moment his tongue swept through my arousal, my bones went liquid.

"Oh God."

At first, I was frozen, my mouth open as his tongue dove into my depths, sucking and then teasing at my clit. Then, as my orgasm swelled in my body, my hips began to move of their own accord, back and forth, fucking his sexy, scruffy face. It felt amazing.

When he moaned, I could feel the rumble vibrate in my core, my insides tightening, so ready to burst.

"Oh, Ben! I'm going to come."

He made a sound that indicated he wanted nothing more than for me to come all over his face, then increased his suction on my clit. I tipped over the edge, cascading down, down as my hips bucked and a howl of ecstasy tore out of my throat.

"Good God," I gasped as the waves calmed. Ben continued to lap at my juices, drinking me greedily as his hands held firm onto my hips. "Oh my. Oh God. *Ben.*" He pushed me almost to the point of torment; then, just when I thought I couldn't stand any more, he flipped me backwards and held himself over me, wiping his mouth.

"You taste *so* fucking incredible. I could eat you all night," he murmured, bringing his mouth to mine before kissing me deeply, sharing my flavour. What stood out most to me wasn't *my* taste but the taste of *him,* the texture —smooth, silken. Addictive.

He moved his hand down and cupped between my

legs, sliding his fingers through my juices, pushing inside as I gasped and keened. One finger. Two. In and out. Three fingers.

Holy fuck.

"Feel good?"

I nodded, words simply not existing in that moment. He was filling me, stretching me, pushing his fingers gloriously deeper as he added a fourth. I felt him to his knuckles and surprised myself by wanting more, curving my hips to urge him on.

"Mmm, she's greedy. Do you want more, Holland?"

I nodded, gasping.

"I didn't hear any words. How do I know what you want if you don't speak?"

I attempted to answer but could barely make my tongue move from what he was doing to me.

"More?" he asked.

"More," I parroted, needing to force out the word as I squirmed against him. "Please, more." I wasn't too proud to beg.

He withdrew his hand and his body, and I whimpered at the loss, but was quickly rewarded with the scintillating view of him unbuckling his belt, then his fly. I licked my lips, focused on the muscular V that pointed to the monster cock I knew he hid inside his jeans. As he shoved them to the ground and stood before me in all his naked glory, I honestly wasn't prepared for the sight. I'd felt it, imagined it, but I wasn't quite ready for the reality of it. It was *huge*. Bigger than anything I'd ever seen—in real life or in porn. My mouth fell open and I sat forwards, inspecting it closer to make sure it was real.

"I, uh… think a baby elephant is missing a trunk somewhere," I commented as I stared at it and tried to imagine how that was going to get inside me. I'd taken four fingers, but they were tapered and easy to insert. This was long, thick all over and slightly curved. I didn't think it would even fit in my mouth if I wanted to suck it—and I had a pretty big mouth.

He chuckled and pulled out a condom, one of those XXL ones that you didn't see sitting on the shelves in stores. Then he tore the packet before positioning it over his tip.

"May I?" I asked, reaching out to take over the job. I was desperate to touch it, to stroke the silken skin before it was sheathed.

"Be my guest." He handed over the rubber circle and I shifted down the bed, sitting in front of him as I ran my hands down his length and back up again. He released an erotic hum as I continued to stroke him.

"You have a beautiful cock," I murmured as I rolled the condom down, touching him way more than was necessary, but seriously, I couldn't get over the size of it. "You should be very proud."

"Thank you." With a laugh, he climbed over me as I shifted back with him on the bed, our mouths finding the other's as he pushed his tip into my entrance. "Breathe and relax," he whispered, his hips moving back and forth in small increments as he slowly filled me, my body stretching to adapt. There was a slight burn initially as I took him in, quickly replaced by a mind-numbing pleasure when he began to slide in and out.

Who knew being this full would feel so damn good?

"Holy fucking hell," I gasped as his thrusts quickened and he gripped at my arse. He swivelled his hips back and forth, deeper, deeper, hissing through his teeth while I was wide-eyed and set to explode. I was *so incredibly full.* Every part of me that could tingle was tingling, every part that could tighten was tightened. I was about to have the orgasm of the century, and I wanted it commemorated with a fucking T-shirt that read 'I heart giant cocks'. I would wear it everywhere, proudly letting everyone know that I'd experienced one. They were fucking magnificent. Every girl should get one. Oh, I could be like Oprah, throwing out giant cocks for an audience of lucky women to try. They'd love me forever. Giant cocks for the win.

"Fuck, Holland, you're squeezing the life out of me," he hissed through his teeth, lifting my left leg as he increased his speed. I looked down between us, watching his shaft as it disappeared inside me, touching me deeper than any man had before. "I need to come."

"Me too," I gasped. "Hold on. Me too."

With the strain evident on his face and in the veins in his neck, he clenched his jaw and thrust harder, faster. "Ohhhhhh."

I tipped my head back and called out so loud my neighbours probably thought I was being murdered. But no, I was simply being shattered by the most powerful orgasm I'd ever experienced.

Ben caught my mouth with his, kissing me passion-ately as he stilled inside me, pulsing into my depths, that satisfied feeling of sated lust flowing between us. "Mmmm, that was…," he started, grinning as he shook his head, words escaping him.

"I know," I gasped, panting beneath him. "You're good at this."

He rolled off me, kissing the tip of my nose. "It takes two to make a spark, gorgeous. Where's your bathroom?"

"Second door on the right."

Pressing another kiss to my lips, he slid off the bed. "Be right back."

Leaning up on my elbows, I watched the muscles in his arse pop with each step he took. I think I wanted to bite that arse too.

"It takes two to make a spark." Did that mean he thought we had something? My mind delighted at the thought. Imagine getting to have *that* in my bed on a regular basis. I'd never wipe the smile off my face.

I didn't want to get too excited, but I was still grinning to myself when he returned. "Something funny?" he asked, lying next to me on the bed and holding out a glass of water. He was so incredibly beautiful to look at. "Thought you might be thirsty." Just as I reached out for it, he pulled it away. "On second thought…." He placed the glass on the bedside table.

"Hey!" My protest caught in my mouth when his sealed over mine and his arms went around my waist, pulling me against him. I felt my body react favourably, getting ready for him all over again.

"I don't think we've worked up enough of a thirst yet. Ready for another round?"

"More than ready," I returned, sliding my hands over his hard pecs as I stared up at him and tried to memorise every little detail of his face. There was no way I was going to forget *this* night in twenty years.

He kissed me again, deeper that time, his tongue becoming more familiar with the work my dentist had recently done. Then he pulled back all of a sudden and looked at me with a question in his eyes.

"What is it?" I asked.

"That sandwich you mentioned earlier."

I frowned. "The ham and cheese toastie?"

He grinned. "Yeah. I really want one of those."

Laughing, I wrapped my arms around his neck. Men were weird. "Right now?"

He looked at me like he thought I was mad. "No way. After. I haven't finished fucking you senseless yet."

"Sure. I'll make you one for each orgasm you give," I replied.

His brow lifted, and then his hand slid down and started working open the hooks on my corset. "In that case, I hope you have a lot of bread, because I don't plan on letting you leave this bed until we've at least hit double digits."

"Double digits?" My mouth gaped as the corset popped open and he flattened his tanned hand against my snow-white belly. His touch felt so good on my skin.

"Do you object?"

"Not at all," I responded. "I was more concerned about having enough ingredients for the toasties."

He pushed himself up so he was hovering over me. "Not enough ingredients for ten toasties? That's it, I'm through." He made as if he was about to get out of the bed, then buried his face in my neck and growled instead. "Forget the toasties. I'd prefer to eat you."

I giggled as he slid down my body and started his feast. Oh, he had a magnificent tongue. We made it to six orgasms before my throat was so dry from all the gasping that I gulped down the glass of water while he removed his second condom.

"Sorry, I should've saved you some," I said, holding up the empty glass upon his return.

He looked from me to the glass and back again.

Seeing him standing naked in my doorway was the last thing I remembered.

CHAPTER THREE
COMPLETE AND UTTER FOOL

I WOKE in a rumpled bed to the sound of birds chirping outside. The sun streamed in through the windows, and my body throbbed pleasantly after the rigours of the previous night.

Wow. Ben is—I turned my head to the side to find a vacated pillow—*gone*.

I sat up straight, disappointment flooding my system as I looked around the room. "Ben?" I waited for a sound. Nothing. "Shit." Even though I didn't want to let myself, I'd still had high hopes for that one.

Twisting my way out of bed, I sat on the edge with the sheet wrapped around my naked frame. I had a pretty epic headache, wincing slightly as it pounded when I moved.

How much did I drink last night? Certainly not enough to warrant this kind of headache. All I could remember was orgasm after orgasm, then getting overwhelmingly tired. *Did I pass out?*

"Ow." My brain felt like it was sliding with each movement. Placing my hands on the wall to steady myself,

I shuffled into the bathroom in search of painkillers. When I opened the medicine cabinet, I found the note, folded and propped against the pack of ibuprofen. **I'm sorry**, it read on the outside. Then I opened it up to the words **You're amazing and I wish things were different. But this is who I am. B.**

"Ugh." I rolled my eyes and scrunched the note into a ball, dropping it into the toilet and flushing it away. What a bloody cop-out. I understood that it was just a hook-up. Sure, I wouldn't have said no if he'd wanted to see me again, but I understood the nature of what we were doing. I didn't need some lame 'It's not you, it's me' note after he crept out during the night while I was sleeping. "Arsehole."

Downing two pills with water, I shuffled to the kitchen and took the bag of coffee beans out of the pantry. I needed it extra strong this morning. Once there was some caffeine in my system, I'd call Alesha and fill her in on the gory details of the previous night's romp. She'd made me promise to tell her *everything* when I left with Ben. At least I had a really good story to tell. She'd never believe how good he was.

Unclipping the bag, I lifted it, ready to pour my beloved beans into the coffee machine. Except when I went to remove the grinder lid, there was no grinder lid at all. In fact, there was no grinder. Or a coffee maker.

What the fuck?

Suddenly wide awake, I looked around the kitchen. All my appliances were gone. "What?" I spun towards my living area—my *empty* living area. "No. No. *Nooooo.*"

This wasn't OK. Where was my furniture? Where was

my TV? My stereo? Where was *every single thing I owned?*

Holy hell.

I blinked twice and rubbed my eyes, hoping this was all some kind of hallucination. But it wasn't. The room was still empty when I looked again. I'd been robbed. I'd been fucked into oblivion, and then I'd been fucked over, swindled, hustled, taken for a ride in every possible way. There was no way he'd done this on his own; there must've been at least one other guy waiting somewhere with a moving truck while I was unwittingly having the most expensive sex of my life.

It cost me almost everything I owned.

Moving across the apartment as if walking through a dream, I couldn't believe this was happening. I checked the room I'd set up as my home office to find it was empty too. My computer, my desk, chair and bookcases, all gone. They'd even taken the books and my teaching manuals. Why? What was the point of that? The only room they'd left untouched was my bedroom.

Or *had* they?

Oh no.

In a sudden panic, I rushed into my room, flinging open my wardrobe to see that it had been completely ransacked. My clothes were still there, albeit on the floor, but my designer handbags, expensive shoes and the big wooden jewellery box that adorned my vanity were all gone.

"No!"

I dropped to my knees, my head falling into my hands as I burst into tears. It was gone. The only keepsake I had of my mother had been in that jewellery box, a mother-of-pearl hairpin that she'd worn on her wedding day. It was an antique—her something old. I was supposed to use it myself one day for that same purpose. Now it was gone, just like she was gone.

How can someone do this? What is wrong *with him?* I could never replace something like that hairpin. I was beyond devastated—I was destroyed.

Oh God. I needed to call the police. I needed to report this. I needed to give them Ben's description so he couldn't do this to some other poor unsuspecting woman. *God,* what a monster! Who fucked a woman and then robbed her, and how the hell did I sleep through it all?

It dawned on me almost immediately—the note was next to the painkillers, meaning he knew I'd wake up with a headache. *He drugged me! But when?* I searched my memory, the expression on his face when he saw me holding the empty glass telling me all I needed to know. *The water. He drugged my water. Arsehole!*

I should've known that a man like that would never be legitimately interested in me. How positively stupid could I be? Beautiful muscular men *did not* go for short round women. I was *beyond* stupid.

Growling at my own foolhardiness, I pulled on a pair of leggings and an oversized shirt, then marched back into my room to get my phone. It wasn't where I normally hooked it up to charge, but then again, I'd discarded my handbag when I'd walked into the house the night before.

Oh shit. He'd taken the handbag. That meant he had my wallet and ID, the keys to my apartment, all my credit cards and my phone.

Nooooo.

Pulling on my runners, I rushed for the front door,

ready to drive to the police station and report this in person. But when I grasped at air where my keys should've been, I knew beyond a doubt that my car was gone too. "Fuck. *Fuck. Fuuuck!*" I screamed, stamping my foot over and over as I hit the wall and cried. "Fuck!"

I dropped to the ground, my hands in my hair as I tried to decide what to do. My eyes burned. I'd fucked a thief, bedded a criminal. I'd been so enamoured by how beautiful he was that I didn't for a second question his motives for wanting me; I simply thought I'd hit the jackpot.

I stretched my legs out in front of me and groaned.

What a complete and utter fool.

"HE ROBBED ME." I stood on the front step of Alesha's colonial-style home in the next suburb over. It had taken me nearly forty-five minutes to walk there, and in that time, I'd decided that I was going to hunt that son of a bitch with the big dick down and force him to give me my mother's hairpin back. Everything else I couldn't give a fuck about; I just wanted that piece of her returned.

"What?" Alesha knitted her brow, perplexed. "Who?"

She stepped aside and I practically charged for her couch, dropping my weight on it and moaning, "Furniture!" I already missed my overstuffed couch.

"What's going on? Did you *walk* here?" She stood in front of me, her arms folded across her chest.

I nodded. "They took my car."

"Who are *they*?" She perched on the edge of the couch as she regarded me.

"Ben and whoever helped him."

"Big beautiful Ben from last night?" Her eyes went wide and her mouth fell open.

"Yes. They took everything, Leesh. All I have left are my clothes and my bed. I don't even have keys to get back in. Please tell me you still have the emergency set I gave you."

"Of course I do. But I don't understand. He took *everything*?"

"Yes. All my furniture, everything in my study, even my fucking coffee maker."

"What? Who does that?"

I shook my head. "Arseholes do," I murmured.

"He seemed so… hot," she said in quiet shock.

"Well, hot guys can be criminals, it seems."

"My God. I can't believe this. Are you OK? Did he hurt you?"

I shook my head. "No. He drugged me." My lower lip trembled, so I clamped my emotions down. I'd given that man all the tears he was going to get already.

"Did he… you know…?" Her brow knitted tight as she let the question hang in the air ominously.

"No. I was awake and willing during that part."

"Oh. Thank God." She sat for a moment with her hands tucked between her knees the quiet stretching before either of us spoke. "Was it at least *good* sex?"

I glanced at her and pressed my lips together, hating to admit it. "Amazing."

"So, he went home with you, you had amazing sex, and then he drugged and robbed you?"

"That's exactly what happened."

"Whoa."

"Whoa indeed."

We sat quietly for a moment, letting the information sink in. I could tell she wanted more details but felt it was an inappropriate time to ask.

"Have you called the police?" she asked after a few beats.

I shook my head. "He took my phone."

"He was thorough. Do you want to call them now?"

"I probably should." She handed me hers, and I dialled, then waited for my call to connect. "He has my mother's hairpin, Leesh." My emotions threatened to spill over again, but I swallowed hard to keep them at bay.

"Oh no. Holland, I'm so sorry." I hadn't met Alesha until after my parents had passed away, but she understood how important that hairpin was to me. She was the first friend I'd made after I'd moved in with my aunt. We'd been through everything together. "Maybe we can get it back. We'll go to all the pawn shops in the city in search of it. It has to turn up."

"I think I'm going to find him and force him to tell me where it is. After that, I'm going to cut off his balls for being a scumbag." And of course, that was the exact moment my call connected. *Fuck my life.*

"Malvern Police, Sergeant Stephen speaking."

"Yes. I'd like to report a robbery."

CHAPTER FOUR
PAYMENT FOR SERVICES RENDERED

"WE'VE COME across this guy before. He preys on lonely women, convinces them to take him home, then drugs and robs them." The senior constable on the scene held his notebook in front of him, shaking his head in pity. Pity that was directed at *me,* the 'lonely' woman. Could I possibly feel any worse? "It's been in the news."

"It has?" I balked. I never was one to pay attention to the news. I preferred Netflix to reality, so I missed it. *Ugh.*

Alesha played with the gold cross at her neck, sliding it from side to side. "You say he drugs and robs them. Does he ever do anything else?" she asked in a small voice.

"Nothing has been reported." The officer's eyes shifted from hers to mine with concern. "Is there something you're not telling me?"

Taking a deep breath, I shook my head. The fact he slept with me didn't necessarily mean anything. Like me, the other women could've been keeping that detail to themselves out of embarrassment.

"They had sex," Alesha squeaked, and I shot her a look

that said *shut up!*

The officer's brows shot halfway up his forehead. "Consensual?" he directed at me.

"Of course. I would be reporting a rape otherwise."

"You'd be surprised by the number of women who don't report sexual assault. He didn't force himself on you at all?"

"No," I insisted. "We met at a karaoke club, we talked, we came back here and... we had *fun*. It was consensual, and I was sober-ish the whole time. Everything was as it should be until I woke up to the empty house."

"Did he use a condom?"

My cheeks flamed. "Of course! I'm not that stupid." I felt genuinely offended that he'd ask such a thing.

"Do you remember what he did with that condom?"

"Threw it out when he went to the bathroom?" I shrugged because I honestly had no idea.

Using two fingers, he beckoned another officer over then asked them to check the rubbish in the bathroom.

"This guy never leaves any prints, so it'd help if we could get a DNA sample to see if he's in the system."

I nodded my understanding then watched the bathroom door to see if they found anything. The officer stepped out and shook his head.

"It was worth a try." The senior constable looked at his notebook then sighed. "You said you were sober-ish. Do you remember much about him?"

"Of course."

"Do you think you could sit down with a sketch artist? We have a very vague description so far. He tends to choose women who've had a bit too much to drink, so their memory is always hazy. They report getting home and offering him a drink, then passing out shortly after. It seems he's changed his MO with you."

"Because he slept with me? Maybe he was just randy last night," I offered, laughing a little even though there wasn't anything funny about the situation. *At least he didn't steal my sense of humour.*

"Your detailed description of him could really help our investigation."

"Of course." I could recall every inch of that man in vivid detail. My cheeks heated as I thought of the most prominent part of his body. I wasn't going to have to describe that too, was I?

We organised a tentative time for me to go to the station and work with a sketch artist, and I gave him Alesha's number since I no longer had a phone of my own.

With a set of keys to my apartment in the thief's possession, I felt it best to stay at Alesha's until I got the locks changed. Once there, the rest of the day was spent cancelling my credit cards and phone, dealing with my insurance company and organising a locksmith. There was so much work involved, so much that needed replacing. If I ever decided to take a man home on the first night again, I hoped someone would slap me in the face to knock some sense into me. There was a reason a lot of girls had a three-date rule.

Alesha set a glass tumbler on the table next to me with orange juice in it. "It's laced with vodka. I thought you could use it." I'd set myself up at her kitchen table with her laptop and phone so I could work through my to-do list while periodically groaning into my hands.

"Thank you," I said appreciatively, gulping at the cool alcoholic beverage and closing my eyes. "I just can't get over it, Leesh. He was... amazing. He said all the right things, did things to my body I never imagined liking. He made me feel special, wanted. But it turned out that all he really wanted was to clean me out." Draining the glass, I set it back on the table. "They completely maxed out my credit cards. There's a freeze on my line of credit now, but still, there could be some woman out there already pretending to be me. I hate that I was so easily duped." I was trying so hard not to cry about it.

She pulled out the chair beside me and sat down, placing her hand in the centre of my back. "He was very convincing, Holland. It could've happened to any one of us."

"But I should've known, right? I mean, you saw him. As if a guy like that would ever be truly interested in me."

"Don't sell yourself so short. You're amazing. Anyone who gets to know you for more than five minutes knows that."

"That's what he said in his stupid note," I scoffed, shaking my head and sniffing, my eyes burning with unshed tears.

"He left you a note?" I nodded. "Why didn't you show the police?"

"Because I flushed it. I was annoyed that he gave me the brush-off in a letter. I hadn't even seen the empty apartment yet."

"What did it say?"

"It said that he was sorry, I was amazing, and he wished things were different but this was just what he did. I took it that he regularly fucked women and then left during the night. I didn't realise he meant that he stole everything they owned."

"Do you think he felt bad about what he did to you?"

"What? Who cares. He still did it."

"Yeah, but he slept with you first. The officer said he didn't do that normally."

"Don't romanticise this, Leesh. Maybe the other women were just keeping it a secret?"

She shook her head. "I don't think so."

"Either way, what difference does it make? Am I to be so grateful for the awesome sex that I view his taking my stuff as payment for services rendered?"

"I don't know, was he *that* good?" Her eyes shone and her mouth twitched on one side. It was never too soon to make a joke about something in Alesha's world.

"Worth the entire contents of my house?" I closed my eyes and thought about how amazing having him inside me had felt, the way my body had shattered from his touch. "Hmm, if he'd just taken my car… yeah. But I think I'd need a bit more from him to make what he took fair payment."

"Still, being worth your car, he must've had a golden cock."

"Not golden. Just huge."

"How huge?"

"Crazy huge." I showed her with my hands and watched her eyes widen.

"Wow. What was it like?"

"Better than I could've imagined. But the memory is just so tainted now."

"He seemed so genuine," she mused, pulling a grape out of the fruit bowl in the middle of the table and popping it into her mouth. "What if it wasn't him? What if he left, and *then* someone came in and robbed you?"

I shook my head. "That doesn't make any sense. Besides, you heard the officer. This isn't the first time it's happened. Robbing desperate women is obviously how he makes a living."

"You are *not* desperate."

"Aren't I?" I locked eyes with her, daring her to object. We both knew my romantic history. I'd had exactly two boyfriends in my thirty-two years: one while I was at uni that lasted less than six months, and one a few years ago when I'd had some weird on-again off-again relationship with a parent of one of my students that ended rather badly. Apart from that, I'd had a handful of sexual partners that lasted anywhere from one night to a couple of months. Primarily, I was single. Painfully single, and longing.

"Are you really going to try and find him?"

"Yes. I need that hairpin back."

"Is that the only reason?"

I stared at her for a long time, annoyed that she was suggesting I could have any other motive. "Of course it is."

"Can't you let the police do their job? I don't think this is a good idea. We don't know if he's dangerous or not."

"The police?" I scoffed. "Considering they've known about him for a while and they haven't caught him yet, I'm not holding my breath."

"Maybe they'll do better with your description of him?"

"And maybe Brad Pitt broke it off with Angelina because he realised he was meant for me. Honestly, Alesha, I don't think they're looking hard enough. You heard the way that officer spoke to me. He made a point of telling me that he preyed on 'lonely' women. He was mocking me. They probably think we get what we deserve for being so gullible."

"He wasn't mocking you, Holland. He was just stating the facts."

"Then maybe they're not looking hard enough. The man is *huge*. Surely he can't be too hard to find."

She sat back in her chair and folded her arms across her chest. "Fine. Let's say you find him. Then what are you going to do?"

"I'll kick him in that big dick of his, then demand he give me the hairpin back while squeezing his balls so hard he cries like a baby." I mimed the motion with my hands, imagining him falling to the ground in pain and promising to do anything I wanted to make me stop. He wouldn't be rocking anyone's world for a long time once I was done with him.

"And how are you going to get close enough to do that? He could see you and run, or he could overpower you, hurt you. You're not thinking this through."

Turning my lips downward, I folded my arms and shrugged. "I could do it."

"Holland, I'm being serious."

"So am I. I could do it."

Pressing her lips together, she released a heavy sigh. "Just consider letting the cops do their job, OK? I don't want to lose my best friend because she went all Veronica Mars on me."

"Hey, Ronnie is my girl. She always comes through. And she's a teenager. I'm a grown woman. I've totally got this." My best friend needed to have more confidence in me.

CHAPTER FIVE
COMFORT FOOD AND FAMILY

"YOU LOOK TIRED TODAY, MISS," one of my year ten students, Emma, pointed out during fourth period. We were rehearsing scenes from *A Streetcar Named Desire*, and I wasn't showing my usual enthusiasm for my work. Honestly, I didn't have a lot of enthusiasm for anything lately.

After three months, I still hadn't found Ben or my mother's hairpin. I spent my nights visiting bars and night-clubs in Melbourne City and the surrounding suburbs, leaving no stone unturned. Not once did I lay eyes on a tall, dark and deliciously handsome man trying to take advantage of *lonely* women—I wished I could get that term out of my mind. The need to hunt him down possessed me, made me restless and agitated. Even singing had lost its lustre; every time I got on stage at a wedding, I felt more like pulling an Adam Sandler and singing about how life sucked instead of the love-soaked ballads the bride and groom had picked. I literally could not stop looking for him everywhere I went.

Every day that ticked by was another drop of disappointment in an already overflowing bucket. I'd even lost
my appetite and dropped *two* dress sizes from not eating.
Seemed the handsome thieving bastard of a man had also
stolen my love of food. What kind of sick monster
did that?

"I'm sorry, girls. I just didn't get a lot of sleep last
night." I sighed, dropping down in my chair and closing
the play book.

"Maybe some fresh air would do you good. We could
rehearse outside," another girl suggested.

I smiled and stood up again. "You know, I think that's
an excellent idea. We can do the final scene at the tables in
the senior area."

As the girls all filed out the door, my mind returned to
my troubles. My insurance company had paid out and I'd
replaced my car, my furniture and most other things I'd
owned before, but there were so many times that I went to
look for something as simple as a book I owned before
realising it wasn't there anymore. It sucked. It made me
angry. Made me sad. Hurt.

Why couldn't I find him? It wasn't like he was a
forgettable character. I'd even started taking the police
sketch around, asking people if they'd ever seen him. The
response I got to the sketch was mixed; some people said
no and others looked at me like I was crazy and laughed.
Weird. But the question remained—how did a man so
large manage to remain so hidden?

I was tired. I was cranky. And I was beginning to lose
hope. But I kept going, searching for him in every crowd.
Stupidly—and embarrassingly—my unconscious mind
couldn't separate my obsession with finding him to get

back my mother's hairpin and the reason my vagina wanted to find him. I'd woken in a panting ball of sweat more times than I cared to admit. Honestly, the fact that he was the best sexual experience I'd ever had really messed with my head. Lust mixed with anger and sorrow—it was a terrible combination.

I wanted to hate him, but I also *wanted* him. *A desperate, lonely woman*. That's why he'd preyed on me, right?

"This final scene really is the most important of the play," I explained to my students as they gathered around the wooden tables outside. "Blanche's behaviour reflects the way being raped by Stanley has scarred her. Think about her earlier scenes in which she *performs* for Stanley's friends, seeking their attentions. But now she's hiding and hoping they don't notice her. She's broken, crazy. Her tenuous grip on reality is long gone, and she spends most of the scene in the bath, preparing for an imaginary meeting with Shep Huntleigh when in fact, she's getting carted off to a mental hospital because her sister would rather believe she's crazy than believe her husband was capable of rape."

I paced back and forth in front of them, the script open in my hand as I stared at the words and stage directions I'd looked at so many times before. The crimes committed against us were different, but I couldn't help feeling an affinity with Blanche Dubois. I was struggling with my own grip on reality after having my illusions torn apart by a man. It was our trusting nature that did us in, our belief that the faces people showed us were honourable and true.

I stopped moving and stood in front of my students, who were surprisingly staring on in rapt attention. "It's the culmination of everything these people have gone through, filled with tension, grief and guilt. I want you all to keep that in mind while we work on this scene, feel it as you deliver your lines, remember it as you interact with the other characters." Placing my hands on my hips, I surveyed the area, deciding how to set the stage. "I want Blanche over there." I pointed to the last table in a block of four. "Stella and Eunice sit here." I pointed to the closest table. "And the poker players sit back there with Mitch and Stanley. We'll keep the doctor and nurse waiting in the wings." I pointed to a patch of grass. "Everyone else sit on the benches and follow along."

As we worked through the scene, my chest grew tight and my blood pumped faster through my veins. Why did men think they could treat women any way they wanted? What gave them the right to take from us without guilt, as if they were literally owed something just for being born? What Ben had done to me shattered my trust in my own judgement. I'd believed him when he'd called me beautiful, was elated when he'd hinted at something more. But it was all a lie, a scam designed to trick me just long enough to clean me out. It made me look stupid, made me feel naïve. More than that, it felt so damn unfair. What kind of a person did that to another? I would never be able to trust a man's interest in me again. Especially if that man was even remotely attractive. I'd always be questioning his motives and expecting the worst. I would never be fooled by a handsome face again.

Emily, who was playing Blanche, paused dramatically, ready to deliver her final line, and I held my breath, wrapping my arms around my middle as I waited for it.

"Whoever you are, I have always depended on the kindness of strangers."

I closed my eyes and nodded. *You and me both, Blanche. You and me both.*

And it made fools out of both of us.

"YOU LOOK LIKE ABSOLUTE SHIT," Aunt Maya said when I turned up on her doorstep after work that night. She was already wearing her pink dressing gown, pantyhose still on her legs but slippers on her feet. Her brown hair was in a neat French roll, and her make-up was almost perfect despite it being the end of the day. She worked as a corporate secretary in the city and couldn't stand wearing her business wear for a moment longer than was necessary. It was my strongest memory of her growing up, looking exactly like this every night. And since I couldn't face another night searching pubs and clubs, finding her this way was a sight for my sore eyes. I needed comfort food and family.

"I *feel* like shit," I sulked, falling into her warm embrace, inhaling her familiar scent—Coco Chanel, her favourite. She'd been with me for every moment since my parents' passing, held my hand through the good and bad, dealt with my teenage drama and listened to my adult woes. She was my everything.

"How about I whip up a batch of my mac and cheese? That always cheers you up."

Pouting, I nodded. She made *the best* mac and cheese, with four different types of cheese, full cream and crispy bacon. It was pure comfort in a bowl. If anything could bring back my love of food, it was Aunt Maya's cooking.

With an easy smile, she gave my shoulder a squeeze and moved aside so I could follow her into the house.

"Want to tell me what's got you so down?" she asked, pulling out pots while I grabbed ingredients from the fridge and pantry.

"It's just the search for Mum's hairpin. It's not turning up anywhere, and I can't seem to find the guy who took it." I set everything on the kitchen counter while she filled a pot with water and set it on the stove.

"I still think it's a terrible idea for you to go looking for him. What if he's dangerous?" Aunt Maya had made it abundantly clear how crazy she thought my idea was when I first told her about the robbery. But she also knew how stubborn I was, so there wasn't much she could do to stop me. She'd learned years before to support my choices whether she liked them or not, knowing I'd just do it anyway. But if she rallied against it, I'd do it and not tell her about it. Supporting me was safer.

"You sound like Alesha. But I really don't think he's dangerous. Of all the things he could've done to me, he chose to rock my world and then send me to sleep. He's not vicious, he's just a thief."

"Still, I don't like the idea of you traipsing around town looking for him. Anything could happen to you going to all those random clubs. I really wish you'd just leave it alone and let the police find him."

Taking a seat on the other side of her bench, I rested my chin on my hands. "*Pfft*. How hard can it possibly be to find a six-foot-six man with bulging muscles? It's not like he can hide in a crowd."

She shrugged. "Maybe you're all looking in the wrong

place. You said he's muscular. Maybe he's hiding in a gym."

"A gym?" *Oh my God.* It was the light-bulb moment I needed.

Nodding, she handed me the block of cheddar and a grater. "He has to get those muscles from somewhere, and if the police sketch has been on TV, he might be lying low for a while—although, based on that sketch, Hugh Jackman should also lie low."

"That sketch *does not* look like Hugh Jackman."

"Yes it does, sweetheart."

"It does?" She nodded. "Well, I guess that explains why people kept laughing and looking at me funny whenever I showed them." I did compare his looks to Jackman's several times during the sketch artist interview.

"You know, he probably doesn't even live around here," she said after she'd finished chopping up the bacon. The pan sizzled noisily when she dropped a handful in.

He doesn't live around here. Why didn't I think of that?

"You are *so* smart, Aunt Maya. I could kiss you!" Suddenly my eyes were open, and I had a whole new method of searching for him.

She laughed. "I'm even smarter than you think. Take a look in that bag over there." Her eyes directed me to the hutch in her dining room.

"What's this?" I asked, pulling out a white box with a small plastic rectangle pictured on it.

"It's a GPS card. You put it in your purse and if anyone takes it, you can ping it and it'll tell you where it is. I thought that since you insist on hunting this man down, there should at least be a way of finding you when I can't sleep because of the worry."

I grinned, then got up and hugged her. "Aw, Aunty, you *do* worry about me."

"All the bloody time, girl. Now get off me and grate that cheese. We'll never eat at the rate you're going."

When I got home, my belly full and my resolve strengthened, I opened my brand-new laptop and channelled my inner Sherlock. I remembered smelling salt air on his clothes, so it made sense that he must spend a lot of time near the sea—that or he had an amazing fabric softener. Chewing my lip, I tried to recall something that would narrow it further…. *His tan!* Salt air plus the outdoors equalled the beach. Tall, muscular, scruffy men who smelled like the sea *and* had a great tan? A surfer. He had to be! Melbourne beaches were fairly sheltered, which meant surfing was non-existent anywhere within Port Phillip Bay. The closest surfing beach was over an hour south, and it made sense that he didn't shit in his own backyard. It also explained why I'd had zero luck searching for him in Melbourne. *He doesn't live here!*

Taking Aunt Maya's advice, I googled gyms in the closest surf suburb I could think of—Torquay. By the end of my search, I'd narrowed my list to fifteen gyms around the two most popular surfing beaches. There were about to be a lot of early morning drives in my future, but it was a starting point that gave me renewed strength and direction.

I slept like a baby that night.

CHAPTER SIX
DUCHESS

NORMALLY I WAS like a ninja at the gym—you never saw me there. But suddenly I was a regular, up at the crack of dawn and driving for over an hour to pound out steps on a treadmill and keep a close watch on the entry doors, later asking the women in the change room if they'd ever seen someone matching Ben's description. I was even more exhausted than I'd been searching clubs and bars, plus my thighs were burning and my runners didn't understand why they were being used so much, but still I persisted. It was as if I could smell him close by.

Sure, I could've searched the beaches to see if he was among the surfers, but since I'd never been on a board before, I didn't think it would look believable if suddenly I turned up with one asking questions. Plus, I'd seen *Point Break*—those surfer groups weren't easy to break into. No, a chubby chick looking to join a gym was much more believable.

"Are you talking about *Nate*?" a tiny girl asked in the ninth gym I'd been to in two weeks. I hadn't even been talking to her; she'd overheard me talking to a redhead and interrupted.

Nate? It was possible he'd given me a fake name.

Frowning, I mopped my overly exerted face with my towel. Cardio was hard. "Is this him?" I pulled out the police sketch and showed it to her.

"That's not Nate. It's a drawing of Hugh Jackman." She looked at me like I was growing a second head before her eyes.

"It's not supposed to be Jackman." I tucked the picture away. I really needed to stop using it as a reference. "But the man I'm looking for looks kind of like him though—a younger version with light blue eyes and dark hair. He's also built like a brick shithouse, and has an American accent... or maybe he doesn't. He might have been putting that on."

"I don't know. I suppose it could be him—he *is* a joker," she said, pulling out her phone and concentrating on the screen. "I think I have a picture here somewhere, but he doesn't have an accent since he grew up around here. He's an Aussie through and through." She swiped for a few moments. "Here. That's Nate there. He's gorgeous, right?" She turned the screen towards me and I stopped breathing. It was him. Under any other circumstance, the picture would've made me laugh. It was of the girl in front of me and a friend posing in front of the gym's mirrors. Ben—I mean Nate had photobombed it by coming up behind them and pulling a silly face with his tongue poking out.

His name is Nate, not Ben, and he doesn't have an accent. He also grew up right here. I knew absolutely nothing about him. For some reason, that revelation *hurt*. I couldn't explain why.

"I actually went to school with him and his brothers," she continued, oblivious to my shock. "The Cartwright boys were always a lot of fun. Lots of parties on the beach and crazy antics." She laughed in a way that told me she had fond memories of them.

As I mutely studied the picture, my heart pounded against my ribcage with a painful thump. I'd finally found him. The realisation made me sick to my stomach.

"That's not him though, is it?" she asked "I mean, I guess he looks a little like Jackman if you squint, but... I don't know. I'm probably wasting your time."

"That's him," I said, my voice just above a whisper as I stared at his face. I knew him intimately, but other than that, I knew nothing about him at all. Emotions I didn't understand came flooding to the surface, my eyes pricking as a result. There was relief, there was fear, there was sadness, disappointment, and that pitiful emotion: desire. I didn't want to feel desire for that man, but there it was, swimming around in my pool of hurt.

"Did...did he *do* something to you?" the girl asked, her brow furrowing with concern. She seemed horrified at the thought, but was enough of a sister to ask anyway.

I took a breath and tried to compose myself while shaking my head. "No," I lied. "I just need to talk to him. Can you tell me when he comes in?"

She shrugged. "He doesn't really have a schedule, just floats in whenever he feels like it. I'm not even sure he has a job." She laughed at that, and I wondered if anyone knew exactly what he was. "But his older brother Toby is more regular. Should be here already, actually. He does free weights downstairs, so if Nate's here with him, that's where they'll be."

I wondered if maybe this brother was the guy who helped him rob me.

"Thank you," I said, feeling as though I should hug her for her helpful information. But I decided that would be a little too familiar and gross considering the sweaty mess I was in, so I just waved, then collected my things and headed for the door.

"Good luck," she called after me.

Taking the stairs slowly due to my thigh pain and the fact that I didn't enjoy sliding down stairs on my face, I followed the signs and walked cautiously around to the free weights area, keeping my eyes peeled for any familiar giant men. I didn't need to look far—the moment I rounded the corner, I landed smack dab in the centre of a broad chest. The scent of him hit me full force, and I didn't even need to look up to know it was him.

"Holland?" A disbelieving voice spoke my name slowly as strong arms wrapped around my upper arms to steady me. *He remembers me?* I forced my gaze to travel up the two-toned tank top that stretched itself across a football field–sized chest. All the while, my heart hammered out a tune that sounded a lot like *'Bow chicka wow wow....'* My God, he was breathtaking.

"*Not-American Nate Cartwright*," I replied when our eyes locked. My stomach threatened to empty its contents, but I clamped it down as something flickered across his expression. It looked a lot like guilt, or maybe it was just worry. I knew who he was.

"What are you doing here, and what happened to the rest of you?" He spoke in a clear Australian accent as he frowned, taking in my smaller figure. I still wasn't thin by any stretch of the word, but I was a lot smaller than I was the night I met him—well, the *him* he'd pretended to be.

"Excuse me?" I needed to make sure I'd heard him right. There I was, the woman he stole from finding out who he really was, and he was asking me about my weight loss?

"Don't get me wrong, you look gorgeous either way. But I really liked those curves." His hand moved from my arm to my waist and he pulled me flush against him, smiling down at me. "I remember those curves *real* well." His hand slid down and settled on the rounded part of my arse, gripping a little tighter, pressing a little closer. "I also remember how perfectly we *fit*."

With our skin brushing, tiny electrical currents passed between us, heating my cheeks and giving me a moment where I forgot the whole point of my being there. I remembered how well we fit together as well. In fact, my dreams wouldn't let me forget. I also couldn't stop thinking about his ripped chest and magical mouth. The whole name change and different accent thing was really throwing me off, but I couldn't deny the impulses of my body.

Why do I hate this guy again? Oh that's right, he lied to me and robbed me.

"Stop." Shaking the lusty haze his closeness created, I pulled away from his grip and took a step back to get some distance and some clarity. "This isn't why I came looking for you."

Even in my confused state, I couldn't help but notice the mega biceps he had going on. He was wearing a grey and charcoal tank top and a pair of black gym shorts. I could see so much of him, and my traitorous nether regions tingled at the memory of what it felt like to touch him. I had to look away before I climbed him like a tree.

He grinned. I loved the way his eyes danced with mischief. *Shut up, Holland!*

"How did you find me, anyway?" he asked.

"I looked."

"For three months and two weeks?"

"That's a very specific number," I commented with a smirk. It was exactly how long I'd been looking.

"I suppose it is." His gaze travelled over my body, and his grin broadened.

Does that mean he was waiting for me to find him? Counting the days we were apart? Was he longing for me, or does he just keep count of the days between one theft and the next? The last one was most likely.

This interaction definitely wasn't what I was expecting when I imagined confronting him. Honestly, I hadn't thought much past jumping out in front of him and yelling, "Ha! The jig is up!"—and I didn't even manage that part. The rest of it I was going to wing. I just hadn't expected him to be *happy* to see me.

A tiny part of me was actually enjoying the flirtation we had going on. I couldn't deny the pull of attraction that coursed between us; it was intoxicating, to say the least. But at the same time, the bigger part of me was flashing warning lights and telling me I was being stupid. This wasn't just any guy standing in front of me. It was a man without morals. Suddenly, all the warnings from Aunt Maya and Alesha lit up in my mind. He was a *bad* guy. I needed to get my head on straight. It was time to ask about the hairpin and get out there.

"Why did you lie about who you were, then take all my

stuff?" I asked, pushing my attraction to him down as deep as I could. I was angry and I felt betrayed by him. I needed to remember that. It didn't matter how gorgeous he was, or how my traitorous body reacted the moment he was near, where I could feel him and smell him and remember exactly what it felt like having his naked skin pressed against mine...

Focus on the anger. Focus on the danger. Stay smart.

His tongue ran along his bottom lip as his expression evened out and he regarded me carefully, his hands resting on his hips. My heart rate kicked up and I realised that I had no idea what my true fight or flight reaction was. What if he really was dangerous? I should run the moment things went bad, but I didn't know if I was one of those crazy people who stood there and fought when I couldn't possibly win? I had never been in the position to find out.

It was at that moment I realised how insane I was for hunting this guy down without a plan. What would my epitaph say now? *Here lies Holland Williams. The wizard should've given her brains instead of courage. She was still awesome though.*

Some guy came down the stairs and brushed past us, nodding at Nate in greeting before he gave me a curious look. Nate stayed quiet until he walked away, leaving my question unanswered. That small act really pissed me off.

"Can we go somewhere else to talk?" he asked, reaching out to steer me towards the exit.

I rolled my eyes. Having me there obviously cramped his style and he didn't want anyone he knew to see me. I supposed it wasn't every day that the woman you fucked over turned up at your gym. Still, it wasn't like any of them knew that. I could be anyone. Maybe he just didn't want his gym buddies to find out he was a chubby chaser. Maybe he just worried someone might listen in on our conversation and find out who he really was.

"What for? So you can take me for another ride?" I spoke a little too loud on purpose.

He leaned in and lowered his voice. "If you want your answers, you'll have to get them somewhere a little more private."

"I don't trust you in private." I folded my arms across my chest, jutting out my chin.

"Not sure I trust myself either." His eyes spoke of hunger as they dropped down to my cleavage and a grin spread across his face. The mischief had returned, and I uncrossed my arms immediately.

"Are you seriously perving on my tits right now?"

He shrugged. "You're the one sticking them in my face."

Without a second's thought, I pulled my hand back and slapped him. Hard. The clap loud enough that other patrons looked our way. "I was *not* sticking them in your face." The flirtation was definitely over on my side.

Recoiling from my slap, Nate grunted then let out his breath before glancing over his shoulder. "We really need to get out of here." Placing his hand on my upper arm, he bustled me towards the stairs.

"Let go of me, you oaf," I called out, slapping his arm with my free hand.

"Please shut up, Holland," he begged, his voice calm and even.

"Why? Will you drug me if I don't?"

"I'm thinking about it." He was much bigger and stronger than me, so I didn't really have much choice as to whether I wanted to follow him or not. I just kept moving along and complaining until we got outside and around the corner where we were alone.

"I *knew* I made a mistake with you," he said when we finally stopped and he released his grip. The flirtation was obviously over for him too. Good. But being called a mistake kind of hurt. A lot. I was an *amazing regret.* Fabulous.

Rubbing at my arm, I frowned up at him. "Which part? Lying to me, fucking me or robbing me?"

A growl reverberated out of his chest as he glared at me, hands on hips. "All of the above."

I mimicked the pose. "Well, the feeling is mutual."

He clenched his jaw, studying me. *Fuck, he's hot.* I winced internally, wishing I'd quit thinking about him in that way. But, it just kind of popped into my head unbidden. "What do you want from me, Holland? Why are you here?"

"I want the hairpin you stole."

He frowned. *"What?"*

"Don't act like it wasn't you. I remember the look on your face after I drank that water. You drugged me and took everything I owned while I was knocked out."

"I'm not denying anything. But I don't do inventory, so I don't know what you're talking about."

It blew my mind that he used a word like 'inventory' as if he worked in some retail store doing stocktake.

"It's a hairpin. It's gold and has a flower made from mother of pearl on the end of it. It was in the jewellery box you took from my wardrobe."

Shaking his head, he lifted his shoulders. None of this mattered to him. "I don't have it."

"Can you at least tell me what you did with it so I can buy it back?"

"What's so important about this hairpin? You had insurance, right? Let it go."

"Let it go?" His words were like a slap in my face and I gasped in response, my emotions getting the better of me. "That hairpin is the *only* thing I have left of my mother. And you took it, you sick, twisted bastard of a man. Don't forget that I know who you are. I could have the cops on you in seconds." Tears sprang to my eyes and I shoved against his chest, angry that I was crying, and furious that he was the reason for it. He'd made me feel special. Then he'd made me feel worthless. And all he could do was stand there, taking the punishment I was dishing out while looking ridiculously gorgeous. I hated that. I hated that he was still so beautiful to me even though I knew he had a criminal heart.

Stepping away, I turned in a circle, unsure of what to do as I raked my fingers through my hair. "I just want it back."

Pressing his lips together, he wiped a hand over his scruff. "I didn't know," he responded.

"How could you have known? It's not like we knew each other. We chatted and we fucked. There were no deep secrets shared. Hell, I didn't even know your real name. Is it really Nate? Or is that a fake one too?"

"It's Nate," he responded, letting out his breath slowly.

"Forgive me if I don't believe you," I scoffed. "Jesus Christ. I can't even... what is *wrong* with you? Do you have any idea how it feels to be your victim? You came into my home, I gave myself to you, and then you took *everything.* I felt used and violated, not to mention stupid and desperate. Do you ever think about the women you fuck over after the fact? Do you have any remorse?"

His hands stayed on his hips as that tongue of his touched his lips. This was crazy. I doubt he felt any remorse. Why should he? He'd never been caught. He'd never been confronted by his victim. No one had ever made his crimes personal. *Why the fuck had he chosen me?* "Listen, if it helps I wasn't supposed to pick you. I was supposed to pick your weird friend."

That made it so much worse. Had I been a backup? Had he seen me and decided I looked far more desperate and easy? I felt ill. "She's not *weird.* She's just awkward around men and painfully honest. Something you could probably learn from. Why did you choose me instead? Decided I was an easier target since big girls are always so desperate?" I had to know.

He took a step towards me, his voice a low rumble when he spoke. "I chose you because you made my dick hard when I watched you swinging your hips on that stage."

That so was not the answer I was expecting. I had to clear my throat and force my voice steady before I could speak. "And I'm supposed to take comfort in that?" Despite my efforts, there was still a slight squeak to my final words.

"Take it however you want. Just know that my dick has been thinking about your snug pussy a hell of a lot since that night. I'm kind of glad you tracked me down." He moved a little closer, crowding my space and making it a little hard for me to focus.

Fuck off, hormones. Don't you dare cloud my mind. He stole from me. He made me miserable.

"Are you trying to flatter me?"

He tilted his head to the side, smirking. "I don't normally sleep with the women I steal from. You were the first." He brushed his fingers lightly against my cheek. I flinched out of the way, but not before his touch left a searing impression on my skin.

"Then I suppose I should be thanking you, huh? What an amazing honour you bestowed upon me." I bowed dramatically and he chuckled. "This isn't funny, Not-Ben."

"It's kind of funny. You've been looking for me all this time. I must've made a big impression."

"Uh, yeah. You seduced me, you drugged me, and then you robbed me. I'd say that's a little unforgettable."

"That's exactly what I did," he said unapologetically. "Although, you kind of drugged yourself. I wasn't going to give you the water, if you remember correctly."

"*Why?*"

"Because I liked you. I was going to give you a pass, but you took the water and the opportunity was there. You had nice stuff." He shrugged like that explained everything.

"No. Why do you rob people?" The fact that he'd just said he liked me didn't escape my attention, although adding that I had 'nice stuff' had thoroughly diluted the effect of such a declaration. *He really has zero shame. He stole from me because he couldn't help it. Bastard.*

For a moment, he looked at me as though he thought I was a little daft. And maybe I was, because I didn't understand how someone could feel entitled enough to take things that didn't belong to them. I needed it spelled out for me. "Because it's what we do. We're the people keeping the insurance companies in business. It's how the economy works. People buy shit and pay premiums to protect it from people like me. Then I take their shit and they get more new shit with their payout. The cycle continues." His eyes did a slow search of my face. "I'll bet you have a whole apartment full of nice new furniture and appliances now—a new car, new phone. Felt good buying all that shit too, didn't it? Unpacking it all and setting it up? We didn't hurt you. We gave you a new start."

"So what? You think you're some kind of glorified Robin Hood?"

"Duchess, I don't give a single cent to the poor. There's no room for sentimentality in this game."

"You're glorifying what you do. That *game* you're playing messes with people's lives and makes them feel afraid in their own homes. I should just call the cops and tell them where you are so I, and all of womankind, can be done with you." I folded my arms across my chest again, then remembered it only served to enhance my bust. I caught him looking and dropped my hands by my side once more, beyond frustrated.

"Call them and you'll never get your stuff back."

"You just told me you don't know where it is."

He bowed his head until he was maybe an inch away from my face, his breath on my skin. "Doesn't mean I can't find out."

"So find out!" I stepped back so I could see him and not be so close that I was affected by him. Even sweaty from the gym, he smelled good. "Do me that one small favour. That pin is the only thing I care about getting back. I don't give a fuck about the rest."

"Fine. I'll get you the pin, and you'll keep the cops out of it."

"I didn't come here to make deals."

"And I'm not helping you without one."

"Well, that depends... Have you robbed any other lonely women lately?"

"You consider yourself lonely?" Our eyes locked and held. I refused to dignify him with an answer. "You were my last," he said finally. "I haven't gone home with a woman since you. The grift was getting too hot."

"Well, don't I feel special? I'm the first you fuck and the last you rob."

"Guess I'll remember you in twenty years too." With his eyes searching mine, and that ever-present smirk on his lips, I felt the air crackling between us. I wanted it to be frustration and anger, but I knew better than that—it was unbridled lust. My private parts were calling to his, saying, 'Hey, remember me? We fit so well together.' I clenched my pelvic floor so hard it almost sealed permanently shut.

"Just get me the hairpin," I whispered, "and I won't call the cops."

"Deal." He held his hand out to shake mine and confirm the pact.

"Nate," a male voice called out from several feet away, snapping us out of the haze we'd descended into, saving me from having to slip my hand into Nate's.

"I'll be right there," he responded, shifting so he was blocking my view. Despite his efforts, I caught sight of the guy, a slightly smaller version of the man in front of me—the older brother, I supposed. They had the same dark hair and a similar build, but the other guy seemed to have lighter eyes.

"Aren't you going to introduce me to your friend?"

"I'll meet you inside," Nate returned, more forceful

that time. The other guy reluctantly headed back into the gym.

Pressing his teeth into his bottom lip, Nate turned back to me and shook his head, biting back a grin as he studied my face. "Is it wrong that I'm totally hard for you right now?"

I lowered my eyes and could see the bulge in his shorts. He reached down and adjusted it slightly so it wasn't so painfully obvious. A sense of longing blossomed in my core, aching to revisit his touch. I wished that circumstances were different. That he wasn't a thief and I wasn't his victim. That we were just two regular people with no baggage or history at all.

"It's wrong," I whispered, hating that I was still reacting to him after everything he did.

"Doesn't feel wrong." He took my hand and placed it on his crotch. I didn't even try to pull away. *But*, I did refrain from stroking it, so I was proud of myself for that even though my whole body shook from the memory of it inside me. I guess I really was desperate, or crazy. Or both.

"So... ah... we have a d-deal?" I stammered, forcing myself to pull my hand back, but he just tightened his grip and held me steady, bringing his other arm around my body. "Nate, please don't." As I said the words, he pulled me to him, his mouth finding mine on a powerless whimper.

He kissed me long and hard, my knees turning to jelly as his tongue pushed inside and explored. It was the most fantastic kiss, one I felt all the way to the bottom of my feet and the ends of my hair. I almost forgot to hate him, lost in the song of our bodies. But it was over too fast, my memories immediately flooding back as he set me on my feet.

"I'll be in touch," he murmured against my lips as I took my own weight.

At first, I couldn't even speak. I just nodded, mute. I'd wanted to come to him and hold all the cards—his freedom —in my hands. Instead, he'd taken complete control, and I was dumbly letting him. And he knew it, based on the wicked grin that curved his full mouth.

I cleared my throat and took a steadying breath, trying to find my wits again. "I'd, uh… give you my number, but I'm fairly sure you know how to find me. I'm the girl living in the apartment you cleaned out."

He looked at me for a long moment, his eyes dancing as if this was fun for him.

One phone call, and I could have him locked up.

I knew I should do it. I obviously couldn't be trusted to think clearly in his presence.

"I remember." His eyes did one last slow sweep of my body. "I remember *everything*."

"Holy hell," I muttered, unable to stop the words from jumping out of my mouth. The things he could do to me with a look. It was sinful—*criminal*. What in the world was I doing getting turned on by him? I came to get my stuff, justice! And yet my attraction to him was undeniable.

With a chuckle, he took a step back. "See you around, duchess."

Then he turned on the ball of his foot and jogged away.

It took me a good ten minutes before my knees would let me walk again. But my underwear, that definitely needed changing. *Damn that man.*

"POPCORN TASTES like butter-soaked cardboard when you're watching a gastronomic adventure through France," Alesha stated, shoving another handful of said cardboard into her mouth.

"This makes me want to travel," I sighed, smiling incessantly throughout the movie so far. We were watching *Paris Can Wait* with Diane Lane, Arnaud Viard, and Alec Baldwin. It was so simple in its storyline, but inspiring at the same time—we all spent far too much time rushing through life without experiencing it. It made me want to sell everything I owned and spend the rest of my years backpacking through Europe.

"Me too. What is it about Frenchmen that makes them so damn sexy?" She tilted her head to the side as she studied the characters on the screen. "I mean, this guy isn't even that great to look at, but the moment he opens his mouth, and the *way* he speaks... I'm getting heart palpitations."

"Imagine his voice in your ear, telling you what to do."

I put on my best French accent. "Oh, Leesha, I want you to remove all of your clothes and kneel on the bed with your derrière in zee air."

Alesha giggled so much she almost choked on a popcorn kernel. "I reckon I'd swing upside down from a chandelier if he asked me with that voice," she said once she'd stopped coughing.

"Maybe I should go for an Italian man. They like big women, don't they?"

"They have beautiful accents too. I also love Spanish accents. Oh, and Irish ones. I could listen to an Irishman read the assembly instructions for a chest of drawers and I'd be hanging on his every word."

"Oh yes, I'll have to add Ireland to my list."

She narrowed her eyes slightly. "Are you serious about this?"

"Travelling? Yeah, I think I am. Besides, that Contiki tour we did in our twenties, I've hardly been anywhere, hardly done anything. I've spent most of my life living in the same city and experiencing nothing. Plus, this place doesn't feel as much like home as it used to." I looked around my apartment, at all the new furniture that was far too modern for my taste but that I'd been forced to purchase mass-produced because my insurance payout didn't cover the cost of my random DIY finds. My place looked like a Harvey Norman showroom.

Sitting up a little straighter, she turned towards me. "Don't you think you'd just be running away then? I mean, I know you're shaken after that Ben-Nate guy came into your life and messed around with it"—I'd told her all about finding my handsome thief and how disappointed I was at my own lack of control around him—"but don't you think you owe it to yourself to stay and sort this out? You can't let him return the hairpin and have that be the end of it. No matter how attracted to him you are, you need to remember that he's a criminal and he needs to be behind bars where he belongs. You have a duty to the other women he might prey on."

To Alesha, the world was always black and white; people were supposed to follow the rules and bad guys got thrown in prison—end of. And while I knew she was right, I also knew that snitches got stitches. I had no idea how deep Nate's criminal affiliations really went. If I dobbed him in to the cops, who's to say some sort of retaliation wouldn't befall me. After all, *they knew where I lived.*

"I know, Leesh. Just let me focus on getting the hairpin back, and then I'll tell the police everything I know. But after that, I think I'm going to travel. I need a change of pace."

After talking some more when the movie finished, Alesha went home with a promise to go shopping with me on the weekend to buy a new outfit for the next wedding I was booked to sing at. I generally tried to match the colour scheme of the event, and this one was mauve and cream. I hoped to find a mauve dress that would suit.

No sooner had I started cleaning up the popcorn mess and our empty Coke cans than there was a knock at my door.

"What did you forget this time?" I asked as I pulled it open, expecting to see Alesha on the other side. She was always leaving things behind that she had to come back for. Just last week, she'd walked out and gotten to her car only to realise she'd left her keys on my counter.

Nate leaned against the door frame, a lazy grin

spreading across his face. "I don't know about you, but I thought she'd *never* leave."

"What are *you* doing here?" I demanded, nerves taking flight in my belly the moment I set eyes on him. "Do you have the hairpin?"

"Not yet." He stood up straighter, filling the entire doorway. "But I did come with a peace offering."

"Oh yeah? What's that?"

"My cock."

The laugh burst from my mouth before I had the chance to stop it. "Your cock? It's a little arrogant to think I still want your cock, don't you think?"

He chuckled. "Oh you want it. But I was joking about that being the peace offering. I actually brought you this." He held out a bottle of tequila, the good kind with the grub at the bottom. The last time I drank tequila, I was nineteen and at university. It was the cheap nasty stuff, and we'd been doing shots with salt and lemon. I'd been so drunk that my hangover lasted a whole week.

"Uh, thanks?"

"You don't like it?"

"I don't drink it outside a margarita, and then only when I'm out."

"So, make us margaritas with it."

"Right now? Despite the fact that I don't have the ingredients, it's a school night. I don't claim to know the hours a thief keeps, but I have work in the morning."

"Come on, duchess. Let me inside. Have a drink with me. We'll drink it straight if we have to." His voice sounded so soft as it filled my ears and wrapped around me invitingly. He was sin on two legs, and anything I had to do with him was bound to lead to trouble. "Please, I drove all this way to see you. And don't think I didn't notice that you didn't shake on our deal. We'll drink to confirm it instead." He flashed me a brilliant smile.

My resolve was slipping. It was something about those eyes and that grin; they held a promise of fun and good times, and I so desperately wanted to be a good-time girl. I was so bored with the ins and outs of my life. I worked, I watched television and occasionally went out with the same people over and over again. I wanted some excitement. And excitement was standing right in front of me.

Reaching out, I took the bottle from his hands. "Why do I feel like inviting you in is going to go bad for me?"

"Because I'm a vampire," he said, snapping his teeth together. "But since I've already been inside, there wouldn't be much you could do to stop me."

"That's true." I stood to the side, shoving my better judgement out the window. "Try not to steal anything this time."

He brushed past me with a wink. "I'm not promising anything."

"Then walk back out the door, Nate."

With a laugh, he ignored me, walking into my kitchen and opening cupboards in search of glasses instead.

Meanwhile, I was still standing by the open door. "I mean it, Nate. There is no deal unless you promise to leave my things alone this time."

Stopping what he was doing, he placed one hand on his heart, then held the other in the air, palm facing me. "I promise not to steal all your stuff. Scout's honour."

I narrowed my eyes at him. "Were you even a Scout?"

"Sure I was. I can build a fire and everything. Come on, duchess. These glasses aren't going to fill themselves."

Pushing the door closed, I took the bottle into the kitchen and broke the seal, pouring a small amount into the two glasses. "Here," I said, pushing his towards him. "You drink first. I can't trust that anything coming from you isn't drugged."

"That's fair," he replied, reaching out and downing the contents of the first glass, licking his lips when he was done. The action sent tingling feelings to my tingly bits.

I pushed the other glass at him. "Drink that too. You're bigger than me, so you'd need more."

With dancing eyes, he held the second glass up to his lips. "Trying to get me drunk so you can have your wicked way with me?"

"I'm fairly sure that was *your* plan." I tilted the bottle of tequila to prove my point.

He downed the second drink, and I felt a surge of longing in my chest as I watched his Adam's apple bob during the swallow. He was just so... *manly*. Everything about him was larger than life. He made me feel small, something I didn't encounter often. "I'll admit that thought did cross my mind." He placed the glass back on the counter and I poured two more fingers.

"Do we toast?" he asked, handing me my glass.

Taking it, I held it halfway between my mouth and the bench. "I thought this was a drink to you finding my hairpin and me not calling the cops."

"I think we can do better than that."

"Fine. What would you like to toast to?"

"You pick."

"I don't know. I'm struggling to find the hopefulness in this situation."

"Why? Do I scare you, Holland?"

I shook my head. "No. But you unnerve me. I don't trust you."

His tongue touched one of his eye teeth. "That's probably for the best." He lifted his glass and held it next to mine. "How about to trusting your instincts? May they serve you well."

"That works," I said, tapping my glass against his and downing the contents. It didn't burn anywhere near as much as I expected it to. "That's not half bad."

He moved closer and I moved back, my arse hitting the counter, halting my retreat. "Only the best for my duchess." He took the glass from my hand and poured some more tequila, handing it back to me and clinking our glasses together again.

I looked at the pale amber liquid. "Duchess. Why do you keep calling me that?"

"I don't know. It's just what I think when I look at you. The way you act, I guess."

"The way I act? You think I have a stick up my arse?"

With a chuckle, he shook his head and rested his finger under my chin. "No. It's more that you seem ruthless, like you always get what you want."

"I *do not* always get what I want."

"You found me when no one else has been able to, right?"

I shrugged. "I suppose."

"Plus, you're kind of unobtainable."

"Unobtainable?" I scoffed. "That is *so* not the case."

"It is where I'm concerned."

"You're standing in my kitchen, not so inconspicuously brushing a hard-on against my hip."

Placing his hands on the bench either side of me, he

lowered his head, and his voice along with it. "Doesn't mean I get to keep you."

Did that mean he *wanted* to keep me?

I turned to meet his eyes, the question on the tip of my tongue, but he kissed me before I could speak. It started out as a simple joining of mouths, then turned into a hungry passion that caused me to forget I was holding a glass, the crash on the floor the sudden reminder it was there. Not that we cared to stop and clean it up. The moment it hit the floor, Nate wrapped his hands around my thighs and lifted me onto the bench, tilting my head back so he could kiss me deeper, pushing my legs open so he could fit between them.

"This is crazy," I gasped when we broke the kiss for a mere second as he pulled my shirt over my head.

"Then let's be crazy," he responded, discarding his own shirt before his mouth returned to mine with a fervour that caused our teeth to clash. His hands were everywhere at once, igniting a raging fire inside me. Before I knew it, I was completely naked and his fingers had slipped between my legs, gliding through my juices. I was ridiculously wet for him.

"Mmm," he murmured next to my ear. "Feels like you've been ready since I walked through the door." With his fingers moving in and out of my pulsing need, his mouth travelled down until he found my nipple, sucking back hard and teasing it with his teeth through the lace of my bra. All I could do was quiver and moan in response.

My God, why am I letting him do this to me? There was barely a moment of objection on my part; I'd just let him into my house and into my body. But why? Because he was hot? Because he had a big dick? Or because I was uncontrollably attracted to him? So attracted that all semblance of logic went flying out the window, along with my self-respect?

As my head dropped back and I clutched at his arms, I knew it was mostly the latter. There was just something about him. "I want you inside me," I gasped. "Please." I'd been dreaming about it, thinking about it, envisioning that feeling of fullness for months.

"I want in that tight pussy of yours. I want to fuck you so hard that even when you open your mouth, you won't be able to scream. You'll be too far gone." He said all of this while opening his jeans and sheathing his cock, readying himself to push inside me. "I can't promise this won't hurt."

"Do it," I gasped, shifting my hips to press my opening against his tip. I wanted it to hurt. I wanted to feel the shock of his intrusion and ache from it the next day.

With a groan, he slid inside inch by inch, stretching me to the point of pain but no further. "There it is," he gasped when he was fully inside. He slid his fingers into the sides of my hair and looked down at me. "That's what I've been wanting." His hips moved back and forth as his fingers tightened against the roots of my hair, pulling my head back as his mouth devoured mine.

I could barely breathe. I could barely think. All I cared about was the coil tightening in my belly, begging for release as his cock stroked my insides. I released a long, low moan against his mouth.

"That's it, duchess. Come hard. I want your cunt gripping the fuck out of my cock while you do."

I was so close, so perfectly ready to explode that when he pulled my bra down and clamped his mouth over my nipple, I did just that—mouth open, head thrown back, the cry of a wounded animal reverberating out of my chest as he moaned and then stilled as he came equally hard, a hiss between his teeth.

"Fuck me," he gasped, taking a deep breath.

"I'm pretty sure that's what you just did to me."

"Mmm," he hummed, capturing my mouth in a quick kiss, breathing me in. "I *really* like fucking you." He pulled out of me and threw his condom in the kitchen bin before tucking himself away and zipping his pants. "If only I'd met you on a different night, different time, different place."

"That wouldn't change who you are, or what you do. We could never be together." Even as the words left my mouth, my heart squeezed. Because what did he really mean by that? Did he regret that he was at that nightclub, that he chose me to go home with, that he chose me to rob *even though* we'd had such an incredible night together? Or was he saying that he wished we'd been given the chance for more, that had his crimes not connected us, perhaps it could have just been our chemistry?

I wished things were different too. *Don't go there, Holland.*

Sliding his hand back in my hair, he kissed me in a way that was deep and tormenting, his tongue taking its time exploring my mouth, stealing my breath. When he released me, he looked into my eyes for a long moment before he lifted his glass of tequila to his mouth. "To the man who steals your heart." Then he drained it, refilled it and held it out to me. "Since yours is kind of smashed on the floor." Wrapping my hand around the glass, our fingers brushed and held for a beat. I couldn't help but feel sad at his toast. *To the man who steals your heart.*

I held the glass to my lips. "That man won't be you." Closing my eyes, I downed the shot of alcohol then released my breath. I didn't know who that man would be, but I knew without a doubt that it couldn't be the one who stood in front of me, no matter how strong our attraction to each other was.

"You should probably go," I whispered as I set the glass back down and pulled my shirt back over my head, righting myself. I couldn't meet his eyes.

"Trying to push me away, duchess?" he responded, leaning down and picking up my panties. He held them out on one finger and waited until I met his gaze. My chest jolted from our unspoken connection. Then annoyance flared when he snatched my panties away as I reached for them.

"Yes," I responded honestly. "This wasn't why I went to so much trouble to find you."

"I know that. You want your mum's hairpin back. I get it. Family is important." He leaned down and slid my panties over my feet, then pulled them up my legs. "How did she die?"

"Car accident. I was eight. My parents were out cele-brating their wedding anniversary and they got T-boned by some jerk who ran a red. None of them survived." I didn't even know why I was telling him, it served no purpose other than to make me look more pitiful than I already was.

"I'm sorry." He touched my chin so I met his eyes.

"Don't be sorry, just give me back what you stole."

He searched my eyes for an uncomfortable moment,

then took a sharp inhale and picked up his shirt, pulling it over his head while he spoke. "I know where the pin is. I'll get it to you, and then you'll never see me again."

I turned away from his gaze. "I think that's for the best."

When he didn't answer or move, I chanced a glance at him and met two very cold and possibly angry eyes. *Why would he be angry at me? He's the fuck-up in this relationship.*

Relationship? I squashed that thought before it had any more of a chance to grow.

"Goodnight, Holland," he said, his voice curt as he turned and walked straight over the broken glass and out the front door. I jumped when it slammed shut, then closed my eyes and tried to ignore the emotion that was welling in them. I didn't know what it was about Nate that had me wanting him when he was so obviously bad for me.

Pressing my knees together and pulling my shirt down, I looked at the mess on the floor. I was still on the bench and had no shoes on. He'd left me high and dry in the middle of a glass-shard minefield.

What a jerk. I was glad he was gone.

I picked up the tequila and took a swig straight from the bottle. At least I'd done something right tonight. I felt weak for having sex with him, but I was proud of myself for telling him to leave.

Sliding down from the bench, I was careful not to get glass caught in my feet while I picked my way across the floor to the cupboard where I kept my mop and broom. As I cleaned up the mess, my head started to ache, a combination of stress, shame and tequila. After a quick shower, I felt even worse. It was like a migraine was coming on, but I'd never had one before.

Feeling the full weight of gravity pulling at my limbs, I climbed into bed, falling asleep the moment my head hit the pillow.

A PAIN on my left side roused me from my sleep. I couldn't remember a time when my mattress had felt so uncomfortable. When I shifted slightly, the first thing I noticed was my lack of a pillow. Opening my eyes, the second thing I noticed was the carpet—right next to my head. I was on the *freaking floor*. For a split second, I hoped I'd somehow managed to fall out of bed, but I knew that was too good to be true. I had knowingly fucked the thief, after all.

Shit.

Sitting up, wincing from my aching body, I looked around my bedroom. It was completely empty. Forcing myself to my feet, I stumbled to my door. A quick perusal of the rest of the apartment showed that it was empty too.

"Fuuuuuuck!" I screeched, stomping my feet and flailing my arms. "Fuck! Fuck! Fuck!" They hadn't even left me clothes this time. All I had were the Kmart pyjamas I had on with sloths on them. God, I wanted the floor to open and swallow me whole. I couldn't believe I'd let this happen again. I *knew* I should've called the police when I found him, but no, I had to be stupid and actually trust that the guy would do the decent thing and give my mother's hairpin back.

Boy, was I a shitty judge of character.

I couldn't even cry this time. I was so damn angry—at myself and at him—that I couldn't do anything except pace back and forth, grunting and hissing like some caged animal. What was I supposed to do? I couldn't walk to Alesha's this time, because not only was I in my pyjamas, but I also didn't have any shoes. *That arsehole!*

With my head aching, both from the stress of the situation and the aftereffects of whatever drug he'd slipped me, I went into the bathroom, hoping they at least had the decency to leave me some headache tablets.

When I opened the cabinet, that's literally all there was. Well, a pack of ibuprofen and an envelope with my name on it.

Picking up both, I swallowed two pills and then tore open the envelope. There was a note, and inside the note, my mother's hairpin. "Oh my God." I hugged it to my chest, giddy with happiness from its return. He'd actually come through. He'd done it in the cuntiest way possible, but at least he gave it back to me. I slipped it into my hair for safekeeping.

Confession time: I lied. I was never a Boy Scout. Stop trusting shitty people. Here is your mother's hairpin. Since it's the only thing you care about, it's the only thing I've left you with. Have a nice life, duchess. You won't be seeing me again. N.

P.S Don't bother looking for me at the gym. I won't be there anymore.

P.P.S I really do wish things were different. I could get addicted to that snatch of yours.

Somehow, I managed a laugh at the last line. He was probably the most self-centred, arrogant man I'd ever met. Still, I wished things were different too. We had a great connection and could've been great together under better circumstances.

Knowing I had to make at least one phone call to deal with the mess I was in, I went next door and asked to use their phone, telling them I accidentally got locked out when I went to check the mail instead of offering the truth. It seemed too ridiculous that I could possibly be robbed again, less than four months after the first time. Although, how they'd managed to move the entire contents of my apartment out twice without anyone asking questions was beyond my understanding.

After my phone call, I returned to my apartment and sat on the floor, waiting for a knock at the door. It came forty-five minutes later, and there Alesha stood, looking perfectly made up for work with a question mark etched into her expression and a bag of clothes in her hand.

"What's the emergency? Everything O—shit." She stepped over the threshold and looked around the empty room. "He robbed you again."

Wincing a little, I nodded.

"Why did you even let him in? Oh no, did you sleep with him again too?"

Full-blown wince.

"*Holland.*" She put her hands on her hips and looked at me like I was a naughty toddler.

"I couldn't help it, Leesh. He makes me feel *so good.* I'm weak. I'm pitiful and weak."

Still looking around the room, she clutched the leather strap of her handbag at her shoulder. "He must be if *this* could happen again. Have you called the police yet?"

"I'm not calling them this time."

"Why? How are you going to replace your things without a police report?"

"I'm going to go get them back myself."

"I'm sorry. You're going to do what now?"

"Aunty Maya gave me this tracking card that's hidden in my handbag. All we have to do is activate it and we can find out where they went. Then we can get a moving van of our own and steal my stuff back." I shrugged as if the idea wasn't even a bit preposterous.

"Why don't you activate the tracker, then call the cops with the location and *they* can go get it all for you?"

"Because it might be too late then. By the time they mobilise units—or whatever they do—Nate and his thieving helpers could've found the tracker and gotten rid of it. We need to move *now*." I pulled the clothes out of the plastic bag she gave me and started getting dressed. It was a pair of black harem pants and a too-small T-shirt with Wonder Woman on the front. It barely covered my stomach, and poor Wonder Woman's face was stretched across my left boob.

"That is the craziest fucking idea you've ever had, and I've known you for twenty-four years. I survived home bleach jobs, crashing parties we weren't invited to, and that time you convinced me to write something nasty about Stacey Ryan in the bathroom stall and I got caught by the vice principal."

"Considering she didn't even know the difference

between 'your' and 'you're', I think Stacey deserved every properly punctuated syllable you wrote about her."

"That's true. But I still got detention over it."

"And it made you badass, so you're welcome."

Shaking her head, she started laughing. "Of all your crazy schemes, Holland, this by far takes the cake. You're not seriously going to try to steal your stuff back, are you?"

"Of course. And if I'm lucky, he'll lead us to where he lives and I can rob him too. It'll be the perfect revenge. Give me your phone." With her lips pursed in disapproval, she did as I asked, and I brought up the website where I could log in and track my bag. It popped up on the screen plain as day in an industrial area in Geelong. "Feel like going on a road trip?" I asked, holding the screen out for her to see.

"Only if you promise not to confront him. If we go, we go in there all stealth mode, locate your stuff, and then we call the cops to do the dirty work. I beg you. We are *not* stealing anything."

"You are one massive party pooper."

She took her phone back and placed her hands on her hips. "Considering you need me to drive you to this place, it's either my rules or we don't go at all."

With a groan, I rolled my eyes. "Fine. You win. Reconnaissance only."

She smiled and handed me the pair of black espadrille flats she'd purchased along with my clothes. "I knew you'd see it my way. Now, call in sick to work. We've got some thieves to catch."

Stuffing my feet into the canvas shoes, I muttered under my breath as I followed her to her car. Stealing everything back and robbing him would've been the sweetest payback for a man like Nate. But Alesha was right—without her help, there was no way I could do anything. I had no transport and no access to my money to rent a moving truck. Watching him get arrested was just going to have to do.

———

"IT'S SELF-STORAGE," I mused as we pulled up to the building the tracking app had sent us to. There were several cars in the parking lot along with signage promising the best rates for self-storage around. "How are we going to know which one it's in?"

"We can't know without going inside. And I really doubt they're going to let us go walking around in there on our own. It'd be a maze. Plus, I'm pretty sure we'd be trespassing, and I'm not paying to rent a storage unit just to give you a reason to snoop. I think this might be where the cops need to be called in."

"I suppose." I pouted, disappointed that we hadn't arrived in time to spot Nate unloading my furniture from a truck. We could've caught him and his accomplice red-handed—and it wouldn't have hurt to watch their muscles bulge as they carried some of the bulkier items while we waited for police assistance either.

Just as Alesha started keying in the phone number, movement in the entry caught my attention and I grabbed her arm. "Oh my God. Look," I gasped, lowering in my seat. A group of four men laughed and messed around, looking completely carefree as they headed towards an SUV parked in the lot not far from us. One of those men was none other than Nate the thief. Another was the brother I'd seen at the gym. I'd never seen the other two before, but they all had similar builds and features, leading me to believe they were all related. *The Cartwright brothers.* The girl at the gym had gone to school with them. It made sense.

"Wow," Alesha breathed, her jaw dropping as we watched them larking about. "That is too much hotness for one group of men." She slipped her phone into her pocket.

The SUV they walked towards started its engine before they'd even gotten to it. "There's a fifth person," I noted as they all piled into the car.

"Another hot guy, I hope." She craned her neck to try and see through the tinted windows as they pulled out of the parking lot.

Is she drooling?

"Follow them," I insisted, leaning over and pressing the button on the dash to start the car.

Her hands gripped the steering wheel, and then she put the car into gear, but we didn't move anywhere. "Wait. This is crazy. Call the cops, Holland. Give them the plate number and let them handle this." She handed me her phone.

"OK, I will. But please, Alesha, they're getting away. Just *follow* them. I only want to see where they go."

She stared at me a moment then released the parking brake with a sigh. "Fine," she said, pulling out and following the SUV into traffic. "But we call the cops the moment we see where they go."

"Of course."

People often called watching TV a waste of time, but this was one instance where all that television watching finally paid off; because of spy shows like *Burn Notice,* we knew to keep a couple of cars back at all times, and not change lanes unless there was an exit coming up. We followed them like pros.

As I expected, they led us to the city I'd found him in: Torquay, a city synonymous with surfing and beaches. It was pretty much a straight shot down Surf Coast Highway until they turned off on Combes Road, then took an immediate left onto Jetti Lane.

"Shit, keep driving," I told Alesha as we watched them turn.

"Why? We could lose them." She craned her neck but drove on like I asked.

"They just turned into a lane—a *lane.* That means dead-end street. If we followed them straight in, they'd notice." I kept my eyes on their car for as long as I could before it disappeared around a bend. "Chuck a U-ey up here. We'll double back and park before the bend."

"And do what?"

"Look for their car on foot." It felt like an obvious next step.

"I don't know. I really think we've narrowed it down enough. We could call the cops now and be done with it." She indicated, then turned into their street despite her protests.

"Call them with what information? They're hiding stolen goods in one of hundreds of storage containers, and we *think* they live on Jetti Lane. We need at least one thing specific, Leesh. They'll never even know we were here." I really wanted to see where they went. We were so close.

"All right," she said, trepidation in her voice as she parked on the side of the road. "But give me back my phone. I'm keeping the emergency services number on my screen in case things go bad."

"They won't. Reconnaissance only. Trust me."

She hit the power button on her phone enough times to bring up the SOS slider. "Doesn't hurt to be prepared," she said, slipping the phone back in her pocket. Then we got out of the car and looked around the long gravel road lined with towering eucalyptus trees. Cicadas sang their ear-piercing excuse for a song against the midday sun.

"Their car went that way," I said, squinting towards the bend in the road.

"OK. Let's go find out what kind of place a group of sexy-as-sin thieves like to gather at."

"JESUS. Robbing people must be lucrative. This place is *huge*," Alesha stage-whispered as we crept along the tree line that surrounded a large white-rendered two-storey house. So far, we'd circled the property and noticed a three-car garage that was separate from the house, an in-ground swimming pool and a tennis court—pretty swanky. It was on a private block of land, well-shielded from street view by the trees we were currently taking cover in. The gardens were well maintained, and the surroundings were so quiet that I doubted any of the neighbours could hear you if you screamed. An unsettling thought.

"They must clean out a lot of apartments," I said. *And some of them twice.*

"They must. I wonder how many rooms it has." She held up her finger and started to count windows.

"Enough for five brothers, I guess."

"You think they're all brothers and they *all* live here?"

"They look like brothers. And why have such a big house otherwise?"

"Maybe this is where they grew up? Or maybe—" Her mouth made an O shape as she sucked in her breath. "Maybe they're *robbing* it."

"They wouldn't fit much in that SUV," I stated, trying to see if there was any sort of movement in the house. "At most they'd be casing it."

"Oh wow. I'm going to find out."

"Reconnaissance only," I hissed as she darted out into the open. What happened to the cautious girl who wanted to stay in the car and call the police? Suddenly she was Veronica Mars willing to risk it all on a case.

With my heart in my throat, I dashed after her, keeping my head down and moving in a half crouch, as if that would make me look less conspicuous as I ran across an open space.

"Are you insane?" I gasped, heaving from the exertion. Even after all my recent gym visits, I was not even a tiny bit fit, and it was possible that I was in the midst of a heart attack. I pressed my palm against my chest and tried to catch my breath.

"Like you said, we need to know exactly what's happening before we call the cops. If they're only casing the joint, they might not be here when the cops arrive, right?" She twisted around, placing her hands on the windowsill and pulling herself up to peer inside.

"Do you see anything?" I asked, keeping my eyes on our surroundings.

"It's too dark in there, and the sun's reflection is getting in the way." She cupped her hands against the glass to cut out the glare. "Wait, I see movement. They're in the kitchen, I think. Looks like they're—"

Yip, yip, yip, yip, yip!

With an ear-piercing squeal, she fell back on the grass while a Boston terrier attacked the window from the other side, barking and scratching, spit landing on the glass.

"What is it, Rogue?" a male voice asked from inside.

"Shit," I hissed, grabbing Alesha's wrist and pulling her against the side of the house. We were crouched under the window, holding our breath and trying to be as two-dimensional as possible when the curtains moved and the dog pawed the window, still barking.

"We need to get out of here," Alesha whispered, to which I nodded and pointed to the corner of the house. The detached garage sat maybe six feet away and would provide our best chance for cover and escape.

"If we crawl, they won't see us."

She gulped, then nodded and closed her eyes in silent prayer.

Say one for me too.

Watching the window carefully, I waited until the curtains closed again and heard, "I can't see anything. Maybe it was a magpie or something?"

"Nah, mate, there was a squeal. Someone's there."

"Go, go!" I commanded, pushing Alesha's shoulder before crawling after her as fast as I could. They had heard her. It wouldn't be long before they decided to do a thorough search.

Yip, yip, yip, yip, yip!

"Faster," I gasped, pushing Alesha on the bum. The barking sounded like it was outside now, and for some insane reason we kept crawling, only faster. I supposed it was the same logic that girls in horror films subscribed to: they knew they're about to get caught, so they just lay there screaming while the killer stabs them to death. In this case, we kept crawling, butts in the air while a small, angry dog ran to catch us. Big mistake. Huge. The second his teeth sank into my arse, I face-planted in the grass, howling in pain.

"Run, Alesha! Save yourself!" I screeched.

Leaping to her feet, she sprinted for the tree line. I'd never seen her move so fast. *Go, you good thing,* I silently urged, lying prone while a terrier tore the butt out of my pants.

"Rogue. Down."

The dog obeyed, sitting on the ground with his mouth open and his tongue hanging out, smiling. *Is that my blood staining its teeth?* I felt faint.

Just as I thought I might swoon, large hands wrapped around my middle and hauled me to my feet. "What do we have here?" a deep voice asked, laughter in his tone. It wasn't Nate. This guy was a little bigger, if that was even possible, and a little more tanned, with fairer hair. Same blue eyes.

Hanging from his hold, my feet off the ground and my heart beating so hard I thought it might crack my ribs, I released a nervous laugh. "Would you believe that my car broke down and I need to use your phone?"

He shook his head.

"I'm looking for my dog?"

He shook his head again.

"How about—I live next door, and I'd like to borrow a cup of sugar?"

"Nice try." He carried me towards the house, and I had little choice but to hang there while my butt cheek bled out from the dog bite. Classy.

At least Alesha was going to get away. She'd call the

cops and I'd be out of here in no time—if these guys didn't kill me first. But were they killers? That was something I didn't know. Stealing was one thing, murder a whole other kettle of fish. I hoped they'd just let me off with a stern warning after I agreed to let them keep everything I owned and not tell anyone I knew where they lived. But that was probably wishful thinking on my part. No, I was in serious shit.

"Go, Toby!" One of the brothers stood just outside the entryway laughing as another—the one I'd seen at the gym —sprinted after Alesha. He was *fast*.

My eyes went wide. "*Noo!*"

The body behind me chuckled as the one called Toby flew through the air and collided with her midsection, tackling her to the ground where they rolled over a couple of times from the momentum.

Alesha had spunk. She tried to fight off her assailant, succeeded, broke free, ran two more steps and then got tackled to the ground again.

"You need some help, mate?" the guy who had me asked. "That tiny girl giving you trouble?"

"Fuck you, Sam," Toby snapped as he picked Alesha up by the waist and threw her over his shoulder. She kicked and hit, but he held her steady.

We were both carried unceremoniously into the house and set on the tiled floor in a light and airy entryway. All five brothers crowded around with Nate standing in the middle, an imposing bunch. I'd be forgiven if I peed a little. They did not look pleased to have drop-in visitors.

"Duchess," Nate said, his arms folded across his middle as he glared my way. "Care to explain what you're doing here?"

"You know this one?" the guy holding me, Sam, asked.

"I know her," Nate stated. "You can let go."

I shook my arms free the moment Sam relaxed his grip.

"What about this one?" Toby asked, still holding tight to Alesha's arm. "You know *her* too?"

Nate looked at Toby for a long moment, something unspoken in their exchange. Then he nodded once. "Let go of her."

Alesha jumped almost a metre away when released. "Fucking jerks," she yelled, shoving at Toby, who laughed like she was a cute kitten with no claws.

"We're the jerks?" Sam started. "We're not the ones skulking around your windows."

Alesha's hands went to her hips, her cheeks bright red as her wide eyes absorbed the giant man standing before her. "No, you're just the arseholes robbing my friend of everything she owns—twice."

"Shit. I thought the big one looked familiar," one of the others said. He was a slimmer version of Nate, with golden-brown hair that hung loose to his shoulders. He had surfer written all over him.

"Who are you calling big?" Alesha snapped. "You look like a girl with your stupid long hair."

The brother closest to him snorted out a laugh. "Told you, bro."

Alesha curled her lip in a way that said, 'See?' I'd never seen her be so forthright before. I suppose her fight or flight had kicked in, and she was definitely a fighter. I, on the other hand, was completely mute. I had no idea what to do or say, and just kept sneaking looks at Nate to try and gauge what he was thinking. His expression gave away nothing. *And my butt is killing me.*

"You're a fucking idiot," Sam said under his breath, directing the comment at Nate as he ran a hand through his thick dark hair. It curled a little at the ends, needing a cut. But the extra length totally worked on him.

Nate worked his jaw in response, his light eyes landing on me, somehow getting darker. "I know," he said finally.

Toby moved towards Nate and shoved him on the shoulder. "You'd better fix this. I told you to leave her the fuck alone, and now she's *here*."

He told him to what?

Nate clenched his teeth. "I will, OK? Just take that one into the other room." He indicated Alesha. "Holland and I need to talk."

"*Don't* let her leave," Toby commanded through clenched teeth as he jabbed a finger into Nate's chest.

"Come on, darlin'," the big burly Sam said, taking Alesha by the arm. "Seems you're gonna be here awhile. You drink beer?"

"Ahhh, yeah," she replied with trepidation as she tottered along beside him. She needed to crane her neck to see his face. The others followed, filing out of the room in a long line. Lord, I hoped they didn't do anything to hurt her.

"What the fuck are you doing here?" Nate hissed after they'd gone. "I gave you what you wanted. Our business relationship has concluded."

"Then maybe you shouldn't have stolen all my shit again. It's like you were begging me to come find you."

He looked away and shook his head. "I was actually hoping I'd never see you again."

"Tired of my snug pussy all of a sudden?" I bit back, his words causing a slight sting to my ego.

His eyes, previously filled with annoyance, shone with amusement as he shook his head. "I never said that. How did you find us, anyway?"

I thought about not telling him, but there was little point. It'd all come out eventually. "There's a GPS tracker in my handbag."

He laughed, but the amusement had left his eyes. "Jesus. So you expected this? What are you, a cop? Is this a sting?"

"Maybe." I shrugged, acting coy.

"Maybe," he repeated, the tip of his tongue running over his bottom lip as he stepped towards me until we were toe to toe. I could smell him, that manly scent mixed with the sea tickling my nostrils and making me heady. I fought to keep my eyes on his, to keep my breathing even, wary because I wasn't sure if he wanted to fuck me or kill me. He was a man who loved sex, but I had yet to see any sort of tenderness from him. I hadn't thought he was capable of hurting someone, but you could only push a man so far before he did things he hadn't considered for self-preservation. Me being there meant I had enough information to send him and his brothers to prison. I was a danger to him.

He was a danger to me.

Suddenly he sprang to life, wrapping his hand around my throat and squeezing. I made a choking sound as I struggled for air, grabbing at his fingers in panic. *Oh God. He's going to kill me.* No more singing, no more teaching, no more good times with friends. It would all be over. Aunt Maya would be beside herself.

His face was right in mine. "You'd better be real fucking honest with me right now, duchess. Are. You. A. Cop?"

I shook my head and tried to say no, but there wasn't any sound besides some strangled gurgling.

He released me roughly and I coughed repeatedly, trying to fill my starved lungs with air. "Shit," I gasped, tears burning my eyes.

"Explain," he demanded, his voice gruff and angry.

"My… my aunt was worried." I paused to cough and clear my throat. "She knew I was looking for the hairpin and bought me the tracker for safety. When I woke up to an empty house this morning, I used the app to find you."

"But your bag isn't here."

"I know. We tracked it to the storage facility in Geelong. You were leaving when we arrived, so we decided to follow you."

"Then you decided to snoop?"

I nodded. "Yes. But we didn't call the cops. No one knows except me and Alesha, I swear to you. Just let us go and no one will ever know anything."

He looked at me long and hard, then took a breath. "Abbot. Kristian," he called over his shoulder, and two younger-looking brothers appeared in the doorway. Twins, perhaps? One had long hair, the other's cropped close to his scalp, but their faces were the same.

"What's up?" the long-haired one asked.

"I need you to drive back to the storage facility. Find the handbag. Inside is a… what does it look like?" he asked me.

"It's small, square and blue." I held up my fingers to show the size. "It's in the pocket on the outside." I felt so stupid explaining this to them. "Oh, and while you're there, can I grab my mobile and wallet please? It was such a pain in the arse to cancel all those cards and pay for a new licence last time. I kind of don't want to go through that again."

The boys looked from me to Nate with an expression that said *Is she crazy?* Nate rolled his eyes and sent them on their way.

"So, five brothers, huh? That must have been crazy growing up." I smiled as if it was a perfectly normal time to make conversation.

"No crazier than most."

"It must be nice. I never had any siblings. What are their names?"

Nate looked at me for a moment, then sighed. "Toby is the oldest. I'm next. Then Sam."

"The other two are twins?"

He nodded. "Abbot and Kristian. Abbot has hair, Kristian has the military do."

"And you all steal together?"

"It's the family business."

"How lovely of your parents to teach you such an admirable vocation." A saccharine smile dripped from my lips.

He looked at me, his eyes hard, arms still crossed over his chest. "Just our mother. None of us knew our father."

"Of course you didn't. And your mother is where? Prison?"

"I'm right here, actually," a female voice said from the foot of the stairs. She had the dog in her arms, and I swear that mutt had a piece of my pants in his teeth. "Care to introduce me to your new friend, Nathaniel?" She was tall and thin, with elegant features and dark blonde hair threaded with grey.

"Holland, this is my mother, Jasmine Cartwright."

"It's a pleasure to meet you, ma'am," I said, opting to be polite to the dragon in its den. I even held out my hand to shake hers. She just looked down her nose at me.

"Don't piss on my feet and tell me it's raining, Holland. There's no pleasure in this meeting."

I lowered my hand and pressed it against the curve of my thigh. "No, I suppose not." What was I even thinking?

"Do you like the house?" she asked. Despite how normal her question sounded, it set me off ease.

"It's beautiful," I stated.

She smiled, but it was too straight and didn't touch her eyes. "Wonderful. Because you won't be leaving anytime soon." My stomach plummeted, landing somewhere in my unsteady legs. I had to force myself to remain impassive instead of dropping to the ground and crying—which was what I really wanted to do. "You've probably guessed, but we don't take kindly to drop-in visitors here. Especially not the kind who seem so filled with information as you and your friend seem to be."

"So, that's it? I'm a prisoner now?"

"Just until we figure out what to do with you." Jasmine waved a hand in my direction, then carried the dog into the other room, leaving me and Nate alone again.

"I can't fucking believe this."

"We can't exactly let you go, Holland. I'm sure you understand that." He actually sounded a little apologetic.

"I understand that perfectly. What I can't believe is that a grown fucking man is still living with his mother."

"*That's* what you're focusing on?" It wasn't what I was

focusing on. Inside, I was freaking the fuck out, but humour was my defence mechanism. I could mock anything. I couldn't help it. "I do have a place of my own. We all do. It's just easier to stay here when we're working."

"Fucking good for you." I crossed my arms across my middle, not giving a shit if he was interested in my tits or not. I was pissed that not only had he robbed me twice, but now I was a captive. And what did 'figure out what to do with me' mean?

"You're pissed," he stated.

"Of course I'm pissed! You can't keep us here. We have jobs and family who will notice we've gone. Alesha's father is the most overprotective man on the planet and will go to the ends of the earth to find her, and my aunt will just use the app for the GPS card to find the last-known location. Then *she'll* call the cops, and keeping me here won't have made a single bit of difference."

He worked his jaw thoughtfully, then pulled his phone from his pocket.

"Abbot?" He paused to listen. "That tracker, put it in an envelope and post it to Guam or something. Also, get Holland's phone and her clothes. She's going to need more than a pair of pants with the arse torn out." He listened for a moment, then disconnected.

"What are you planning to do now?"

"Nothing different. I'm still planning on keeping you here. You're just going to make a few phone calls using those acting skills of yours. You can make everyone believe you've gone on an impromptu holiday, can't you?"

"I don't know. Maybe I'm no good. Did 'Oh, yes! Nate!' sound believable to you?"

His eyes narrowed as the echo from my fake orgasm made the high-ceiling entryway even quieter once it stopped.

"On second thought, maybe we should get you to send a text."

I frowned. "Excuse me?" It was some of my finest acting. I'd go so far as to say I gave Meg Ryan a run for her money.

"Duchess, I've heard you come so hard that your voice didn't even register, felt your juices pour into my mouth while your clit pulsed under my tongue. Standing here pretending that was all fake is the biggest joke I've ever heard, not to mention the worst acting I've ever seen."

My mouth fell open and I really wanted to stomp my foot, but didn't. "It wasn't meant to be great acting," I lied. "It was meant to be an insult. And I do not *pour* when I come."

Folding his arms across his chest, he smiled. "Oh yes, you do. You're a gusher, Holland."

I gasped, my cheeks heating. "I am not."

He stepped closer. "You are. And it's so fucking hot, I get hard every time I think about it."

My eyes travelled down. Yep, he was hard. My tingly bits tingled. My breathing shallowed. It wasn't a response I wanted to be having when I was in the midst of a hostage situation, but my body had a mind of its own. Traitor.

Swallowing hard, I forced myself to meet his eyes while jutting my chin out defiantly. "Maybe I have a bladder control problem." I knew I didn't have a bladder problem, but as I already mentioned, mocking jokes were my first line of defence. "Maybe I didn't ejaculate at all. Maybe you drank pee instead."

His eyes twinkled. His mouth twitched. Then he threw his head back and roared with laughter.

Swiping his thumb across his eye to catch a mirth-filled tear, he finally got control of his bouncing shoulders. "You really are a shitty actor, duchess."

LAUGHTER FILTERED up the hallway as Nate led me to the back of the house. It was there we found Alesha playing pool with Sam while Toby and Jasmine watched. They were hanging out and having fun like it was a normal Friday night and they were just friends instead of captive and captors. It was a surreal scene to walk in on, especially after the tension-filled altercation I'd just come from. To make things even more cozy, they all had beers in their hands and immediately offered one to Nate and me when we entered the room. I declined. I was never accepting another drink from a Cartwright again. Also, I tended to not feel like socialising when I was being held against my will.

"Ha! Suck on that!" Alesha hollered, shooting a fist in the air after she managed to sink three balls with one shot. *Glad she's having a good time.* I wondered if she fully understood the mess we'd landed ourselves in.

"She's good," Sam said, jerking his thumb over his shoulder to a pleased-as-punch Alesha, who was draining her bottle of beer while fighting a grin. *Maybe she's drunk? That might be why she seems so happy right now.* I couldn't get over what I was witnessing. Not only was Alesha acting as though we were simply hanging out with a bunch of guys, but she was *talking* to them. There wasn't any of that stammering messiness that normally jabbered out of her mouth. She actually appeared to be having *fun.*

"I am kicking your arse," Alesha crowed, gladly accepting another bottle of beer from an amused Toby. He met my eyes, something unknown flickering across his expression as he transferred his attention back to the pool game. He unsettled me. It was like there were waves of anger coming off him, but only towards me. To everyone else, he seemed fine.

Jasmine cocked her head to the side and looked between Nate and me. "You two get everything straightened out?" she asked, her eyes watching the room with hawklike attention as the devil dog sat obediently at her feet, licking its chops every time it glanced my way.

Nate nodded once. "I just need to have a chat with the queen of the pool hall here. Then I think we'll all know where we stand."

"Oh, I know where we stand," Alesha said, chalking her cue. "We found your hideout and your base of operations, and now we're not allowed to leave. I've watched enough TV to know how these things work."

"And you're not afraid?" Toby asked, amusement in his tone as he watched her line up a shot.

"Why would I be afraid? I stand in a refrigerated room and put make-up on corpses for a living. This is the most excitement I've had in years. There's hot guys and beer, and *bonus,* my dad can't come and haul me off to confessional every chance he gets. This place is like a resort to me." She grinned, then took a shot.

The family all exchanged silent conversation while I just stood there with my mouth open, wondering what the hell happened to my nervous best friend.

Jasmine placed her half-empty bottle of beer on the grey marble–topped bar that was built into the cream-coloured walls. "Can I see you in the office?" She directed her question to Nate, not waiting for a response before she walked across the terracotta tiles, her feet bare and Rogue the Boston terrier clicking along behind her.

Nate followed without a word, leaving me alone with his brothers and Alesha. Toby looked at me head to toe and then back up again. Was that disdain in his eyes? "You're trouble," he stated, sucking back on his beer.

"*I'm* trouble?" I pointed to myself. "I'll have you know my life was nothing but simple up until the moment you lot came into my life with your five-finger discounts."

"Insurance companies need us to stay in business," he stated.

Before he could go on, I rolled my eyes and added, "People wouldn't insure if people didn't steal, keeps the economy going, yadda, yadda, yadda. I've already heard the spiel. You're still a bunch of criminals."

"Holland!" Alesha reprimanded me. "Don't be so rude. We're guests here."

"They are *keeping* us here, Alesha. We *aren't allowed* to leave. How are you OK with this?" There was a shrill sound to my voice.

She shrugged. "What do you want me to do? Cry? Scream? Shake and rock in the corner? They're not going to hurt us."

"What makes you so sure about that?"

"I think the fact that I'm standing here playing pool instead of being tied to chair with a gag in my mouth might be a pretty good tip-off. Plus they've had ample opportunity to hurt you, in particular, and so far you've just had sex—sex so good, I might add, that you went back for a second round, which is what landed us here in the first place."

"So this is my fault?"

"Yes, Holland," she asserted. "This is *very much* your fault. We might as well make the best of it."

"But we *can't leave*."

"So? What are we going to go back to? Netflix and no chill? Your apartment is empty. Mine is filled with religious paraphernalia. I *like* it here."

"B-but…," I spluttered, trying to come up with a reason why she should be feeling as indignant as I was. "But they're thieves."

"The economy needs thieves," she parroted. She'd obviously taken a really large gulp of the Kool-Aid.

Sam walked over and slung his arm over her shoulders, completely dwarfing her with his size. "She learns fast, this one. You might want to take a few pages out of her book, Holly." His blue eyes landed on mine as he drank from his bottle in silent warning.

"Don't call me that," I growled.

"I think I'll call you whatever I want." He took a step forwards, but Alesha grabbed his forearm.

"Just not Holly, OK, babe?" *Babe?* "It's the pet name her parents gave her. She hasn't let anyone call her that since they died."

One of his eyes twitched slightly and his lip curled in a

sneer. "Then I'll call her hole. Since that's all she is to my brother anyway—a hole to fuck."

My eyes locked with Alesha's. There was compassion in hers, but I was surprised she hadn't jumped to my defence. *Ouch.*

Toby chuckled. "By the expression on her face, she'll likely become a black hole to destroy you, Sam."

Sam growled and turned away, hooking his arm around Alesha's waist and tugging her with him.

I pressed my lips together, my stomach twisting in discomfort. *I'm living in the Twilight Zone.* How could Alesha be so accepting? It was obvious they were dangerous. We were a threat to them; we had the power to bring the police right to their door. At what point would they decide it would be easier to drop us in a ditch than it would be to keep us quiet? The thought hurt my head.

Alesha returned to playing pool, innocuously joking around with Sam while my stomach grew tighter, my chest began to ache. I felt claustrophobic even though I was in an open space.

What have we gotten ourselves into? Why didn't I call the cops when I had the chance?

As my eyes searched the room, analysing all points of entry and exit, I caught Toby staring at me, his eyes cool as steel. There was something unrestrained about him that set all my nerves on edge. If there was any real danger in this place, it would come from him.

"You might want to do something about that bite on your arse," he said after a moment. "Dogs' mouths aren't the cleanest things."

I twisted my hips and fingered the tear in my pants,

noting the stickiness of the drying blood. "Am I allowed to use a bathroom?"

He nodded and pointed to a door off the games room. "There's a bathroom in there. And don't even think about climbing out the windows. They're all alarmed."

Walking cautiously towards the door, I turned the knob, pushing it open to reveal a bedroom with grey carpet, white walls and timber furniture. The bedspread was several shades of grey with silver thread and beading. Above it, a framed black-and-white picture of a silhouetted girl looking out at the setting sun. Besides a few decorative pieces, there weren't any trinkets around, no signs that anyone occupied it. A guest bedroom, perhaps? I continued through and entered the en-suite bathroom, almost falling over when I caught my dishevelled appearance in the mirror. There was dirt on my cheek, grass in my hair, and my complexion looked bright red and patchy.

There's no way Nate would want me. Not looking like this. I looked like a homeless person.

I stopped myself, frowning at the thought. Why would I want Nate to want me? After everything he'd done, how could I possibly be holding out any hope that he'd want me? I should *hate him*. I should want his head served to me on a platter, his balls delivered for my lunch.

Yet there I was, looking at the mess in the mirror and the first thought I had was 'Does he still think I'm pretty?' God, I was a sad and sorry excuse for a self-respecting woman.

Turning on the tap, I used the hand soap to wash my face before I finger-combed my hair and tied it back into a ponytail. Opening the cupboards, looking for any first aid supplies, I found cotton pads, Dettol and some Band-Aids. That would have to do.

Wetting a flannel, I pulled my pants down so they were just below my arse cheeks, then tried to angle myself so I could see the damage that little dog did. My skin argued against the coarse cloth as I cleaned the tacky blood away, and I winced a little from the pain. I was *not* looking forward to using the antiseptic.

Just as I was rinsing the blood from the flannel, a large semi-familiar figure filled the door frame, causing my insides to flip excitedly, nervously. He held a first aid kit.

"Looks sore," Nate said, eyes on my bare arse.

"That little dog has a good set of jaws," I replied, trying to keep my voice even as I continued to clean myself up.

"Let me help you." He stepped closer, setting the first aid kit on the vanity. The moment he was in my space, I could feel the pull of his body calling to mine, stealing my breath. I wasn't sure I could be trusted alone with this man.

"I can do it myself."

He wrapped his hand around mine and pried the flannel from my grip. "I wasn't asking permission."

Placing a hand on the top of my arse, he pushed my T-shirt a little higher, then crouched so he was level with my injury. Gently, he wiped at the small puncture marks.

"I don't think they'll need stitches. The bleeding has already stopped." He took the cotton pads and Dettol from where I'd placed them and saturated the pad, pressing it against my arse cheek.

"Fuck," I hissed, the pain like needles in my brain.

"Almost done," he said, his voice soft as he dabbed at the area.

I leaned forwards, gripping the edge of the basin as I tried to focus on anything but the sting from the wound. "Everything sorted with your mother?" I asked through gritted teeth, thinking that maybe conversation would keep my mind off it.

He blew gently on my skin. "She's angry. Rightly so. I messed up."

"Because of me?"

"Mm-hmm." He opened the first aid kit and took out a large adhesive plaster. "I put my desires ahead of the job. And now we have two extra people to worry about."

"You think we'll go to the cops." It was more of a statement than a question.

He laid the plaster over my wound and smoothed it with his hand. "Wouldn't you?" He looked up and met my eyes.

"If you hadn't caught us... probably."

"So now we have to work out what we're going to do about that. Do we keep you?" He grabbed the waist of my pants and pulled them down my legs. My insides tingled while at the same time I tried to hold them up.

"Don't," I argued.

He only tugged harder. "Do we let you go and hope for the best? Or do we make you disappear and our problems along with it?"

I closed my eyes. I didn't want to disappear. "Nate," I whispered, pleading in my voice.

He wrapped a hand around my ankle, lifting my leg as he pushed my shoe off and fully removed my pants leg, then did the same on the other side.

"Please, Nate," I whispered. "Just let me go. I won't talk."

"*She* was leaning towards getting rid of you. There's a lot of vacant land around. It'd be hard to find someone if we buried them deep enough...."

My eyes pricked with tears and my throat tightened. "Wh-what did you want?" I asked, breathing hard as his fingers danced over my skin, heading towards my apex. I shifted away, not wanting him to touch me while we were having this conversation.

"To keep you. My desire for you is, after all, the reason we got into this mess."

"And you still desire me?" I already knew the answer to that. This thing between us was inexplicable. My brain said to hate him, but my body cried out with joy whenever he was near.

"Very much." His fingers brushed lightly against my outer lips. "All I can think about is being inside you."

My hands tightened on the basin in front of me and I gasped. "And she... she agreed to let you k-keep me?"

"She thinks I should be punished for putting the family in danger. Getting rid of you would serve that purpose." He pushed a thick finger inside me, his breathing kicking up a notch as he pressed his lips against my arse, just below the sticking plaster. I wanted to cry out in fear but also surrender to the ecstasy.

"Oh God," I gasped, overwhelmed by the opposite emotions. They swirled uncomfortably in my gut and made my body shake. "Don't do this."

"I talked her out of it." He moved his other hand to the front of my thighs, sliding up until his fingers found my clit and gently teased. "I reminded her that we were thieves, not murderers. We've come to an... arrangement of sorts."

"Arrangement?" I was shuddering over him, my mouth open as my need swelled and my objections melted away.

"Mm-hmm." He added an extra finger, working me until I was on the brink. "I get to keep you, but...." He paused as I came undone, my insides tightening around his hand as I pulsed against his fingertips, my hips rocking. "My God, duchess, I love watching you come." I felt the heat of his breath against my bare cheeks. "You're so responsive to my touch. So warm. So wet." He stood and unzipped his pants, leaning me forwards as he positioned himself at my entrance. "My cock is aching to be inside you."

"What happens if you keep me?" I urged, my voice barely audible as I fought to remain standing and focused. It would be easy to get caught up in his dirty talk and let my worries fly further away with every orgasm he gave me. But it wasn't just my possessions at stake this time—it was my entire existence. Still, my pussy pulsed in antic-ipation.

"I have to marry you." With that, he pushed inside, filling me so swiftly that my eyes bugged out.

"What?" I gasped, freaked out by his words while his thick cock did magical things to my insides. "I don't... I don't want...." I could barely speak with him inside me. It felt too good and robbed me of my senses.

"You don't want to marry me?"

I shook my head and he continued thrusting, his hand on my back, the other gripping my hip.

I don't want to have this conversation while you're fucking me.

"I'll admit that I wasn't too keen on the idea either," he gasped. "Marriage wasn't something I ever considered.

But then"—he quickened his pace, thrusting deeper, harder —"I thought about having unlimited access to this." He rammed his hips against me, grinding, sliding a hand under my shirt and cupping my breast, twisting my nipple until I cried out. "And I thought it might." *Thrust.* "Just be." *Thrust.* "Worth it." He slammed into me, the strain evident in his last words as he came inside me, spilling his seed into my depths. "You feel so good, duchess. Even better when there's nothing between us. So yeah, you get to be my wife. I get to fuck you whenever I want, and you can't testify against me if I'm ever arrested. It protects us both."

He pulled out and flipped me so I was facing him, cupping his hand between my legs and catching his cum as it spilled out. "Looks like we both get what we want, huh? You get to live, and I get to watch you come for the rest of our natural lives. You excited?" He grinned and then pressed his mouth to mine, forcing a kiss.

At first, I didn't want to respond. I was shocked and angry, confused and raging. I'd given up on the idea of marriage when I hit my thirtieth birthday and had yet to have a serious boyfriend. Then suddenly, this guy comes along and *tells* me that I have to marry him or I die. It wasn't exactly the romantic proposal I'd envisioned as a child. It wasn't even the amicable agreement I'd thought might happen as I got older. This was plain-as-day caveman bullshit that gave me limited choice. *Death or marriage, death or marriage... ummm, I suppose I'll take marriage since I'm not too keen on the whole being dead part just yet.*

"Come on, duchess." He sucked on my lower lip. "You can't honestly tell me there isn't at least some part of you excited about this. You and me, fucking and fighting,

fighting and fucking. It'll be beautiful." The moment I opened my mouth to respond, his tongue stole my words like the thief he was. As he twisted my head to the angle he wanted and deepened the kiss, I lost my fight. Releasing a tiny moan and wrapping my arms around his neck, I surrendered, so horribly weak where this man was concerned. All he had to do was touch me and I was his. It made me sick in a way. In another way, it made me a *very* satisfied woman.

"Wait. What happens if we get married and then you decide you don't want me anymore?" The thought struck me the moment our locked lips parted.

He leaned over and turned the tap on, washing his hand and collecting a fresh flannel. "If my dick is as good a judge of character as I think he is, we're gonna be fine." He pressed the clean flannel between my thighs and cleaned me up. "He likes you a hell of a lot. The rest, as my grandmother used to say, will come out in the wash." He dropped the flannel back into the sink. "You know, another thought crossed my mind as I was fucking you. Those hips look like they can carry big children. I wouldn't mind an heir."

What?

"An *heir?* You just *informed* me that we're getting married and now you want me pregnant with your kid so you can what, teach him or her to steal like you do?"

"Every family has their particular skillset."

I ran my hands over my face and shook my head. "This is the craziest fucking proposal I've ever heard."

"Not a proposal, duchess, a certainty. This is your life now."

"No, my life is teaching and singing. It's being a friend

and a niece, *not* an accessory to crime and raising children destined to populate the prison system."

"Cartwrights don't do time. We work smart and we stay safe."

"Then why do I have to marry you?"

"So you can live. So I can keep an eye on you. So that on the off-chance I do ever get caught, *you* won't be the person to put me there."

"I could still be an informant."

"Are you trying to blow holes in my argument? Do you want me to let Jasmine *dispose* of you and your friend?"

I sealed my lips shut and shook my head.

He leaned forward and pressed a kiss to the top of my head. "That's what I thought. Now get dressed. I put some clothes on the bed for you. We have an engagement to celebrate."

Never one to stay quiet for long, I opened my mouth to release the words that were bursting to get out.

"What about Alesha? What's happening to her?"

He leaned against the doorway. "Same deal."

"This is bullshit. You fuck me like that's the solution to all our problems, but you're taking away my choices and are completely unapologetic about it. Now my best friend is caught up in it too. You caused this, Nate. You preyed on me. You took everything I owned. Now you're taking the only thing I have left. You're taking my freedom."

"You're wrong, duchess. I'm giving you a life you never dreamed of. I'm saving you."

With that, he left the room, leaving me with nothing but a confused mind and my reflection staring back at me.

CHAPTER ELEVEN
THERE'S ALWAYS A CHOICE, DUCHESS

WITH EVERYONE around me acting like it was normal to celebrate a forced engagement with an impromptu Friday night BBQ, I was beginning to wonder if I'd somehow stepped into an alternate reality, like Alice falling through the looking glass. None of this could be real.

Except it was. I'd pinched myself enough times to know that I was awake and present. Still, I struggled to believe it.

In front of me, a squeal sounded. Alesha was in the pool frolicking with the twins and Sam. Kristian had just catapulted her through the air and she'd landed sideways with an almighty splash in front of Sam.

"You OK?" he asked with a laugh when she surfaced looking like a drowned rat. She nodded and he collected her in his arms, then said something to her I couldn't hear as he pushed her hair back from her face. She smiled and nodded again, and then he hugged her against his big chest. It was a picture-perfect moment. And if it had happened at any place or time besides this, I would've smiled and hoped my best friend was going to fall in love. Instead, I sat and scowled, hating myself for bringing us here. I'd messed up, and the only way I could combat that feeling of inadequacy was by sucking down vodka mixers and hoping I'd pass out soon so my brain would quiet. I didn't know what else to do. It seemed to me that I was stuck without much choice.

Maybe Alesha had the right idea with her joyful acceptance of the situation. Her behaviour seemed crazy and asinine to me, but maybe it was her way of dealing. Maybe she was so frightened that she felt only complete submission would assure her survival. Although, from her position on top of Sam's shoulders, she certainly didn't *look* scared. I honestly didn't know what to think. I was better off drunk.

Shifting my gaze across the yard, I could see Toby and Nate inside the house, deep in conversation with Jasmine. Nate's back was to me, but Toby and Jasmine kept a careful watch over the rest of us, giving me an unpleasant feeling whenever I caught their eyes.

Chewing the straw that had almost drained my fourth vodka mixer, I closed my eyes, feeling sick from the alcohol and lack of food—I'd refused to eat at dinner—but mostly from the worry seeping into my core. They wanted me to call my aunt and tell her I was going on a spontaneous vacation to the Cook Islands. I was to make up a story about being stressed and needing some time out. I didn't know if I could pull it off. The last time I'd lied to her was in year ten at school when I told her I was sleeping over at a friend's house, when in fact Alesha and I had snuck out to see a band. I never discovered how she figured it out, but she'd showed up at the venue, gotten them to stop the show and call us out of the audience. It was positively mortifying and meant that I *never* attempted to lie to her again.

"Nathaniel tells me that you aren't too keen on your impending nuptials," Jasmine said, taking the seat beside me. She held out another vodka mixer, which I gladly took but didn't thank her for.

"Being told I'm to marry someone so I won't be killed isn't the romantic proposal I'd envisioned."

"We take what we can get, I suppose."

I regarded her with a frown. "I don't know if you're insulting me or insulting Nate."

She sat up a little straighter and inhaled a steady breath. "If I'm honest, this whole situation is a fuck-up. I don't know what it is my son sees in you, but he's jeopardised the safety of this family with whatever game you two have going on. That tells me his interest in you runs a little deeper than a simple fuck. And since he won't let me do things my way, we have to get creative." Placing her elbows on her knees, she leaned a little closer and lowered her voice. "But mark my words. You refuse to go ahead with this wedding, and I *will* end you. I've been in this business all my life, and you don't get to where I am without getting your hands dirty. Right now, the *only* reason you're still alive is because of Nate. I suggest you keep him happy. He wants you. He wants children. *I* want grandchildren. Make being a wife and mother your focus and we'll get along just fine. But if you fuck up, if you refuse him or try to leave or talk to *anyone* about our business, I will end everyone you love. Then I'll slit you from ear to ear and make you watch yourself bleed out in a mirror. And there won't be a thing my son can do to save you."

I looked at her, my horrified heart beating wildly in my chest. *She would slit me ear to ear? End everyone I love? Lord, save me. Who says stuff like that?*

She sat back and smiled, seemingly pleased with my reaction. "Glad we cleared that up," she said, patting my thigh in a motherly way that was completely at odds with the monster she'd just shown me. "There's plenty more of those in the bar fridge." She pointed at my drink. "Feel free to help yourself."

I grabbed her arm to stop her leaving. "Can't you at least let Alesha go? She won't cause any trouble."

Still smiling, she glanced at her sons and Alesha in the pool. "She fits in well here. I think we'll keep her. You know, I offered her Toby, but she wanted Sam. I like a woman who knows what she wants and isn't afraid to ask for it." There was real pride in her voice.

"What about Sam? Doesn't he want to find his own wife?"

"Relationships are hard to sustain in our line of work. Best if he has a woman who already knows what she's walking into. Look at him, he seems pleased enough."

"So your sons just do what you say?"

"If they know what's good for them, they do. Alesha will make a good wife and daughter-in-law. I can already see that. You, on the other hand." Her eyes moved over me with disdain. "You're a complication. And I don't like complications, Holland. But fall in line and we won't have a problem. The choice is yours." Then she turned and walked away, leaving me alone with my self-pity and a bottle of alcohol.

TIRED, drunk and emotional, I made my excuses and was directed to a room upstairs where the twins had put my luggage when they returned from the storage unit. I had yet to speak to Nate, who'd retreated somewhere inside the house after his discussions with his mother and Toby. Doing what, I had no idea.

Toby had come out though, and he'd spent the evening watching—well, glaring—at everyone. Particularly me. I got the impression that he shared Jasmine's sentiment and would rather do me in than welcome me into the family. Perhaps that would be for the best. I couldn't imagine anyone would be particularly happy in this situation. Except Alesha and Sam, of course. They were acting like they'd won Lotto.

Perhaps this is all a dream.

Sitting on the end of a king-sized bed, I closed my eyes and clicked my heels together three times. "There's no place like home." *Click, click, click.* "There's no place like home."

Waiting for a breath, I cracked one eyelid open and allowed the room to come into view. I thought that if I willed it hard enough, I'd be sitting on the end of my own bed and not in a strange room in a strange house where I was prisoner. But alas, in front of my eyes was that cream fucking wall, grey carpet beneath my feet, a pale blue comforter beneath my arse. I was still in Torquay, also known as my new messed-up reality.

I sighed and pressed the heel of my palms against my eyes. *I will not cry. I will not cry.*

The door to the room opened and Nate stepped in,

somehow moving quietly despite his bulk. I couldn't help but notice that he didn't need to stoop to enter. Custom-made door frames?

"I thought you were avoiding me," I said as he took a seat next to me and leaned forwards, his forearms on his thick thighs.

"Just had shit to do. There's a lot to organise."

"Guess you never thought you'd be planning a last-minute wedding in the Cook Islands when you met me that night." I tried to smile, but my lips wobbled and tears filled my eyes. I looked up to the ceiling and sniffed to drain them before they could fall.

"No." He focused on his hands, thumb massaging the opposite palm. "But I reckon we could do worse for ourselves."

I released a burst of air from my nose. "I could've chosen a contract killer to bed, I suppose." The moment the words left my mouth, I felt awful. "I'm sorry," I back-tracked. "I shouldn't put you down like that. I just... I don't get it. How do you wake up every morning knowing that what you're doing is illegal? Aren't you afraid of getting caught? Don't you feel guilty?"

Taking a deep breath, he laid back on the bed, his arms stretched out and folded behind his head. "You make it sound like I'm a bad guy, duchess."

I twisted slightly, tucking my knee beneath me so I could face him. "Aren't you?"

He shrugged. "I don't feel bad. We're not physically hurting people. Sure, they get a shock when they discover their shit is gone, but that's what insurance is for."

"So you just explain everything away like that and your conscience is clear?"

"Not clear. I know what we do is wrong, but at the same time I don't really care. I've tried the straight and narrow before and honestly, it shits me. Working a nine-to-five while some other bastard gets rich off my back, that isn't for me. I don't want to live like that."

"So you live on the run instead?"

"Who's running?"

"I just can't wrap my head around it. Your mother raised you all to be a band of thieves. Who does that?"

"A person who grew up in a 'band a thieves'. This is the life she knew and it's the life she taught us, the one we've all grown accustomed to. You'll grow accustomed to it too. You'll see."

"What if I don't want to see? What if when we stand in front of the altar, I refuse to say 'I do'?"

His tongue slid out and wet the seam of his lips as he stared up at me, not speaking for a long moment. "Is the idea of a life with me really that terrible?"

"It's not about *you*, per se. It's about having a choice."

"There's always a choice, duchess."

"What, marry you or die? That's no choice."

"There are worse choices."

I looked at him, confusion knitting my brow. How was he so calm about this? Surely he wasn't actually *happy* about our impending nuptials. "You can't honestly tell me that I'm the woman you want to spend the rest of your life with. Marriage is supposed to be between two people who love each other, Nate. The only things I know about you are that you have a big dick and you rob people to make a living. That's not a firm basis for a relationship. And what do you know about me? I stretch enough to fit your big dick, and I figured out where you stash your loot and hide out."

He chuckled.

"Why is that funny?"

"Loot." He smiled. "You make it sound like we steal bags of cash with a big dollar sign on them."

"Well I'm glad you find this so amusing. Meanwhile, I'm here having my life turned upside down."

Reaching out, he wrapped a hand around my arm and pulled me towards him. "Come here," he said, his voice soft as he urged me back on the bed. With a sigh, I joined him, lying on my side to face him.

"Let it be known that I'm lying here because I'm tired, not because you told me to."

"Sure thing, duchess." He placed a hand on the curve of my hip and looked into my eyes. "Listen, I'll admit that getting married at this point isn't what I'd planned, or something either of us wanted. We hooked up a couple of times, had crazy-good sex, and then I was less than gentle-manly in my exit."

"You cleaned my apartment out. Twice."

He chuckled again. "Yeah, and I would've loved to have seen your expression when you woke that second time. Shocked the hell out of you, right?"

"Of course it did. You're a shit-stirrer. When the hell did you manage to roofie me, anyway? We were drinking from the same bottle, same cup."

He lifted his hand and brushed my hair back from my face. His fingers grazing my skin felt ridiculously nice. "When I offered you my glass after you'd finished screaming my name."

"I didn't even see," I whispered, my eyes fluttering just a little.

"Sleight of hand," he stated, holding his pinched fingers to me, my gold earring between them.

"How?" My eyes went wide as I sat up on my elbow and touched my earlobe. "I didn't even feel it."

Sitting up with me, he gently placed the earring back through my ear. "It's an essential skill in my line of work."

"Your line of work." I closed my eyes. My brain felt like it was vibrating from the stress of my situation. The alcohol really hadn't been enough to take the edge off. It just made me feel sick, tired and even more troubled. "Tell me something about yourself. Something that doesn't involve your... work."

"I can cook," he offered. "I make a really mean salmon dish with green beans that just melts in your mouth. Plus, I can make any kind of breakfast you want."

"Can you make pancakes?" The idea of food made my stomach grumble. I still hadn't eaten.

He smiled. "I'm told they're the best around. Want me to show you?"

"Do you have Nutella and strawberries to go with them?"

"Jasmine keeps this place pretty well stocked, so I'm sure you won't be disappointed. Wanna go see?" He sat up and held his hand out to me. Then my stomach growled so loudly that I felt compelled to take it.

"Just because you're feeding me doesn't mean I'm suddenly OK with all of this."

"Understood. But I won't allow my duchess to waste away. You can be pissed and well fed."

When he led me down to the kitchen, the area was dark except for the light over the stove.

"Looks like everyone's gone to bed," I noted.

"Good. I was only planning on cooking for you, anyway." He pulled ingredients from the pantry and placed them on the bench: flour, sugar, baking soda and salt. Then he dug a little farther and came out with a jar of Nutella. "Looks like we're in business. Sit." He pointed to the stools on the other side of the bench.

Doing as I was told, I climbed onto the stool and watched him move about the kitchen, pulling the last of the ingredients from the fridge: eggs, milk, butter, strawberries and... *lard*?

"You put *lard* in your pancakes?"

He winked as he started dumping ingredients into a bowl. "Trust me."

I didn't know why my mind didn't instantly object to that request. Perhaps it was because the topic was only pancakes, but it made me realise that for some reason, unknown even to me, I did trust him. He may have stolen from me, but he was doing everything in his power to protect me. I had no doubt that I'd be dying in a ditch somewhere if he hadn't stepped in.

"Thank you," I said suddenly, the realisation of an alternative fate hitting me in the chest.

"Save your thanks for the final product," he replied, flicking the whisk around the bowl like a pro.

"Not for feeding me. For saving me. I'm still pissed at you, but that doesn't mean I don't fully understand the gravity of what you're doing for me."

He set the bowl to the side and placed a pan on the stove, clicking on the gas flame before he met my eyes.

"I'm just glad you said yes. It would've been a bit of a hit to the ego if the first girl I asked to marry me chose death instead." He was so candid with his words. Whether he was joking or just being matter-of-fact, I didn't know. Either way, calling this what it was made things a lot easier for me.

"I don't recall being asked."

One side of his mouth kicked up as he dropped a nob of butter into the heating pan. The scent and the sizzle took over the air. "How about you tell me something about yourself that I don't know yet," he said as he picked up the mixing bowl and tipped enough batter for two large pancakes into the pan.

"You know everything there is to know already. I'm a drama teacher, I sing, I can make a joke out of just about anything, and I have exactly one good friend. I lead a pretty sad life."

"What do you like to do when you're home alone?"

"If you're hoping my answer is 'masturbate', you'll be terribly let down. I like to binge Netflix while eating junk food. Or I like to read in bed while also eating junk food. Food kind of goes with everything, but it's savoury for Netflix and sweet for reading. Oh, and I'm a terrible cook. I pretty much live on takeaway food. Uber eats is the biggest blessing of my life."

"Can you chop?" He lifted his brow as he slid an egg flip underneath a half-cooked pancake and flipped it.

"Of course I can chop—as long as you don't mind a little blood in your food." He stopped what he was doing and looked at me, a question in his eyes. I laughed. "That was a joke. I guess I'm not very funny tonight."

He moved slightly to his right and handed me the

punnet of strawberries, a small knife and a cutting board. "Think you can manage to keep all your fingers intact?"

I picked up the knife and a strawberry. "I'll try."

As I sliced at the small red berries, using the knife as a weapon to escape crossed my mind. But the moment the idea entered my thoughts, I squashed it immediately back down. To do that, I'd have to hurt Nate. And despite everything he'd done, hurting him was the last thing I wanted. So I finished slicing the strawberries and then put the knife back down, realising that he'd been right earlier—there were always choices.

"All done," I said, pushing the cutting board towards him.

He looked at the knife, then back at me and said, "Thank you." I had to wonder if he'd been reading my thoughts.

When he set the plate of hot pancakes and melted hazelnut spread in front of me, my mouth watered at the sight. I almost drooled when the scent hit my nose. "This looks delicious," I said, licking my lips as I picked up my knife and fork and cut into it. "You're not going to join me?"

He leaned on the bench and shook his head. "They're all yours. Eat up while they're still hot."

Loading up my fork, I took my first mouthful and moaned. They were the lightest, fluffiest, most delicious pancakes I'd ever tasted. "Oh my God."

He seemed genuinely pleased by my reaction and smiled. "Glad you like them."

"Like? I love them. In fact, I think I could marry these pancakes." I took another mouthful and closed my eyes. They were so good.

"Technically, you *are* marrying those pancakes," he pointed out, moving around the bench so he was standing beside me.

"Sure you don't want some?" I offered, holding up my fork loaded with more than was polite to put in one mouthful.

"I'm not hungry for food." His eyes swept over my body.

"Oh." I stuffed the forkful in my mouth and chewed quietly, understanding exactly what he was insinuating. Once again I tingled, my nipples pressing against the fabric of the lace bra I was wearing, straining behind the sundress. Suddenly I wasn't so hungry for food either.

He was by far the sexiest man I'd ever seen. He and his brothers were the kind of men other men developed crushes on and women swooned over. So, the question begged to be asked, "Why do you want me, Nate?"

"Why wouldn't I want you?" he responded.

"Well, I'm not exactly model material." I gestured with one hand to the entirety of me.

"I'm not interested in models."

"So you're a chubby chaser?"

He laughed. "No."

"Then why me? Why are you so into this that you're willing to marry me? Is it just to ease your conscience?"

He ran his thumb over the corner of my mouth. I closed my eyes at his touch, and even though I could feel he was wiping away a stray bit of Nutella, I wasn't embarrassed. It was hot as hell.

When I opened my eyes, he was sucking his thumb into his mouth. "That was really sexy," I whispered, to which he chuckled, then leaned forwards and kissed me by sucking against my lower lip.

"I think *you're* sexy," he whispered against my lips.

"Why?" I simply couldn't wrap my head around it. He could have anyone. If he wasn't a chubby chaser, then why would he choose me?

"How about I tell you how I feel when I'm with you?"

"That might help."

"Found," he said, his voice soft and low as his fingers danced across my skin, touching my face, my neck, brushing through my hair. "Weak." He collected my hair in one big hand and wound it around his palm, tugging so my head went back. "Strong." He pulled so I was forced to tip my head back, and then he lowered his head so his lips brushed lightly along my jaw. "Hard." He whispered that last word in my ear, then held my earlobe between his teeth.

I released a slight gasp as my head swam with the desire he drew from me, uncontrollable.

"When I see you, I want you." His lips moved down my neck and over the skin exposed by my dress. "When you aren't around, I want you even more." He brought his mouth back to mine. "And I know you want me too."

"I do," I gasped just before he sealed his mouth over mine and kissed me, his tongue claiming ownership over mine. My bones turned to liquid and I almost slid off the stool when he released me. Four words. The first two more profound, of course. *Found.* By me. *Weak.* Because of me. Was this even real?

"Finish your food. You'll need plenty of energy to feed my hunger."

I downed the last of my pancakes in record time.

UNLIKE THE LAST time I fell asleep beside him, when I woke up during the night, Nate was still there, still draped over me. Emotion surged through me, a mixture of relief, desire and devastation. I was upset with myself for wanting him, for feeling comfort in his arms, in his body. I should've been fighting against him, not finding reasons to like him. I was a prisoner, for fuck's sake. Was I so desperate for love and attention that I was willing to go along with this instead of looking for an opportunity to escape? What was wrong with me? I was turning into Alesha.

Needing a moment to myself, I tried to move from beneath him but his grip tightened, possessive in his sleep.

"Where are you going?" His sleep-thick voice sounded too loud in the quiet room.

"I need to pee," I whispered.

With a grunt, he lifted his arm, and I slid out from under him, picking my dress up off the floor and tugging it over my naked body.

"Don't be long," he told me as I padded across the plush carpet.

"It'll take as long as it takes," I snapped.

"Back to being pissed, huh?"

"Of course I'm fucking pissed!"

"What's the point? It's not going to change anything."

"I know. I fucking know. But you can't just feed me and fuck me and then expect everything to be fine. You dragged me into this. You had to *know* I'd find you again. But you took my shit again anyway, taunting me, *luring* me here while knowing your family would never let me go."

He dropped his head against the bed and groaned. "That's a huge leap, duchess. You're giving me far too much credit here."

"No I'm not. It makes sense. You orchestrated this whole fucking thing."

"Holland," he said, a slight warning in his tone. "Come back to bed."

"You trapped me."

His blue eyes met mine as silence enveloped the tension-filled air. "Not consciously."

"So you admit it."

He ran a hand through his bedraggled hair. "I don't know what I thought was going to happen with you. But I think we need to accept that we were both playing a dangerous game. We both did things to make my world and your world merge."

"*This* isn't what I wanted."

"Really?" He got out of bed and came towards me. I'd be lying if I said my eyes didn't drink in his naked form. "Then what the fuck are you doing here?" He towered over me, his eyes flashing. "You could've called the cops and had them storm the storage facility and the house, but you chose to come here yourself. Tell me there wasn't a tiny part of you that hoped my dick and your vagina could get down and dirty together. Tell me you didn't want more from me."

"I...." *Had* I hoped that? I'd been so focused on finding him that I hadn't even considered my reasons. I'd thought it was to catch him and then call the cops, but I could've called them in the beginning as Alesha suggested. They could've followed the GPS card, and she and I could be sitting in her lounge room gorging ourselves on take-away pizza while watching the latest Zac Efron movie. I didn't need to come here at all.

"You wanted this," he whispered, sliding his hand around my waist and flattening me against his chest. "Admit it."

"I...." I shook my head, losing my mind a little as his closeness did magical things to my body.

"Admit it, duchess. You're as crazy about me as I am about you." *Wait. He's* crazy *about me?* "You wanted me to catch you. Wanted me to fuck you again and again." He punctuated his final words by thrusting his hips against me, his long, hard arousal pressing into my stomach.

I shook my head. "I'm not that shallow."

"We're all that shallow, duchess," he murmured, lowering himself to his knees.

"What are you doing?"

He slid his hands beneath my dress and rested them on my hips, bunching the fabric beneath his thumbs so my sex was exposed. "We're all slaves to our impulses and desires." He leaned forwards and flicked his tongue between my legs. "There's no shame in it, no shame in admitting that you wanted me." He licked me again. "Just like I want you." My body shook as he sucked back on my clit, burying his face between my legs. I could barely stand as the ecstasy his mouth provided surged through my body. Why was he able to do this to me? I could be angry and screaming, hurt and crying, but one erotic touch from him and I was a quivering mess, a slave to my own desire.

"Ohhh." My hands went into his hair as his tongue brought me to the edge. Then stopped.

"Duchess."

"Don't stop," I gasped. God, what was I saying? What was I *thinking*?

"Then admit you came here wanting me to fuck you."

"Huh." I wasn't in a state to form words. I needed him to finish what he started.

"Say the words."

"Words?" *What are they again?*

"Say 'I want you to fuck me.'"

"I do," I gasped, moving my hips.

"The words, duchess. I need the words."

"I want you to fuck me," I parroted, hating myself for being so ruled by my desire that I gave in. But he was right. I did want him to fuck me. I wanted him to fuck me over and over again in every position possible, and I didn't want him to stop. He was all I thought about.

"That's what I thought."

When his mouth closed over my clit and his tongue dove into my depths, I whimpered. I may have also cried a little. How could I want him so much while hating myself for that very same fact? I was a good, law-abiding citizen. He was an unapologetic criminal. I was supposed to be smarter than this, to be more in control. Yet there I was, surrendering to him and moaning uncontrollably as he coaxed orgasm after orgasm from my body. It was seriously messed up.

When it was over, I placed my hands over my face in shame as he stood over me, panting and out of breath.

"Don't cry now, duchess. If you're honest—*really* honest—with yourself, you'll find that you wanted me to keep you too."

Lowering my hands, I felt the cool air wash over my wet cheeks as I looked up at him and frowned. *I also want the fairy tale. I want love.* "I might want you, Nate, but I didn't want you like this. Not when there's no free will. I could never love you after this."

A half-smile pulled up his lips. "Who said anything about love? Lust is what got us here."

With hot tears clouding my vision, I lifted my hand and slapped him, my palm stinging as I turned and fled into the adjoining bathroom.

Sitting on the toilet, I placed my face in my hands and let my tears flow. I felt on edge, like a wild animal caught in a cage. There was this thrumming underneath my skin, an insistence that whispered one word over and over: *run.*

But where? How? They had Alesha, and if Jasmine was to be believed, they'd go after Aunt Maya too. This was my punishment for being wanton. I should've had a three-date rule like other women. Then I wouldn't be in this mess.

Finishing my business, I headed to the basin to wash my hands and splash water over my face. My eyes were puffy from crying. I looked awful.

"I don't want you to hate me," Nate whispered,

appearing behind me and moving my hair over my shoulder, pressing his lips to the back of my neck. Instantly, my skin felt alive and my breathing quickened. *Traitorous body.*

"Then don't force me to marry you."

"What would you have me do instead? You're aware of the ultimatum I was given."

"I know the options, Nate. Marry or *die*. It's so fucking ominous and stupid at the same time. Can't you just, I don't know… threaten my life so I don't talk and then send me on my way?"

His breath washed over my back as he let out a sigh. "You don't think I suggested that?" He slid his hands around my middle and pulled me to him, his eyes meeting mine in the mirror. "I suggested about ten different scenarios before this became an option. I know it's not ideal, but it's the best I've got."

"Making me a member of the family that wants me dead is the best you have?" I actually laughed.

"Well it worked in *Outlander*."

My heart jolted a little and I met his eyes in the mirror. "You watch that show?"

"I read the books."

He watches Pitch Perfect*. He reads romance. He's marrying me to save my life.*

That little voice in my head was at it again.

Not to mention he's amazing in bed. Maybe I could learn *to love him in time.*

Turning in his arms, I studied his face: merry blue eyes, strong straight nose, full lips and solid jaw. I couldn't have imagined a more beautiful man if I tried. And as luck would have it, this man was willing to offer his hand in order to save me.

Perhaps there really is honour among thieves.

"You really suggested the whole marriage thing to keep me safe?"

He clenched his jaw, then nodded and lowered his forehead until it touched against mine.

"What happens if it doesn't work out? What happens when you don't want me anymore?"

"Then we go to a fucking marriage counsellor and work our shit out like everyone else. You are my duchess—my queen. I've never wanted a woman more than I want you."

Grabbing my hands, he took a knee, his eyes on mine. "I know this isn't anything like either of us imagined, but I'd still like to do it right." He held up a ring, an emerald-cut diamond of at least a carat, surrounded by smaller brilliant-cut diamonds set in a rose gold band. It was beautiful —and probably stolen. "Will you marry me, duchess?"

I didn't have any real choice in the matter, but the sentiment touched my heart nonetheless. On his knees before me, with a serious look in his eyes, I couldn't deny him. *He was beautiful. And he wanted me.*

"Yes, Nate, I'll marry you," I whispered, emotion overwhelming me as he slid the ring on my left hand and smiled up at me.

Placing my hands on either side of his face, I ran my thumbs against the stubble on his jaw, then lowered mine to his. For the first time in our short courtship, I kissed *him*. Sweet, soft, and sensual.

"I do need to know one thing though," I whispered as our lips parted but our noses still touched.

"What's that?"

I moved back until his features came into focus. "Where the hell were you hiding that ring just now? You're completely naked."

With that boyish grin that had been the reason I was drawn to him in the first place, he winked at me, then stood and lifted me off the ground. "Sleight of hand, duchess. I'll teach you sometime, but first, let me show you how we play hide the salami."

———

THE NEXT MORNING brought with it a flurry of packing before our journey to the Cook Islands commenced that evening. Alesha was the happiest I'd seen her in years, and when I managed to get a moment with her alone, she assured me that she was fine. "It's kind of like an arranged marriage. Statistically they work out way better than love matches do, you know." Was it possible that the stress of the situation had broken her mind? I knew Alesha was a romantic at heart, but how could she possibly be OK with marrying into a family of thieves? I was so confused by her happy acceptance. The nervous and cautious woman I knew seemed to have slid off her body like a mask that didn't belong. It didn't make sense.

Everyone in the Cartwright family was joining us on our trip. All except for Toby, who was staying behind to watch the dog and 'keep an eye on things'—whatever that meant. I just thought he was so angry about not getting to kill us that he couldn't stand to bear witness to our impromptu nuptials. His death stares across the room were enough to make me sure that I was right. His cold eyes as he looked between Nate and me sent shivers down my spine.

Laughter erupted as Kristian and Abbot burst into the living area, half wrestling, half racing to do God only knew what. Their mannerisms, voice and expressions were *exactly* the same; Abbot's cropped hair and Kristian's golden locks were the only things keeping me from mixing them up.

"Take it outside," Jasmine yelled, shooing them away as she shook her head, then gave Nate a meaningful look. "We're leaving in thirty minutes. Toby, there's food in the fridge. *Don't* order in every night." You could be forgiven for thinking this was any other family preparing to go overseas. There was crazy commotion, suitcases lined up at the door and instructions being yelled.

The illusion was quickly realigned when Nate moved to stand in front of me, holding out my phone. "Call your aunt," he said. It was the last thing I had to do. We'd already emailed our employers telling them we were taking extended leave. That had been easy, now we needed to inform our families. The Cartwrights wanted to make sure no one would come looking for us.

Glancing between the phone and Nate, I swallowed hard. He was wearing a pair of worn-looking jeans and a T-shirt that hugged his chest like a lover. We'd had sex half a dozen times the night before, but I was jealous of that T-shirt. I'd much rather be hugging his chest than contemplating the call I was about to make.

"She'll know I'm lying," I told him honestly, taking the phone.

"Then you'd better use your acting abilities to convince her it's the truth."

"You know full well there's a very good reason why I'm a high school drama teacher and not a highly paid actress."

He grinned, then leaned down and bit the end of my nose playfully. I laughed with surprise, then rubbed where his teeth had been. "Then tell her the truth. Tell her you've met the man of your dreams, and you're going to run away and marry him."

"Man of my dreams?"

"You telling me you haven't been dreaming about me since that first night?"

The blush in my cheeks answered for me.

"Me too, duchess. Every fucking night." He reached down and adjusted his cock.

I licked my lips, wondering if it was possible to fit that thing in my mouth. I was planning on finding out soon.

"I'll tell her you're whisking me away. But I can't tell her about the wedding or she'll want to come. And she'll be hurt when I say no."

"Whatever works."

Unlocking my screen, I pulled up Aunt Maya's number, then waited for the call to connect. When I put the phone against my ear, Nate looked at me and shook his head. A quick glance around the room told me I had an audience, so I put it on speaker so they didn't think I was sending some secret code.

"What are you doing in Torquay?" Aunt Maya asked by way of greeting.

I couldn't help but laugh. "Tracking my whereabouts, Aunty?"

"I haven't heard from you in days. Of course I'm checking up on you. What are you doing down there?"

"Last-minute getaway. It's kind of what I called to talk to you about."

"Oh yeah? Want your aunt to come and join you? I still look pretty good in a bikini, I might say."

"I wouldn't doubt it, but no, that's not what I was calling about. Alesha and I, we've met some, uh, brothers down here."

"I'm interested. Keep talking."

"Well, they're really nice...."

"Are they hot? Good in bed?"

I met Nate's eyes. He was smiling.

"You taught me not to kiss and tell, Aunty."

"To others, not me."

I chuckled. "Yes to everything."

"Ohhh, I want details."

"Another time. Perhaps when I get back."

"Come for dinner tomorrow night. I'll make chicken provençale."

"I can't tomorrow, Aunty. I... I'm going away for like a whole week?" I frowned because I had no idea how long I should tell her or how long it would be before I would see her again.

"You *are* away."

"I know, and this is the crazy part. We've all decided to fly to the Cook Islands to bask in the sunshine and drink too many cocktails."

"Are you high?" She tittered like an old lady pulling uncomfortably on her pearls.

"No." I laughed. "I'm just doing something crazy before I get too old to do it."

"Who are you and what have you done with my niece?"

Jasmine and Nate shifted on their feet. Toby had his hands on his hips and shook his head. Nate turned his finger in the air, signalling for me to wrap it up.

I laughed her comment off. "I'm just finally taking your advice, Aunty. I thought you'd be happy."

"Oh, sweetheart, of course I'm happy. Go, have fun. Oh, and have lots of sex. Don't forget your birth control."

Tears sprang to my eyes as my love for this woman and the sadness I felt from misleading her descended on my shoulders. "I will, I promise. I'll call you when I get back, OK?" My voice cracked.

"I can't wait for all the juicy details. Have a wonderful time, my love."

"I will," I whispered. "Love you, Aunty."

"Love you too."

Jasmine reached out and disconnected the call, removing the phone from my grip. I hadn't even noticed her move so close. I squeezed my eyes shut and wiped at them, looking around the room to find wary faces on the brothers but a smile from my friend. Alesha gave me a thumbs up, and I nodded my thanks.

"It's your turn now," Jasmine said, directing Alesha into the next room. The brothers followed, as did that evil little dog.

"You did good, duchess," Nate said when they left, wrapping an arm around my neck and pulling me against him. "Oscar-winning performance."

It didn't feel good. It felt like lying.

I hated lying.

CHAPTER THIRTEEN
AIR TO BREATHE

"ARE YOU NERVOUS?" I asked Nate as we sat beside each other before take-off. We were sitting in business class, which was just as well because there was no way men the size of the Cartwright brothers could fit in economy seating. As it was, Nate's knees jutted out into the aisle, and he looked almost too big for his seat. On the other hand, I was comfortable in my window seat with my extra legroom and soft blanket.

"Not really. I've already done the hard part."

"Oh yeah? What part was that?"

"Getting you here."

A blush crept into my cheeks. This man had really been turning on the charm since his naked proposal in the early hours of the morning. Maybe this whole marriage thing wasn't going to be so awful after all. I mean, people got drunk and married strangers in Vegas all the time. Sure, most were annulled fairly quickly, but the rest of them figured their shit out and made it work. Nate and I could do that. There would be a *lot* to work out, but we had that spark that people would sell a kidney for the chance to experience. So we were ahead of the curve in that respect, I supposed—or at least that's what I was telling myself to keep from throwing up. I was nervous as fuck.

"How about you?" he asked after watching me fidget. We'd begun to taxi along the runway and I'd checked my seatbelt about five times, read the emergency card and fiddled with the air vent, all the while bouncing my knee.

"Nope. I'm just fine." I nodded, trying to convince myself more than anything. I wished I had Alesha's blissful outlook. She seemed so at peace sitting next to Sam and talking quietly—giggling, even. And Alesha didn't giggle. I needed some of whatever she was on.

Adjusting in his seat slightly, Nate sat back and chuckled. "You're shitting your pants."

"No. I'm possibly a bit nervous about flying, but that's only because I've never flown any farther than Sydney." That flight was only an hour and a half, and I'd done it when I was twelve and Aunt Maya had to attend a conference. We'd gone to see the ballet at the Opera House and ridden the ferry to the zoo. I'd thrown up over the side and she'd laughed it off, telling me the fish would be grateful for the extra treat. I'd cried harder because we'd been eating fish and chips. I didn't want the fish to be cannibals.

I wished she was here now. She'd help me reason this out—or she'd convince me it was crazy.

"I know a way to take your mind off things." Nate smirked, a lascivious glint in his eyes as he reached over to take my hand, bringing my fingers to his lips. He nibbled lightly on them one by one, my breath quickening.

"Oh yeah? Does it have the words 'mile' and 'high' in the title?"

"No. I'd thank you to get your mind out of the gutter, duchess. This is a reputable airline." With a cheeky grin, he leaned a little closer and wrapped our fingers together so our fists were joined side by side.

"You kind of baited me with the way you said it," I argued, watching as he positioned my thumb so it was lying next to his.

"I know." He smiled and met my eyes. "I like it when you're thinking dirty things. Makes your cheeks pink."

"They do not go pink," I retorted, knowing full well they did, if the burn on my face was anything to go by.

Seeming happy with our hand placement, he said, "OK, do you know how to thumb war?"

"Uh, can't say I do."

"So you start with your thumb up like this." He lifted his thumb straight into the air. "Then you move it side to side." He tapped it on my hand and then his, adding, "One, two, three, four, I declare a thumb war. Then you try to capture the other person's thumb and hold it for the count of three to win."

"You have enormous hands. I feel like you have the advantage."

"You wanna play or not?"

"I'll play."

We tapped our thumbs four times, saying the little rhyme before wrestling with our hands to be the one to catch the other's thumb. He won almost every time, but there were a couple of times that I beat him—although I was fairly sure he let me. Still, with all the laughter and focus on competition, I didn't even realise we were in the air until it was announced that we could take our seatbelts off.

"Huh," I said, looking around the cabin as the flight attendants started moving around and offering refreshments. "That's a pretty neat trick."

"You know what else is a neat trick?"

I grinned. "What's that?"

"Fucking in an airplane cubicle."

"I take it you'd like to give it a try?"

"Hell yeah," he nodded.

With a smile, I stood up and slowly climbed over him, pausing a moment so I could lean close to his ear. "You know what else would be a neat trick?" He shook his head and waited for my answer. "Fitting that whopper cock of yours in my mouth and swallowing it down to the base."

I felt the cock in question stand to attention immediately. "Can you do that?"

"I have no idea, but it'll be fun trying to find out."

So it turns out I can't deep throat. I read about these women being able to control their breathing and take a man down their throat to give him the best blow job there is, but my gag reflex was just too strong; I couldn't even get the damn thing deeper than a couple of inches without dry retching. Not my sexiest moment.

Nate had found the whole experience absolutely hilarious and was crying with laughter after the fifth attempt, pulling me to my feet and kissing me as best he could through his mirth. "I love that you tried, duchess. That was fucking brilliant."

I felt like a total disappointment, but when he sent me soaring way higher than a simple mile, I wasn't thinking about *anything* inadequate.

"I've got to tell you, duchess, this pussy is my *favourite* place to put my cock," he rasped, driving into me against the wall as I moaned uncontrollably. With the amount of time he liked to spend in there, I was inclined to believe him.

I know what you've been doing, Alesha teased, sending a message via the plane's entertainment hub once we'd returned to our seats.

Wouldn't have a clue what you're talking about, I returned.

Her: **Mile high, mile high! That glow on your face tells me you're a card-carrying member. Plus, we could kind of hear the banging. Well done.** 😂

Me: **Bullshit! We were NOT that loud.**

Her: **Haha! Made you admit it!**

Me: **Cheeky.**

Her: **And you were totally that loud.** 😶

Me: **OK. So why don't you and spunky Sam go in there and show me how it's done?**

Her: **Oh no. We're waiting til the wedding night.**

I sat back in my seat, surprised that she was adhering to *any* kind of tradition.

Her: **I'm nervous. What if he thinks I'm no good?**

Me: **He's a red-blooded male and you're a gorgeous woman. He'll think you're amazing no matter what you do.**

Her: **I'm worried he'll think I'm too inexperienced.**

Me: **Don't be worried. You're perfect and he's lucky to have you.**

Her: **Thanks.** 🩶

Me: 😬 **Are you sure you want to go through with this? We could fake our deaths and disappear...**

Her: **I'm sure. It was love at first sight. Sounds corny, but he believes it too. I'm ok. You'll be ok too. Nate adores you.**

I smiled to myself and tapped out a final message.

Me: **We'll see. But I'm happy if you're happy.**

Her: **I'm ecstatic, honest.** 😄

Why didn't her saying that make me feel better? I'd accepted that this wedding was happening, but was I happy about it? No. I liked Nate, loved fucking him, but I wasn't ready to marry him despite all the things he made me feel.

Glancing over at him, I watched the rise and fall of his chest as he slept peacefully, resting after our cubicle gymnastics. I couldn't help but smile as I studied his sleeping features. He really was beautiful, and Alesha was right, he did seem to adore me. Why, I didn't quite understand, but there we were, flying to a tropical destination to elope.

Under any other circumstance, I'd feel like the luckiest girl alive.

The tiny hairs on the back of my neck stood on end, causing me to lift my gaze to seek out the source. It wasn't difficult. On the other side of the plane, a set of pale eyes watched me. I locked glares with Jasmine. She resented this entire trip, I could tell that much. I'd know it even if she hadn't told me that she'd rather kill me than have me marry her son. Her baneful scrutiny really did put a dampener on any sort of loved-up feelings I was starting to have towards Nate. Her mere presence was a threat. And when she smiled and nodded at me, I felt like I was being cajoled by a wolf, her grin nothing more than a curving of lips with no real feeling behind it. Did she hate *me*, or did she hate the situation?

Moving my gaze to where Kristian and Abbot sat watching in-flight movies, I wondered if their presence was a threat too. Were they there as witnesses or bodyguards? I had no doubt that despite their goofy demeanours, they were more than capable of menace. I'd even seen a glimpse of that in Nate when his hand had closed around my throat at the mention of cops.

I turned my attention back to the in-flight screen and typed out another message to Alesha.

Me: **These people scare me.**

Her: **Focus on Nate.**

Me: **I can't pretend he isn't one of them.**

Her: **Just do what you're told and everything will be fine. I promise.**

Do what I'm told. She made it sound so easy. I let out a sigh and leaned back, closing my eyes to try and sleep away some of the ten-hour flight, but a new message ping made me open them again.

Her: **Don't message me anymore. He's waking up, and I don't want to rock the boat.**

Me: **See you at our wedding, then.**

Her: ☺

She made a good point. I held my finger against the screen and deleted our entire conversation.

"What are you up to?" Nate asked, his hand resting on my thigh as he adjusted his chair to sitting.

"Just playing around with the entertainment system.

There are games on here as well as movies," I fibbed, tapping the games icon to show him classic options like Tetris, chess and solitaire.

He looked on with little interest. "Maybe you should try and catch some Zs, duchess. There's not going to be much time to rest before the ceremony, and afterwards... well, it's our wedding night, so there won't be a lot of resting going on then either." He dropped his eyes to my breasts, just in case I didn't catch his meaning.

"I have no illusions of sleep in the foreseeable future, or at least until that appetite of yours is sated some."

He leaned back again and closed his eyes. "Never. I think about you and I'm hard. In fact, that bathroom seems unoccupied right now." He looked at me hopefully and I laughed, shaking my head.

"How about you save just a little for the wedding night, big boy? I want you at your satisfying best."

"Me too, so sleep, duchess. Your husband-to-be commands it."

Commands it.

Just do what you're told and everything will be fine.

Without an extra word, I reclined my chair and closed my eyes, doing exactly as I was told. Not that sleep was willing to come. I lay there in closed-eyed worry instead as questions swirled about in my mind. *What is my life about to be like? Will they allow me to go back to work? Will they make me their accomplice instead? Will they let me visit my aunt?*

With every question that popped into my mind, another ten seemed to follow until I couldn't even close my eyes anymore. I stared at the ceiling of the plane, willing the emergency oxygen system to activate and drop down in front of me.

I needed air.

I couldn't breathe.

ON THE COOK ISLANDS, hotels offered elopement packages that took care of every need a couple might have. You could book everything online, then step off the plane to an island paradise where people were ready to cater to your every whim.

"Welcome!" A woman with a toothy grin, caramel-coloured skin and bleached-blonde hair introduced herself as our wedding planner. "We are so lucky to have you. The sun is here in your honour after terrible rains these past few days. Come." She didn't relax her smile once. "There is much to do before this evening's ceremony."

Alesha and I were whisked away in one direction, the grooms in the other. Jasmine followed us, as did Abbot. *It's like they think we might run.*

"Everything you asked for is here," the wedding planner said, gesturing around the room. There were dresses in garment bags, along with facilities for complete hair and make-up. "There is also complimentary champagne." She offered us all a glass, which I drained rather rapidly as a team of women filed in the room. "And here are your helpers."

I'd known this was happening, knew full well that we had made this trip in order to get married. But seeing those dresses and actually getting ready for our nuptials, was a completely different story. Nervous butterflies did an insane dance throughout my entire abdomen. Suddenly this was all too real. I needed more alcohol.

Champagne was now my favourite. Every time I emptied my glass, a lovely Polynesian woman would refill it for me while another piled my long blonde hair on top of my head and a third pinned flowers inside the coils. There was one more applying my make-up while the wedding planner gave orders to the two teams.

Alesha was talking a mile a minute; I don't think she'd even sipped from her glass. "This feels like a fairy tale, don't you think? Whisked away to an island to get married, best friends marrying brothers. You can't make this stuff up and have it be this perfect."

Jasmine smiled as if she was being polite while a snot-nosed child attempted a violin concerto when they were barely capable of "Twinkle Twinkle Little Star".

For the most part, I sat silently, biting my tongue. There was no point in specifying the flaws in this grand fairy tale of hers. Not only were Jasmine and Abbot watching on, but Alesha quite simply didn't seem to care. A gorgeous man wanted to marry her. It was all of her adolescent dreams come true. What they did for a job and the reasons we were there seemed inconsequential, so I kept my lips sealed and let her have her moment, promising myself that I'd be there to hold her when the reality of this new life came crashing down. Things would never be the same again.

"Maybe we'll have kids together too, Holland," Alesha chatted on. "We could live next door to each other and they could grow up just like we did."

"Sure, Leesha," I murmured, staring into my glass. "Whatever you want."

I'd been drinking too fast, stressing too much. My mind started swimming from all the champagne, and I was losing my focus. Alesha's voice became a distant hum. Numbness was only a few more drinks away. I closed my eyes and drained my glass, holding it out to be refilled as I blew out my breath. "Thank you," I said to my server as I took another calming sip. *I can do this. I can marry a thief.*

"You might want to lay off the champagne a little, Holland." My silence would've continued had Jasmine not decided to intervene and ruin my plans for being so drunk I could barely stand at my wedding.

"I'm fine," I retorted.

With a cool smile, she reached out to take the glass I had clutched between my fingers. "We don't want you falling over at the altar."

"Ah, uh, uh," I said, pulling it from her reach. "This is my potion of courage. Didn't you hear? This is a *fairy tale.*" I opened my eyes wide, saying the words in an exaggerated whisper.

"You're drunk," she stated, catching my arm and forcing the glass out of my grip.

"No!" I wrestled her for it, and the golden liquid splashed up and went all over both of our hands.

"Now look what you've done." She pursed her lips, looking for something to clean herself up while I let my tongue do the work for me, licking at my hands like a kitten.

My head feels so fuzzy.

"Get her some food or something, will you?" Jasmine instructed Abbot with a sigh. "She's a mess."

Abbot left the room and Jasmine glared at me for a long moment. Like the grown-up I was, I poked my tongue out at her.

"Give us the room," she commanded, and just like that, all of the helpers vanished from their stations, Alesha staying put. "What is wrong with you?" she hissed, leaning over me, her pale eyes freaking me the fuck out in my drunken state. She reminded me of a wraith.

"I… I'm getting ready for—*hic*—my wedding. Itsh going to be beaut-ful," I slurred, waving my arms to punctuate my speech, or perhaps conduct an orchestra, I wasn't exactly sure what I was doing. *How much have I had to drink?* I squinted over to the table to find the champagne bottle turned upside down in the ice bucket. *Oh, all of it. Whoops.*

"You might not be taking this seriously, Holland, but I assure you, the rest of us are. And if you ruin my son's wedding, I will—"

"Ruin me!" I stuck my tongue between my lips and blew a raspberry. "I know. I *know.* You'll kill me and everyone I care about, then put us all in a ditch for the dingoes to eat us." I cackled at that, for some reason finding the whole thing absolutely hilarious. Drunk Holland was not a clever Holland at all. Despite the fact that there was steam coming out of Jasmine's ears and Alesha was sitting across the room in abject silence, I continued anyway. "You don't scare me, Jasmine. If you hurt me, your son is gonna *hate you.* Because his dick loves my—"

I didn't get to finish—which was just as well considering where that was going—because the back of a hand clapped against the side of my face with such force that it sent my head spinning. Even through the numbing effects of the alcohol, my jaw hurt.

"Don't test me," Jasmine spat, pointing in my face.

"Or what?" I laughed as I tasted blood, then spat some down my chin, smiling red. I really was a terrible drunk. It was why I was normally careful not to drink more than I knew I could tolerate. But forced weddings were the exception to my rule.

"Holland," Alesha interjected, her voice sounding like that nervous thing I'd grown up with. I was wondering where she'd gone. "Let's just get ready, OK? We're about to become sisters." She smiled, trying to spin this in the most positive light as she moved closer and kneeled in front of me. She was already wearing her dress, a simple white slip that fell to the floor and made her look like an angel. Holding up a napkin, she wiped it across my chin, cleaning up the dripping blood before murmuring, "We're going to be OK. Don't fall apart on me now. I can't do this without you." It was then that I saw it, the fear in her eyes. She was as freaked out over this as I was; she was just a better actress. *She's worked out how to play the game—I haven't even worked out there are rules to follow—that's how she's coping.* Somehow, that realisation gave me comfort.

"Oh, Leesh," I whispered, flinging my arms around her and holding on to her tight. "I'm so sorry. This is all my fault."

She gripped me by the shoulders and held me at arm's length. "Everything is going to be OK," she repeated. "We just need to get you sobered up. Maybe some coffee?" She looked past me to where I knew Jasmine was standing, probably glaring down at me with disdain.

"I'll call for it," she said. "Abbot should be back shortly with some food."

"See? It's going to be fine," Alesha whispered, brushing at the stray strands of hair the slap had knocked loose. "You need to be strong, Holl. This isn't the end of the world. It's just the beginning of a different one."

Lifting my head, I looked at myself in the mirror and took a steadying breath. "Well, someone's gonna have to get those make-up girls back in here to add some blush to this side to balance things out." I was sporting a rather solid welt where Jasmine had backhanded me.

Alesha laughed a little. "Or I could slap you on the other side, knock some sense into that stubborn head of yours."

With a little laugh, I leaned forwards and pressed my forehead against hers. "I might need it," I whispered before adding, "Don't leave me again, Leesh."

"Shhh," she returned, pulling back and meeting my eyes. "They're always listening. Just focus on the good. Focus on how you feel about Nate." Then she stood, and someone thrust a cup of coffee and half a sandwich in my face. I was made to finish both before anyone would continue.

I was suddenly *very* sober.

Just as I slipped my foot into the second sandal, there was a knock at the door.

"The grooms are growing anxious," Kristian informed us, looking like a feast for the eyes in a pair of fawn pants and a white linen shirt with a purple orchid pinned to the pocket. "There, uh, might be some heavy drinking involved too." He looked a little sheepish adding that last part.

"You can't be serious," Jasmine snapped, excusing herself while telling the rest of us to stay put.

Kristian stepped into the room and let out a low whistle. "Looking good, ladies."

I smiled at him as I straightened up, both sandals now on my feet. I was wearing a cream wraparound dress that had pink printed flowers on it that matched the flowers in my hair. I felt like a movie star as it flowed around my body. I also felt like shit because as the alcohol wore off, my jaw ached, along with my brain.

"Are they both drunk or just one?" Alesha asked, slipping her earrings in.

Kristian took her in appreciatively. He licked his lips, then wiped a hand over his face. "Both."

"Champagne?" I asked, fighting a smile while feeling glad I wasn't the only one who took in a little too much liquid courage.

"And rum." He grinned, and I noticed he had a slight dimple. Cute.

My smile only broadened. "Can they stand up?"

"They'll be fine."

"Cartwrights can hold their liquor," Abbot added, crossing his arms as he gave me a pointed look.

"You're talking like I threw up everywhere," I retorted.

"What did happen to you?" Kristian asked. "Half your face is swollen."

When my eyes met Abbot's, I didn't find warning in them, so I didn't think he'd hold it against me if I told the truth. But I chose to lie anyway. *Snitches get stitches.* "Too much champagne. I slipped."

By the way he and Abbot looked at each other then stood up a little straighter, I knew Kristian didn't believe me.

"Should we go?" Alesha piped up, grabbing our matching bouquets and handing mine to me. "The longer we stand around here, the drunker they'll be, right? Might as well get this done before anyone else *falls* over." With her lips pursed, she aimed that last part at me.

"Lead the way?" I said to Kristian at the door.

He held his arm out for me to take. "My pleasure, gorgeous. Let's get you and your golden cunt hitched."

My eyes widened at the crass comment, but I didn't dare question the reason for it. I already knew what he meant.

CHAPTER FIFTEEN
IT MIGHT WORK

"DO YOU, Samuel Cartwright, take Alesha Ward to be your lawfully wedded wife?"

The humid air made my skin clammy as insects chirped and bit. This was what last-minute nuptials got us, a ceremony beside a waterfall surrounded by soft spongy grounds and croaking frogs, the scent of warm damp earth tickling our nostrils.

Alesha looked about ready to pass out. She was the only one of us who hadn't been drinking, but I had a feeling the less-than-ideal setting had shattered her fairy-tale focus. All that was left was a marriage to a man she barely knew.

"I do," Sam forced out, his voice choked.

Please don't throw up.

He managed to swallow it down and smile at Alesha, whose eyes were rimmed red from her struggle not to cry.

"And do you, Alesha Ward, take Samuel Cartwright to be your lawfully wedded husband?"

Her mouth opened and she blinked rapidly, words

failing her. All eyes focused on her and waited. "I... I... I do," she forced out, sucking in a huge relieved breath of air. It was then that a bug took the opportunity to investigate her tonsils by flying right down her throat. Her eyes went wide as she coughed and leaned forwards, grabbing Sam's shirt as she tried to spit the offending creature out.

"Whoa!" Sam grabbed her elbows, trying to steady them both as the spongy ground provided little grip for their smooth-soled shoes. They tilted forwards, then back, legs scurrying against mud like a couple of cartoon characters before they went down with a squelch.

A collective gasp went up and no one dared to react—well, except for me. It was wrong to laugh, but that's exactly what I did. The moment I saw their legs fly up into the air, I couldn't help it. We were all so maudlin standing in the oppressive heat while a celebrant read our wedding vows that the sight of them falling was more than I could bear. My laughter bubbled up and I gripped my stomach, letting out a loud whoop as I pointed at Alesha and shrieked, "You should see your face!"

At first, she looked a little like she might burst into tears, but then her shoulders started to bounce and the only tears rolling down her cheeks were tears of laughter.

I leaned back, pointing at her sitting in the mud, howling at the sight of our filthy bride. Then, as luck—or fate—would have it, gravity attempted to take me down too.

"Careful." Nate caught me before I could hit the ground, but Sam decided to lean over and grab Nate by the ankle, pulling him and me onto the damp ground with them.

"Why don't you join us, brother?"

We were a mess. A howling, crying, laughing mess.

"All right. Enough," Jasmine called out, trying to put a stop to our raucous laughter and get the ceremony back on track.

I wasn't sure who it was—Alesha, perhaps—but someone sent a ball of mud flying in her direction. It landed smack against the left side of her face, getting her eye and the corner of her mouth.

Everyone went silent as she pressed her lips together, then scooped the goo off her face. "That does it," she said, and I thought we were all about to get our ears clipped. Instead, she slapped the handful of mud on the side of Abbot's face and burst into laughter. "Take that!" she yelled, showing that she actually did have a sense of humour as she dove for cover behind Kristian.

Before I knew it, balls of mud were flying while everyone laughed and yelled. I was on my knees, grabbing at the ground and flinging it every which way while I tried to shield my face from the onslaught.

"It's in my mouth!" I heard Alesha squeal, right before another lump splattered on the side of her head.

I pointed and laughed, opening myself up to a mud pie right in the centre of my forehead, delivered by my husband-to-be.

"Brown is your colour," he said as he wrapped me in his arms and pressed his mouth to mine.

"No kissing in a war zone!" Kristian yelled, tackling Nate around the waist and slamming him to the ground. Splatter shot up and went all through my hair, so I figured 'what the hell' and jumped on top of both of them.

By the time we got ourselves under control, we were all completely covered in stinky brown mud. Our white clothes would probably never be the same again, but as I stood in front of the muddy celebrant holding muddy hands with a muddy Nate as his muddy family looked on, I wasn't upset or nervous anymore. In fact, I was smiling.

"Wait," Nate said when the celebrant started reading our vows. "I almost forgot." Dropping my hands, he dug into his pocket and pulled out a piece of fabric, kind of like a glasses cloth. He opened it carefully, trying not to spread the mud too far, and held it out to me. "I thought you'd want to wear this." It was my mother's hairpin. I thought I'd lost it.

Tears sprang to my eyes as I nodded. "Thank you," I whispered, holding still while he slid it into my hair.

"Now she's here with you." He took my hands again, kissing my knuckles even though they were covered in mud while I cried happy tears. It was the nicest thing he could've done. *"Focus on the good. Focus on how you feel about Nate."* I felt good when I was with Nate. He made me feel special, made me feel alive.

"Can we proceed?" the celebrant asked, looking a little pissed because some of the mud had splattered him. We both nodded while I wiped at my eyes—not that it mattered with the amount of mud covering our faces.

Line by line, we went through our vows, our eyes locked and our hands linked. Even covered in mud, Nate was the most beautiful man I'd ever set my eyes on. And he was about to become mine.

When the celebrant asked me that all important question, I didn't even hesitate.

"I do," I said with a wide smile.

Nate leaned in and kissed me too early while everyone

else clapped. Sam followed suit, bending Alesha over backwards as he kissed the life out of her.

"This is the most unorthodox wedding I've ever officiated," the celebrant muttered before he pronounced us husband and wife and walked away in disgust. It was seriously the best wedding I'd ever attended.

———

"Wait, wait." Nate stopped me at the door of our suite, then leaned down and scooped me into his arms. "I have to carry you inside."

Balancing me with one arm, he slipped the key card into the door only to hear a negative buzzing sound instead of the agreeable beep and click we'd been expecting.

"What the hell?" he muttered, trying the card again.

"Maybe you should've opened the door and *then* picked me up," I suggested, my arms wrapped around his neck as he tried over and over to no avail. "Are you sure we have the right room?"

"I'm sure. The damn key just won't work. I hate these fucking cards. What's wrong with actual turning keys?" Using the wall and his thigh to keep me off the ground, he inspected the key card and found the problem: we'd smeared mud on the magnetic strip.

"Bloody hell." There wasn't a single bit of clean fabric on either of us to wipe off the strip, so he settled for squatting deep and rubbing the card clean on the hallway carpet.

I giggled. "You could put me down."

"Not on your life. This is tradition, and your feet won't touch the floor until we're on the other side of that door."

Still in a squat position, he reached up and slipped the

card in the lock. When it beeped and clicked, he grinned. All I could see was dried dirt, white teeth and blue eyes. He looked like something out of *Lord of the Flies*, and I was sure I looked no better. We were leaving our mess everywhere, but we didn't care. We'd just become Mr and Mrs Nathaniel Cartwright while covered in the stuff. It had turned into a pretty fantastic day.

"Let's get you into a shower, duchess. As much as I like my woman dirty, this is taking it a little far," he said, rising and lifting me without the slightest bit of strain.

"I like you muddy, but I'm looking forward to getting you into the shower and washing off all those muscles of yours. Rubbing my hands over your soapy skin." I lowered my eyes. "And... other areas."

His eyes darkened as he stepped through the door and released a soft rumble in his chest. "We only have an hour to get down there for dinner."

"They can wait," I whispered, pulling at his bottom lip with my teeth. "There are things I need to do with my husband first."

He kicked the door shut and walked me into the large bathroom. "Mmm, husband. I like the sound of that."

"Yeah? Call me your wife."

He brushed his lips against mine and set me on the tiled floor. "My wife, my duchess, my queen." He started peeling my clothing from my body as his hands explored my abundant skin.

"You make me feel beautiful," I whispered in amazement as my dress dropped heavily at my feet.

"That's because you are."

"Not to most, but I can see that I am to you. I believe it

when I see the way you look at me, and I don't know why."

"Do you need me to spell it out for you?" Reaching out to turn on the rainfall shower, he took my hand and pulled me into the cubicle with him.

"Yes, I think I do."

"You're *my* kind of beautiful, Holland. All I see when I look at you is perfection, and I've got to tell you, my dick thinks you're amazing. He was the driving force behind this whole trip."

I couldn't help but smile. "But why? You just married me, Nate. Why am I that important to you? You hardly know me."

Steam surrounded us, muffling the air and encapsulating us in our own private world. A world that felt safe because it was only him and me. I wasn't afraid when it was just us.

"I don't really know where to begin." Lifting one of the hand jets from its hook, he started washing the mud from my body, his brow knitted in thought. His hands felt so good against my skin.

"Begin wherever you want. Just make me understand how this happened, from your point of view."

Pressing his lips together, he poked his tongue out slightly, then pulled at his bottom lip with his teeth. "I've never had any kind of serious relationship before, duchess. The family always came first, and anyone who tried to get close was cut loose before they could learn anything real about us. It was safer that way, but when you hit thirty-six, meaningless relationships start to be just that—meaningless."

Thirty-six. I probably should've discovered that sooner.

"I didn't even know I wanted anything serious. I just knew there was this discontent inside me. And then I saw you up on that stage." A smile spread across his face and his eyes danced. "Boy, were you something. I would've paid good money just to sit there all night and watch you sway those hips and belt out those tunes. It sounds corny, but I couldn't breathe watching you, and that feeling I'd been having, I knew that if I could have you, it would go away. I figured that if someone could sing with such fire, such power, she had to have something real special inside her. *I wanted that. I wanted you.* As luck would have it, you came and stood right next to me at the bar, like it was my destiny to get you that drink. Then you took me home, and the rest is world-rocking history."

"Why didn't you just date me? You didn't have to rob me, you know. I probably would've hunted you down just for another taste." My eyes lowered to his impressive appendage.

He chuckled and relinquished control of the jet so I could rinse his deliciously smooth skin. "I don't know, duchess. The boys were expecting a haul, and I knew that my world and relationships didn't work. So, I showed you who I was straight up, thinking that'd be the end of it."

I rubbed his shoulder, spraying the mud to reveal tan skin that I couldn't help but kiss. "Then you did it all again. Why a second time?" I ran my tongue along his collarbone.

"Jesus," he moaned, his hands landing on my hips. "I can't think when you do that shit to me. Turn around." He steered me so my back was against his front, then took the jet and rinsed off my back while pulling pins out of my hair, taking care to make sure my mother's pin was set on the soap tray so it wouldn't fall.

"Are you going to answer my question?"

"I don't know, duchess. Why do men do a lot of stupid things? I hadn't been able to get you out of my head, and you showed up with your sass and demands and fuck, you got my juices flowing. I suppose I was trying to teach you a lesson while at the same time goading you to come find me again. I wasn't expecting you to turn up at the house though."

"But you wanted me to know who was boss?"

Satisfied the pins were all out, he aimed the water against my scalp and rinsed the mud from my hair. "I guess. But I think we both know that I'm a fucking slave to you, duchess. You might not realise it, but you own me."

"*I* own *you*?" That revelation shocked me greatly; I was under the impression that it was the other way around. So many decisions had been taken out of my hands.

"Yeah, you do." He squirted shampoo in his hand and began massaging it into my hair and scalp. I leaned back into his touch, my eyes closing in bliss.

"So, um... this whole thing sounds a lot like love at first sight. I mean, I'm not trying to say that you're in love with me, but it just sounds like something happened when you saw me.... I don't know, it sounds stupid when I say it out loud." I needed to learn to keep my mouth shut—I'd already gotten myself into enough trouble by saying and doing whatever the hell I wanted—but I really wanted to understand this man's motives.

"I know that I had *want* at first sight, but *love*... that isn't really something I have a lot of experience with. I know I love that you're so fearless and smart. You didn't quit looking till you found me, and I know that isn't an easy thing to do." He rinsed the shampoo from my hair, running his hand over my back to wash away the suds. "I love the way your skin feels and smells." He placed the jet back on its hook, then slid his hand over my stomach, lower, lower, until his fingers found my sweet spot and his mouth pressed against my ear. "I love that you're always so ready for me when I want to fuck you." He teased my clit, then slipped a finger into my depths. I rested my head against his shoulder and released a moan. "And I can't get enough of the way you moan uncontrollably whenever I'm inside you. I love that." He ran his tongue down my neck, sucking on my skin as he added a second finger and teased my insides. I quivered in his arms. "Love, want, call it anything you like. All I know is that you own me through and through, duchess. I don't know what it is about you, but for the first time in my life, I want more than the haul. I want *you*."

Lifting my arms above my head, I slid my fingers into his hair and pulled, turning my head in a desperate need to kiss him. "I can't even begin to tell you how much I want you," I whispered in a rush as his fingers brought me to climax and I shook in his arms.

With his mouth on mine, he turned me to face him, then lifted me off the floor and pressed me against the tiled wall, positioning himself at my opening before sliding inside me. I moaned as I sank down his length.

"You feel so good," he gasped, hips swivelling, mouth tasting. "So, so good."

It took great effort to allow a man of such size into my

body, and every part of me trembled as he pushed and pulled at my insides with each overpowering thrust. I had to relax my body and allow him total control or he simply wouldn't fit. The experience of making love to him was a test of my limitations, but the reward was an overwhelming, soul-shaking orgasm. I never wanted to stop fucking this man.

"Duchess," he moaned, his fingers digging into my flesh as he drew closer to climax, bringing me right along with him.

"Oh God, Nate," I gasped, shaking around him, feeling the pulse as his release filled me. I could barely breathe when we were done, and I could tell his knees were shaking. "Do you think they'd miss us at dinner?" I asked when I'd caught my breath.

"Something tells me our absence would be noticed."

I leaned forwards and ran my tongue lightly over his jaw. "It's just… I'm only hungry for one thing."

"Oh Lord, duchess. We will never leave this suite if you start using your tongue like that."

"I can't help it," I whispered, clenching my core around his girth, only slightly softened inside me. "I want to taste every inch of you."

"Maybe they *won't* notice," he said, swallowing hard as I ran my fingernails up and down the firm muscles of his back before resting them at the top of his arse. "And seriously, who gives a fuck if they do? We aren't leaving this room."

Pulling out of me, he set me on the floor and kissed me passionately, his fingers on my face, my breasts, my arse. "I'm going to fuck you every way we can think of. And when we run out of ideas, we'll google more. I hope you aren't planning on walking straight tomorrow."

"I wasn't planning on getting out of bed tomorrow." My answer was given without thought. Although it didn't surprise me, in bed, Nate was Nate and I was me—his duchess—the outside world didn't matter. I wanted to pretend that this was OK for a while.

With an approving smile, Nate scooped me in his arms and carried me to the bed, dropping me on the plush mattress before climbing on top and kissing me languidly, his mouth moving down my neck, licking and sucking at my skin. My fingers went into his hair as I wrapped my body around him. "I thought I was the one who wanted to taste all of you," I gasped when he sucked on one of my nipples.

"You want me to stop?" he asked, a wicked glint in his eyes as his tongue teased me.

"No." I shook my head from side to side. "Don't stop. Please don't stop."

With a chuckle, he closed his mouth around my other nipple and sucked, swirling his tongue around the sensitive tip.

"I'm going to make you come just by doing this," he whispered, twisting one nipple in his fingers while he drew the other in his mouth. I moaned, excited by the possibility. I didn't know if coming from nipple stimulation was a possibility, but if anyone could do it to me, it would be him. "I fucking worship your breasts." He sucked a little harder and I writhed beneath him, taking immense pleasure from his play, the intensity from his licks, sucks and squeezes increasing until suddenly I exploded.

Turned out I *could* come from nipple stimulation alone.

I learned I could come a lot of different ways that night. My husband was a sex god.

My husband. The man who thinks *I* own him through and through. The man, who for the first time in his life wanted more. Wanted *me*. The idea seemed crazy, but who knew?

It might just work.

CHAPTER SIXTEEN
NO ONE TOUCHES MY WIFE

"DID I DO THIS?" Nate's fingertip feathered over my cheekbone as his brow knitted intently.

"Do what?"

"There's a bruise blooming and it looks swollen. Did you hit your face on the headboard? Was I too rough?"

My hand went to my cheek and I looked away, unable to meet his eyes. I had all but forgotten about the slap from his mother, and we'd been too nervous, covered in mud, or lost in ecstasy for him to notice sooner.

"It's nothing. I just, uh... I fell a little earlier. Too much champagne." Based on the way Nate looked down at me, he didn't believe me any more than Kristian had.

His jaw clenched. "Who hit you?" he demanded.

"Hit me?" I tried to laugh it off. "I just told you, I fell."

"You really are a shitty actress, Holland."

"I'm not lying," I insisted, not wanting to cause any waves in his family when their tolerance for me was already so tenuous.

"Tell me who the fuck it was." He shot out of bed and

unzipped his bag, pulling out a pair of jeans and slipping them on.

"Nothing happened, Nate. I'm fine. Please just come back to bed."

Pressing his lips together, he shook his head. "No." He pulled a white T-shirt over his head, then buttoned his jeans.

"What are you even doing?"

He shoved his feet into his shoes. "Since you won't tell me, I'm going out there to get to the bottom of this. No one, and I mean *no one* touches my wife."

"Nate!"

Grabbing the key card, he stalked out of the room, slamming the door of our suite behind him

Shit. If his family didn't hate me before, they certainly will now.

I HAD BEEN EXPECTING an empty bed when I woke up the next morning. I'd sat awake for hours, biting my nails, anxious about what was going on with Nate and his family. I didn't want to be the source of any more animosity between them, and finding out his mother had slapped me wasn't going to sit well with him, nor would it sit well with her or his brothers—they'd think I dobbed when I'd done the exact opposite. Eventually though, I must've fallen asleep, because when I opened my eyes, light was streaming into the room and a warm body was pressed against mine.

"Morning, duchess." His lips pressed against my naked shoulder, his arm wrapped around my middle.

"What happened last night?" I asked, slipping my fingers between his and bringing them to my lips. It was then that I noticed his knuckles were bruised. "Oh, Nate," I whispered, kissing the damage. "What did you do?" I turned quickly, half expecting to see a swollen eye, but his face was as perfect as ever. I felt awful, especially considering who might've been on the receiving end of Nate's fist.

"Nothing that wasn't needed." He leaned in and kissed me, inhaling deeply as he pulled me against him. "But what I really need is you."

I placed my hand against his firm chest. "Please tell me you didn't hit your mother."

He stopped kissing me. "What?" he asked against my lips.

My heart leapt into my throat. "What?" I responded, pulling back and trying to act dumb. He obviously didn't know she was the one to hit me.

"My mother?"

"What? I didn't say anything about her. That would be odd to talk about your mother while we were kissing, right?" I sat up and laughed. "Should I call down for some breakfast? I'm starving." I reached for the bedside phone, but he leaned over me and placed his hand on mine, stopping me.

"My *mother* is the one who did that to you?"

"Who... who did you think it was?" I squeaked, glancing down at his bruised fist.

"Abbot and Kristian backed up *your* story. This is from punching the wall."

"W-why did you do that?"

"As a warning." He narrowed his eyes, studying me. "I

told them it would be their faces beneath my fist if I found out they were lying to me."

I pulled back the sheet, the dressing scene from the night before playing out again in front of me. But this time I needed to stop him. "No, Nate, please. Please don't go and hit your brothers. I lied. They just told you what I told them. Please, they already hate me. Don't give them a reason to hate me more."

His pants were on, but his fly was still open when he paused and pointed at me. "They knew. I could see it in their lying fucking eyes. And that woman." He ground the last word out through gritted teeth. "How fucking dare she."

I jumped out of bed and pressed myself against the door. "Don't do this," I begged. "It wasn't her fault. I goaded her. I said horrible things because I was drunk. Please, Nate, I beg you. Drop it. Please. For me."

His jaw worked from side to side as he stood there, taking in my naked version of a human barricade. The moment I saw his shoulders relax, I knew some of the anger had left him. He walked towards me until we were toe to toe, then lifted his hand, cupping my cheek as he leaned down and kissed me. "Duchess," he whispered. "I can't let any of them get away with hurting you. It doesn't matter why it happened. It's the principle. I chose you, and they need to respect that choice."

My shoulders sagged. "I really wish you'd drop this."

His thumb moved against my cheek. "I can't." He pressed his lips against my forehead. "Now, get dressed and make sure everything is packed. I'm getting you out of here as soon as I get back."

"Where will we go?"

"Home." Stepping away, he grabbed the rest of his clothes. "Lock the door after me," he instructed, his knuckles brushing lightly against the cheek that had caused the problem.

"Promise me you won't hit any of them," I whispered, gripping his wrist before he walked out the door.

He pressed his lips together, his eyes focused where his fingers touched my skin as he shook his head. "Go take a look in the mirror, and then tell me why I shouldn't be angry."

Padding across the carpet, I entered the bathroom, the tiles cool against my feet. Nate flicked on the light that illuminated the mirror. "Oh God," I gasped, not quite expecting what I saw. There was a dark misshapen bruise spanning the apple of my cheek, but that wasn't what had shocked me. My eye was also bloodshot, with one big blotch in the lower right corner and lots of angry little spider veins shooting off it. *Bitch!*

"No one touches my wife," he growled. Then he turned around and stalked from the room.

That time I didn't even try to stop him.

CHAPTER SEVENTEEN
A SENTIMENTAL SOD

"THIS," Nate started as he pulled up in front of a large one-storey farmhouse, "is my pride and joy."

I looked out the window of his slightly beat-up Ford Ranger and took in all that surrounded me. "Wow." It seriously took my breath away. And it wasn't that the house looked quaint and romantic, it was that it was situated in the centre of a massive block of land with panoramic views of world-renowned Bells Beach. "This is *yours*?"

"Ours now," he said, unclicking his seatbelt and getting out of the car. "Come on. I'll show you around."

"I can't get over this." I gaped, turning in a slow circle on the dirt drive. "I expected an apartment, maybe a town-house. Not this." The air was fresh and clean when I inhaled. I'd been ready to pass out after travelling for more than half a day to get back from the Cook Islands. After Nate had confronted his family, he'd whisked me away and we hadn't stopped since. But now, looking over Nate's land in wonder, I had caught my second wind. It was sea breeze, and it licked my skin.

"Let me show you inside," he said, taking my hand and leading me to the long veranda that spanned the front of the house.

"How much land is this?" I asked, craning my neck to take in all the green grass that surrounded us. With the sea and the setting sky as a backdrop, I felt like I was standing in a painting.

"Eighty-six acres," he said, unlocking the front door. "The guy before me raised cattle. I still lease the paddocks out to a couple of hobbyists. Helps keep mowing to a minimum." He shot a grin over his shoulder, then pushed the door open. "Welcome to your castle, duchess."

Curious to see the inside, I stepped forwards only to be swept up in his arms and carried over the threshold.

"I see you learned from our last experience and opened the door first." I smiled, pressing my lips to his as he lowered me to the floor. His mouth was beginning to feel like home.

"I'm not just a pretty face."

"Oh, I already knew that," I commented, dropping my eyes low on his body.

"Always in the gutter," he muttered with a smile and a shake of his head. "Make yourself at home while I grab our bags. There are four bedrooms." He pointed in their general direction. "The master is the first door right there. Bathroom is right next door. Kitchen is there, lounge, dining, rumpus through there… and library in there."

My eyes lit up. "You have a library," I whispered, my hand shooting out to pull at his shirt. "Does it have a ladder so I can re-enact that scene from *Beauty and the Beast*?"

He chuckled. "No, but I can make you one. I think I'd

like to see that." He kissed me briefly, then headed outside to collect our things from the back of his ute.

"Wow," I said again, only that time to myself. All around me was a mixture of rustic farmhouse and surf-shack décor. It felt a lot like the shabby-chic look I'd loved in my own place before my *husband* stole it all from me.

And that was when I started to see it. Some of the furniture in the house—the repurposed sideboard, the distressed coffee table, the mismatched chairs around the kitchen table—was all mine. He'd brought some of my things into his home.

What did that mean? I wasn't sure if I should be touched or slightly creeped out. He couldn't have done this knowing I'd come here and see it. He must've done it in the months it had taken me to find him, after that first time we'd met. Had he been watching me?

I walked through the house room by room, finding a little piece of me in every one of them. I even found my books in the library. When Nate found me, I was kneeling on the floor, holding my dog-eared copy of *A Streetcar Named Desire*. "I'm teaching this to my year ten class at the moment," I mused, running my fingers over the pages that were covered with my notes. "At least, I'm supposed to be..." I let the comment hang in the air. I had no idea what was happening with my job, and after *telling* my boss via *email* I was taking leave without a reason, I might not even have one to get back to.

"Thought I might find you in here," he said softly, leaning against the door frame and crossing his arms across his chest.

"This was my copy from when I performed it at school," I said, showing it to him. "I played Eunice."

"You would've made a great Stella." Shifting to kneel in front of me, he took the book from my hands and slid it back into the shelf where it belonged, his movements almost reverent.

"I thought I was a terrible actor."

"You're not so bad."

"My things are in your house," I stated, meeting his eyes, a little in shock.

"Yes." He sat on the floor with a sigh, leaning against the bookcase.

"Why? Have you been planning this all along? Have you been stalking me?"

He laughed in a way that told me he thought I was being absurd. "As I've told you, I couldn't stop thinking about you. After we took it, every day I found myself driving out to the storage unit and bringing things back. At first it was your books—we weren't going to sell them, I told myself. Then it was the chairs—they didn't match, so no one would want *them*. I had a reason for taking every item, but it was really just a way of being close to you, even though I didn't ever think I'd get to have you."

"But here we are," I responded, twisting around so I was sitting on the floor beside him.

He ran his fingers through my hair. "Here we are," he repeated, his voice soft and low.

"You're a bit of a sentimental sod, aren't you?" I teased, my concerns about any sort of creepy motive getting fuzzier by the second. He had a way about him that always seemed to put me at ease. My morality detector would go into overdrive, but then he'd explain everything away until I just wanted to hold him or be held. The gift of the gab, my aunt would call it.

"Don't tell anyone." He winked. "I've got a reputation to uphold."

I looked around the room. "It's kind of weird that you did this."

"It's kind of weird that you hunted me down and then married me, but I'm not holding it against you." He gave me a sidelong glance accompanied with a smirk.

"I'm not holding the whole 'you have to marry me or my family will kill you for finding our secret hideout' thing against you either."

He laughed at that, then took my hand, kissing the back of it. "I'm glad."

"You don't want to know why?"

"I already know why."

"You do?"

He nodded. "Because you know that I did this to keep you safe. And I did it because I want you more than I want anything else in this world."

"Do you want me enough to quit your current job?" It was probably too soon, but I had to try.

"That's another thing I don't really get a choice in." *Interesting. Does that mean he feels like a prisoner too?* It was an intriguing thought that I found myself pondering while we sat in companionable silence.

"I think your home is beautiful," I told him after a while, giving his hand a gentle squeeze.

He seemed to startle slightly, either tired from the travel or just in deep thought. "It's more beautiful now that you're in it."

"Who would've thought you'd be such a romantic?"

He smiled and took my hands, pulling me up until we were both standing. "How about I make us a romantic dinner, then? I'll bet you're starved after barely eating the last couple of days."

"Famished," I responded, leaning against him. "I'm fading away."

He slid his hands down to my arse, gave it a squeeze and grinned. "We can't have that. I like my woman's curves." Then just as fast as it appeared, his grin disappeared, his brow knitting as he brushed the tips of his fingers against my cheek.

"What's wrong?"

"I hate that a member of my family struck you. Every time I look at it, I get so fucking angry. It will *never* happen again, duchess. Never."

"I believe you." There was such sincerity in his gaze and his words that I knew them to be true.

He pressed a gentle kiss on my cheek then took my hand. "Food."

I grinned. "Food."

Following him into the well-appointed kitchen, I cut up ingredients for a salad while he fried some lamb cutlets and cubed potatoes. We topped it off with a bottle of cold Pinot Grigio, then ate outside on the porch, the sound of the ocean providing music. The conversation flowed easily, the same way it had on that first night. He was surprisingly open and told me all about growing up in a house of five brothers with no father figure around, learning how to steal cars and pick pockets. In return, I told him about life after losing my parents, growing up with my aunt and wreaking havoc in the eyes of Alesha's super-strict dad.

"Sounds like you were a bit of a terror," he said during a pause in the conversation.

I smiled at him and took another sip of wine. "No more than most. I certainly wasn't out there robbing people."

His gaze focused on his glass. "You've never taken a single thing that didn't belong to you?"

"Never."

"No one is that pious, duchess. Everyone's taken something—a pen, extra change, a chocolate bar as a kid or an item that didn't scan as an adult. There isn't a single one of us able to cast a stone on that one."

I thought back to the times when I left stores, then found items in my grocery trolley that I'd forgotten to pay for. "I suppose you're right," I said quietly.

He leaned back in his chair and stretched his long legs out in front of him. "There are worse things to be in this life than a thief."

Mirroring his reclined position, I looked out to the water, watching a flock of gulls diving to feed on a school of fish. "Better than making your money being a contract killer."

"There you go." He looked over at me and smiled.

"Or a gun smuggler. I would really hate that."

"Or a people smuggler," he added.

"Oh, you're right," I gasped. "That would be horrible."

"See, there are worse things." He took my hand, lacing our fingers together as we both stared out at the setting sun.

"Or a drug dealer. I'd *really* hate it if you were that."

"More than if I was a contract killer or people smuggler?"

I nodded. "Yes. Alesha's mother is a victim of the drug trade. She had nerve damage and got hooked on her pain meds, which turned into an opiate addiction, and then suddenly she was gone. She went from doting mum to full-blown junkie in less than twelve months."

"She died?"

"We have no idea. She just left when we were in grade six and never came back. Alesha's father won't even speak her name."

He lifted my hand and pressed a kiss against my centre knuckle. "I think everyone has a story of someone they knew who took things too far. Jasmine has always been adamant that if we're caught using, we're out of the family. She has zero tolerance for users."

"That's the first thing I've ever agreed with her on. Although, I have to ask, why do you call her Jasmine instead of Mum?"

"It's just something we've always done. Especially where jobs are concerned, we don't wanna be yelling 'Mum' when we need to run."

"She does jobs with you?"

"Sometimes. Mostly she holds down the fort and deals with the business side of things. She was great in her day though. Never caught, and only questioned twice."

"Sounds like you had a good teacher."

"That we did." Something about the way he said it and the silence following made me think that she was a much better thief than she was a mother. But then, I'd been spoilt growing up. I'd had two wonderful mothers—my own, and my aunt after. I never wanted for love or attention. Perhaps that was the difference between growing into a criminal or a model citizen.

There was so much more I wanted to know about him. He'd lived a life far removed from my own experience, and I wanted to know every single detail. But as the silence between us extended, I knew that those questions would have to wait for another day.

"You know, I never did get a look inside the master bedroom. Want to show me?"

His head whipped around and his eyes lit up. "Is that your way of propositioning me, duchess?"

I stood up and peeled my shirt off. "Maybe," I said coyly, swinging my hips as I headed for the door. The moment I stepped through, I removed my bra and tossed it out for him to see. I'd barely taken two steps before he collected me in his arms and ravished me with his skilful mouth.

I saw a lot of the house that night, but it wasn't until much later that I saw the master bedroom, falling into the massive mahogany bed, exhausted and aching all over in the most delectable way. I listened to the ocean's lullaby singing me to sleep through the large floor-to-ceiling windows that covered the outside wall. It was picturesque, perfect, the fairy tale Alesha had been talking about.

For a brief moment, I wondered how she was now that the wedding was complete and she was married to her own thief. But then Nate pulled me a little tighter, pressing a kiss on my shoulder as he whispered, "Sweet dreams, duchess." I let out a contented sigh, my eyes heavy as I snuggled a little closer. And it hit me then. I was content. A few weeks ago, I'd considered throwing my *normal* life aside and travelling the world for a while. Perhaps I had been feeling discontent then. I wasn't sure. But I was sure that just as Nate had said he'd felt found in me, I was beginning to realise that I felt found in him too. *I could get used to this.*

CHAPTER EIGHTEEN
NO FUCKING CLUE

WAKING up in Nate's arms and knowing there wasn't another soul around to interrupt or influence our day was the slice of heaven I didn't realise I'd been craving. I drank him in, my eyes feasting on his large muscular frame and that beautiful yet still manly face. *How in the world did this happen? How did my life go from perpetually single to married in the snap of two fingers?*

"Good morning, husband," I whispered, sliding my hands over his muscled chest.

He grinned, his eyes still closed as I nibbled the skin at his neck. "Morning, duchess."

As my hand crept lower, I noticed the sheet tent just below his waist. "Looks like someone else is very happy to see me," I said, taking in all that hard, smooth flesh that made up the man I could now call my husband. *Husband...* I didn't know when that would sound normal to me. My life had now become some insane and unbelievable plot for a movie—but the view was fantastic.

"Enjoying yourself down there?"

Glancing up at him, I pressed my teeth into my bottom lip and grinned. "I think I might need to do a little more *thorough* inspection of the merchandise," I said, pulling back the sheet and climbing over him so I was straddling his waist, my back facing his chest, his proud cock standing up in front of me. I used two hands to lift and stroke it. It was heavy.

"Mmm." His hands settled on my hips. "Inspect away."

I leaned close, using a finger to trace over his veins. "How do you not pass out from a lack of blood flow when this thing is erect?" I asked, enjoying the way he twitched when I pressed against the main vein that ran the length of it.

"Thing? I'm not sure he likes being called a *thing*, duchess."

"Hmm, then what would *he* like to be called?" I continued gliding my hands up and down his length as I thought out loud. "I think calling him Little Nate would be insulting."

"Well, he ain't little."

"That's my point. You know, you could make an excellent living in the porn industry with an appendage like this. It's so big that you could conquer cities of tiny women with it. Oh, I know! Goliath, we'll call him Goliath."

When he laughed, I bounced along with him. "I've never had a name for my penis before, but sure, Goliath, it is."

"Does Goliath want to roar?" I teased, gripping a little tighter and sliding my hands up and down his shaft.

"Oh yeah, he does," Nate moaned, his washboard abs tightening beneath my butt. I may not be able to deep throat his oversized appendage, but I could give a great handjob.

Pressing the sweet spot on his shaft, I rubbed up and down. Leaning forwards, I took the tip in my mouth, using my tongue to tease the rim. His hips rolled and his breath hissed. I sucked a little firmer, pumped a little faster. Then I massaged his balls with a light touch. That was all it took.

"Holy fuck, duchess," he grunted, then stiffened as hot cum erupted from his tip. I swallowed it down while I slowed my movements and kept him riding that glorious high.

"Well done, Goliath," I teased when his shudders subsided, stroking it gently as Nate chuckled.

"OK, that's enough of the Goliath talk for now."

I twisted my body and smiled at him over my shoulder. "All right, just don't go getting any ideas over that whole porn industry comment. This might not be your traditional marriage, but I still don't want other women having access to my husband's talents."

He slid his hand up the centre of my back, wrapping his fingers around my long hair before he pulled back so I fell on the bed beside him. He flipped over and held himself over me. "This marriage, duchess, is everything a marriage is supposed to be. Don't for a second be thinking otherwise. I expect you to behave the way a wife should, and in return, I'll behave the way a husband should." He moved his hips slightly, the tip of his cock gliding over my favourite tingly bits, making me gasp.

"Behave the way a wife should? I don't know if I have it in me to be that kind of girl. I don't know if you noticed, but I'm not easily controlled."

His mouth twitched at the corners. "Then I may just have to fuck you into submission." He dipped his head and moved down my neck, kissing and licking as he reached down and gripped his cock, guiding it so it rubbed back and forth against my sex, silky soft as it teased my clit and opening.

"Ohh, I think I like this kind of control."

"I'll chain you to this bed, make you my sex slave."

"You don't need to chain me. I'm willingly here."

He paused and met my eyes. "Are you?" There was something in his gaze that made my heart flit about in my chest, a hopefulness that showed me just how vulnerable he really was.

Is he afraid I'm going to leave him?

I ran my fingers through his thick hair and down along his jaw until I was touching his lips. "Yes."

The moment the word left my lips, he closed his eyes and pushed inside, his features softening in relief as he wrapped his arms around me, then rolled us so I was on top. He'd never given me control like that before, like perhaps he was worrying that if he wasn't pinning me down, I'd get up and run away. But how could I? There was something about Nate that anchored me to his side, called to me like a siren in the sea whenever we were apart. I'd spent months hunting him down, knowing in the back of my mind that I wanted him for far more than simple recompense.

I'd wanted *him.*

Just like he'd told me that I owned him, he also owned me. That part about our relationship was incredibly clear. The rest? Well, that was a huge fucking mess. But we'd work it out. Somehow.

With our hands joined, I rode him, sliding up and down his shaft, taking him as far into my body as I could. We kept our eyes locked, waiting for that moment when we would both find our release and fall just a little further into the abyss of our emotions.

When our bodies shuddered and he came inside me, I leaned down and kissed him with passion and sincerity. I felt closer to him than I'd ever been to anyone in my life. But at the same time, my mind reeled with a thousand different questions about how we were supposed to work as a couple outside this seaside home. We worked *together*, that much was clear; our bodies were completely in sync, and when we were alone, everything in the world felt right. But just outside that door, past the long dirt drive, there was an entire world we had to navigate. It was a world filled with danger and secrets, one I didn't know if I could find any kind of happiness in, let alone bring a child into.

It was something that kept ringing in my ears. The expectation to produce a child had been spoken of more than once, and I honestly didn't know if I wanted one under normal circumstances, let alone under these. When I thought about my future with Nate, every scenario ended with me sitting on the other side of the Perspex sheet in a high-security prison, unable to touch him and only able to speak via phone. The idea made tears spring to my eyes.

"My duchess... my queen," Nate whispered, sliding a hand against my cheek as we rolled again and he kissed me languidly, caressing my face in the most loving way possible. He didn't ask me why I was crying. It was possible that he already understood, or perhaps he just didn't want to know, didn't want to face the reality of our problems.

Reality was something I wished I could switch off so I could just enjoy this honeymoon period with Nate. At face value, he was everything I'd ever dreamed of having in a mate: smart, sexy, gorgeous and funny. He likened life to movies and books, and made me feel like a beauty queen every time his gaze simmered against mine. He didn't give a fuck about my excess curves, loved my slightly over-bearing personality, and even tolerated my incessant questions. He defended me fiercely against his family, and as long as I promised to stay by his side, it seemed I could do no wrong. But there was a lot that *was* wrong. More than I could ignore. So much that I knew it would eventually come between us. This bubble of bliss couldn't last forever.

I had to face facts. He was a criminal. Everything beautiful that surrounded us was attained by criminal means. Even the seemingly romantic gesture of merging his things and mine had happened because of his illegal activities. I couldn't turn a blind eye to that. The big, beautiful, sweet man who made my heart and body sing was not a good man by any stretch of the imagination. And he was completely unapologetic about it because it was all he knew. This life was his *normal*. I didn't know if it would ever be mine. From that point forward, I'd have to lie to everyone and anyone in order to protect him and myself. Could I do that? Did I feel enough for him to put his safety above my own? To *lie* for him?

I'd have to lie to my aunt about who he was. Sitting at the table talking about his latest haul certainly wasn't going to be appropriate dinner conversation. And that wasn't the least of it—what about my job? I didn't want to sit around a house raising a bunch of thug kids while my husband was off robbing the rich to make his own family richer.

None of that sat right with me. No matter how lust-filled I was in his presence, I just couldn't stop that little voice in the back of my head, saying, 'What about...? What about...? What about...?"

Because I didn't know. I had no fucking clue.

CHAPTER NINETEEN
BEGGING DUCHESS

"WHAT ARE YOU DOING OUT HERE?" I asked, entering the shed that doubled as a workshop. I'd been in the bath reading a book about rock stars when I'd heard banging and drilling in the distance. It continued when I'd climbed out, and since I couldn't find Nate inside the house, I'd slipped on a dress and some shoes, then followed the sound to investigate.

"It's a surprise." He looked at me and grinned, a light sheen of sweat coating his skin. *Is it weird that I want to lick it?*

Curiosity drew me closer. "A surprise? For me?"

He continued sanding a piece of wood, the muscles in his arms and back rippling with his movements. He wore a pair of jeans and a faded red T-shirt that clung to his sweaty body. It all looked enticing to me. I loved a man who knew how to use his hands.

"I'm not surprising myself," he teased.

I looked over the items on the workbench, taking in the two long and narrow pieces of wood and the many smaller ones. They all seemed cut from larger branches that I figured had come from trees on the property. I had a fairly good idea what it was, and I already loved it. "Can I try and guess?"

"That would defeat the purpose."

I ran my hand over his warm back and peered around him. "I'm going to guess anyway."

He dropped what he was doing, catching me by the waist. "Mmm, you smell good."

I ran my hands over his chest. "And you smell like work."

"Is that a good smell or a bad smell?"

I made a show of sniffing him, pulling at his damp shirt. "It's a good thing. You smell like you and…." I sniffed again. "The ladder that you're making for the library."

"There goes my surprise." He laughed, dropping a kiss on the tip of my nose.

"I love it."

"It's not finished yet."

"I don't care. Just the fact that you came out here to build something I suggested off the cuff is the most beautiful thing a man has ever done for me."

"I guess you haven't been hanging out with the right men."

"Aren't you glad?"

He grinned, dipping his head towards mine. "Very." He slid his hands down to grip my arse and his mouth connected with mine, kissing me in a way that was softer and more sensual than before. The kind of kiss that made you feel like the centre of the universe, the epicentre of his world.

"I want you," I gasped, pushing his shirt up his chest so I could feel his skin beneath my hands. "Right now. Right here."

"I'm filthy, duchess, and you just got out of the bath."

"Then make me dirty again. We can wash off together."

He responded by taking his shirt off. "Better?"

I licked my lips, then nodded and ran my tongue just between his pecs, the taste of salt coating my tongue.

He groaned, his fingers gripping tighter against my arse, his hips pressing against me as his erection grew. "Want to play a game, duchess?"

My tongue continued up his throat to the curve of his jaw. "Uh-huh."

Walking me backwards until my arse hit the workbench, he caught my hands in his, lifting them over my head. "It's called 'Begging Duchess'."

I liked the sound of that. "And how do we play that game?"

"Do you trust me?" Holding both of my hands in one of his, he pulled down a piece of cord and held it in front of me.

I nodded. "Yes." It was crazy but true. I trusted him with my life.

His eyes smouldered as he wound the cord around my wrists, then secured it to a bracket that housed a shelf of surfboards above my head. "Too loose?"

Pulling against the cord, the boards above me rattled but didn't shift. I hoped they wouldn't fall and tugged a little harder. When all seemed secure, I shook my head.

"Good. Now stay put while I finish making this," he said, stepping away and immediately restarting his work.

"Nate! Don't you dare leave me here." I pulled against the cord, twisted my body and tried to kick out at him.

He ignored me and kept sanding, leaning down to blow away the dust and inspect his work.

"Nate." There was a tone of warning in my voice.

"Duchess." There was amusement in his.

"Get me down."

Placing a rung in the vice, he secured it, then picked up a wood plane.

"Please, Nate, please. This isn't funny." The direct route wasn't working, so I tried a little sugar in my voice.

He immediately stopped what he was doing and looked my way, a giant grin curling that sexy mouth of his. "I guess round one goes to me."

He made me beg. *Cheeky bastard.*

Putting down his tools, he walked over to me, a swagger to his step as he wiped his hands on a rag and threw it aside. My entire body reacted to him. *So incredibly sexy.* "I really like it when you beg. It gets me all *hard* knowing what you want from me." To punctuate his words, he slid his hand into his jeans and grabbed his cock. My insides clenched from wanting.

"Is there any way that I win at this game?" I asked, a smile tilting the edge of my mouth as I realised how easily I got played.

"Beg for the right things and we both win, duchess." His voice took on a gravelly tone as his eyes dragged down my body, obviously enjoying seeing me tied up.

"OK. I think I get this game now. I tell you what I want, and you'll do it, but only if I beg." He nodded, licking his lips in that sexy way I loved. "What if I tell you to do something and you do it without me begging? Do I win then?"

He chuckled slightly. "Sure, you'll win if that's what you want."

"Drive you so wild that you can't help yourself? Of course I want to win." His eyes met mine, filled with interest and desire.

"What is it you want, duchess?"

"I want you to unzip your jeans so I can see your hand wrapped around Goliath."

His eyes glittered, enjoying his game. "That didn't sound like begging."

"Please, Nate. Please, I *need* to see."

He did as I asked, unbuttoning his jeans to release his erection. I gasped at the sight, his hand wrapped around his girth, gliding back and forth. So erotic, so manly, it made my core throb in anticipation.

"You like this?"

My breathing quickened as I watched his masculine strokes. "Yes. Keep going, please."

Heat rose in my cheeks and his tip glistened in a way that made me lick my lips. He groaned at my slight movement.

"Have you ever done that while thinking about me?"

His grip tightened. "Every fucking day since we met. I'd think about that sweet cunt of yours and I couldn't help myself."

"That's a filthy word."

"I'm a filthy guy."

Our eyes locked. *He certainly is.*

"Take off my dress so you can see."

His hand slowed while he spoke. "I'd have to cut you loose."

"You don't want to see my *sweet cunt*?"

"Oh, I wanna see it."

"Then please, I beg you. Strip me."

With his breathing laboured, he released his cock and picked up a utility knife from his workbench. When he stood in front of me, he lifted his hands above my head, his cock pressing into my stomach. Then he stilled just before he cut the cord.

"Wait. I have a better idea," he said, lowering his hands so he held the knife at my chest. A sliver of fear flickered through me, but then he pulled the neckline of my dress back and cut into the fabric, gliding the knife all the way down to the hem until it fell open, exposing my naked body. "Mmm, no panties." He rose to his feet and cut the straps, causing the dress to drop to the floor.

"That was one of my favourite dresses," I gasped, my chest heaving. I was so turned on that I could feel the cool air touching my juices.

"You begged for me to remove your dress. I obliged." He grinned and stepped away from me, disappearing farther into the shed.

"Where are you going?"

He was barely gone a minute before he returned with an adjustable stool.

"Just adding a touch of my own." He positioned the stool under my arse, then flicked the lever until it was high enough for me to sit. "Now, spread your legs," he commanded.

"I didn't hear you beg," I responded with a coquettish grin.

Placing his hands on the inside of my knees, he pushed my thighs wide apart while brushing his lips against my mouth. "That isn't the aim of the game."

He had me there.

My eyes locked with his, I placed my heels on the foot hold, then opened my legs as wide as I possibly could. "Is that what you want?"

Stepping back, his eyes swept over every part of me, lingering on my exposed pussy. His cock twitched, and then his hand caught it. I just about came from the bolt of arousal that shot through me.

"Show me," I whispered. "Show me what I do to you. I want to watch you come. Please, Nate, show me." I was really enjoying this game, more so when his hand began to stroke, his speed and grip increasing along with his rate of breathing while I whispered encouragement and squirmed in my seat.

"Fuck, duchess," he hissed. "I'm gonna come."

"Then do it on me," I gasped. He stepped forward, and with a couple more strokes, he unloaded a hot stream of cum on my chest. He caught my mouth in his, kissing me thoroughly as his cock twitched against my stomach.

"Looks like I won that round," I said when our lips parted. "I didn't beg."

His shoulders shook with amusement as he kissed me again. "Oh, I'm gonna make you beg, duchess." He dropped to his knees and flicked his tongue over my clit. My legs shook. "By the time I'm finished with you, you'll be screaming so loud the surfers on the beach will hear you."

"YOU'RE PROBABLY GETTING REALLY TIRED of my questions at this point," I started as I stood at the sink in Nate's rustic kitchen. The ladder still lay in pieces on Nate's workbench, my dress in tatters on the floor, all left behind in favour of sexual games until our need for food forced us to be domestic.

He leaned against the glossy timber bench top drying a plate. "But you're going to ask anyway." He grinned as he met my eyes. I loved the way his sparkled with happiness. I wanted some of that for myself, wanted to feel as sure about this as he did.

If only we could exist in this house on our own forever. If only we could shut out the world.

"I love my job, Nate. I love teaching, and I love singing. I'm booked to do a wedding in a few weeks, and it would be so hard for them to find someone new at this stage. Plus my class is in the midst of rehearsals for a play we're putting on. I don't want to walk away from that. It's bad enough that I've already walked away for two weeks without notice."

It had been exactly that. Two weeks into my marriage and my new life as wife to the loveable rogue standing beside me. I'd never had so much sex in my entire life. The man was insatiable in his need to torture every blissful moan from my body. A satisfied smile had become a permanent fixture on my face. Thankfully the bloodshot eye and bruised cheek had faded, leaving the unpleasant memory of his mother's temper right where it belonged— in the past. I had no doubt that Nate's wrath was fierce and his family would think twice before even looking my way again. Not that we'd heard from his family since we'd arrived back in the country, but I knew they were there, waiting in the wings. We couldn't ignore them for long.

"That sounds more like an essay than a question, duchess." He set the plate on the shelf, then took the wet one from my hands. "Why don't you just ask exactly what's on your mind?"

"Will I be allowed to go back to work?" I held my breath as I watched his face for a reaction.

"Barefoot and pregnant in my kitchen isn't your life-long dream?"

I released a sigh. "No, it isn't. And if I'm perfectly honest, I don't feel that bringing a child into your world is the right thing to do."

"My world? Look around you, duchess. This property is worth millions. You don't think I could provide a good life for my children?"

"I don't doubt your ability to provide things. I doubt your ability to provide a safe environment."

"Because there are bullets whizzing past your head every time you step outside?"

"You know that isn't what I mean."

"Then what do you mean? Spell it out."

"I don't want to have children with you while you're still involved with your family."

His expression darkened as he set the dry plate back on the shelf, working the tea towel between his hands. "I've already told you that going straight isn't the life for me."

"And being crooked isn't the life for me. I like my job. I like following the rules. I don't want to worry every time I see a cop that they're after you. I don't want to have kids who need to visit their father through a set of bars."

"Cartwrights don't do time," he said through gritted teeth.

"So you've said. But all it takes is one slip-up, one set-up, one crumb to lead back to you and this is all over."

"That won't happen. We're too careful."

"You have to at least admit it's a possibility! Jesus, Nate, what happens to me if something happens to you?"

"You'll be taken care of," he replied quickly.

"No, Nate. What happens to *me* without *you*? Don't you get it?" Frowning, he shook his head. I ran my wet hands through my hair. "I've fallen in love with you, you dopey fuck. And the idea of losing you scares the living shit out of me." I threw the dishcloth over the tap and stomped out of the kitchen, shaking my head as I breathed deeply to calm down. I'd said it. I loved him. I'd sworn I wouldn't do it, but I did. I fell. How could I not fall for him? Despite his profession, he was the man of my dreams, my soulmate.

A few moments later, he slid his hands around my waist from behind. "Love, duchess?" he asked, resting his chin on my shoulder.

"Surprise! I'll bet you didn't expect that to come out of my mouth so soon." Tears threatened the backs of my eyes.

He ran his fingers through my hair, brushing the tangled waves. It felt wonderful and helped calm my stormy mind. "I wake up every day afraid that you've left during night. But when you're still asleep in my arms, I fall a little deeper each time. And when you wake, I get a little more lost in your eyes, your smile, your smell." He inhaled deeply. "I don't know if that's love or need or if it's because you cure my loneliness, but whatever it is, I'm thankful for it. I'm thankful for you. I don't regret a single moment since bringing you into my life. As for kids, I want them, but I can wait. I want you to want them too. I'm not that much of an arse."

"And what about my work?"

"Go and do it. I'll drive you there myself."

"What about *your* work?"

His jaw clenched. "I can't walk away from the family."

I turned in his arms, tired and drained after my outburst. "Look around, Nate. Don't you think we have enough? Don't you think you could retire now and still be a wealthy man?"

His brow furrowed as he peered down into my face. "It isn't that easy, duchess."

"Could you at least promise me that you'll think about it?"

He studied me for a moment, then nodded.

"Thank you." Wrapping my arms around his waist, I buried my face against his chest.

I felt him sigh before his big arms surrounded me. "Love, huh?" he asked again, as if he couldn't believe it.

I nodded and he squeezed a little tighter.

"Love."

"MISS FOSTER!" Emily practically yelled when I walked into the drama room the next Monday. "We thought you might never come back."

"And the sub was awful. We watched the movie more times than we rehearsed. I think she has a crush on Marlon Brando," another girl, Jade, said.

"Pity he got so gross when he got older," a third piped up. The rest of the class laughed until I lifted my hand, a sign they knew meant they needed to settle down.

"How was your holiday?" Emily asked the moment things quieted, bringing the attention back to herself as she was wont to do.

I smiled as I held out my hand for them to see. Besides Alesha, these girls were the closest things to friends I had. Sad, I know, a grown woman considering sixteen-year-olds as friends.

"Is that a ring on your finger? You're engaged?" The girls rushed the front of the room and gathered around me to get a closer look at my bling.

"Married, actually," I said, making them gasp even more.

"We didn't even know you had a boyfriend."

I just smiled and shrugged, knowing that any further details would be highly inappropriate in the current situation.

"So, it isn't Miss Foster anymore?"

"No. Now it's Mrs Cartwright." I said it with pride. Finally, I wasn't the sad, fat and single girl anymore. Now I was a married woman. I never realised how much I'd wanted that title until the moment I said it out loud.

Mrs Nathaniel Cartwright.

WHEN NATE PULLED up outside the school to pick me up from work, there was a gaggle of teenage girls trying to get a glimpse of him. Word had spread pretty quickly around the students and even the faculty that I'd run off and gotten married. That's when the speculation began about what he looked like, whether he was big like me, and the most offensive one—whether I'd paid for a mail-order groom. I couldn't wait for them to eat their words, but at the same time, I kind of wanted to keep Nate to myself and rushed towards the passenger door so we could leave without satisfying their curiosity. I had more pride than that.

Although, the decision got taken out of my hands when he got out of the car to open my door for me. A collective gasp rose from the peanut gallery.

"Oh my God. He's so tall. And *hot*!" I heard one girl exclaim, like it was such a shock that I could land a man like Nate.

"I don't believe it," another said.

The whispering that followed made me a little snappy, and I almost told them all to fuck off before one girl from outside the group, a girl named Edith who was little and round like me, moved in front of me with her hands clasped together as she looked between me and Nate. She whispered, "Congratulations, Miss," before scurrying away. If she'd been a cartoon character, there would've been love hearts in her eyes. Just seeing her reaction was all I needed to cool my jets—now she knew that big girls scored hot guys too. I was the best role model ever.

"Your fan club, duchess?" Nate asked as he leaned past me to open my door. The girls all kept staring, so he smiled at them and gave a little wave.

"More like sceptical spectators," I muttered as they made gasping noises.

"Then let's give them something to gossip about," he said, wrapping me in his arms and kissing the life out me as the girls cheered him on with squeals and giggles. It felt like I was on the red carpet with a movie star.

"You're going to get me sacked." I laughed as he stood me back up. "I'm lucky they let me come back as it is."

"That's an idea," he said, waggling his eyebrows. "Then you'd have more time to devote to me."

With a playful slap against his chest, I slid into the passenger seat and waved goodbye to the girls. Some of them looked as though they might combust if Nate hung around much longer. *Take that, skinny bitches.* It was the most cathartic experience of my life, and I needed to remember to put a photo of Nate and me on Facebook so all the snooty bitches from my high school days could drool and be jealous at the sight of my gorgeous husband. Which reminded me…

"Do you think we can we stop in at my aunt's before we drive all the way back? I've only spoken to her once since the wedding, and she worries about me. Plus I really would like it if you'd meet her."

Pulling away from the curb, that tongue of his moved over his lips. "Will she recognise me?"

"Recognise you?"

"Yeah, from the detailed description you so helpfully provided the police sketch artist."

"Well no, I don't think so. No one recognised you from that sketch. The likeness wasn't really the best, was it? Don't think recalling details is my greatest strength. The sketch looks more like Hugh Jackman than you." I chuckled.

"I don't look like Hugh Jackman?"

"Well, er, no. There are similarities, which is why I kept likening you to him when I was describing you to the sketch artist. I *do* think I went a little overboard though. Now poor Hugh is probably wanted for burglary."

"Poor Hugh," he repeated with a chuckle before asking for Aunt Maya's address.

"So, yes?" I clapped as he steered in the right direction.

"Yes, duchess. I'll meet your aunt."

"She's going to love you."

"I DON'T TRUST HIM," Aunt Maya said the moment we were alone. "He's too good-looking, and what do we *really* know about him?"

"Aunt Maya," I warned, pulling mugs from the cupboard to make tea.

"You have to ask yourself these questions, Holland. He married you after what, one weekend? What if he's after your money? That inheritance from your parents isn't small."

"He's not after my money, Aunty," I responded in a hushed tone. "He doesn't even know about it."

"Are you sure? There are all those cyber hackers these days."

"I'm sure. Is it too much to ask for you to just be happy for me?"

"Of course I can be happy for you. But I'm going to look out for you too. You're my number-one priority in this world, not some muscle-bound surfer type. He is a surfer, isn't he? He looks like he'd be a surfer."

"I haven't seen it yet, but yes, he does surf when the desire arises."

"See? I can pick a man just by looking at him," she insisted.

With my lips pressed together, I shook my head as I regarded her. "I love him. I want to be with him," I told her, just as I heard the water turn on in the bathroom. Nate would be back out in a minute. "Please, Aunty. Be nice." I gave her a pointed look. She held up her hands and went back to preparing tea.

"Anything I can help with?" Nate asked when he returned, dropping a casual kiss on the side of my head.

"That depends," Aunt Maya said. "Did you wash your hands?"

"Sure did," he said, holding them out palms up. "Want

to sniff them to make sure they smell like soap?" He wiggled his fingers.

"I think I'll pass," she retorted, although I was sure I saw her lips twitch.

"Then what can I do?"

"You can get the milk from the fridge."

Nate fetched the milk while I placed teabags inside each mug and Aunt Maya poured the water.

"So, tell me, Nathaniel," she asked when we were seated around the dining table, a plate of chocolate biscuits between us all. "What is it you do for a living?"

I almost choked on my biscuit as soon as I bit into it. Why hadn't I thought about this part? We hadn't discussed what he was going to say.

With a charming smile, Nate finished his sip of tea, then placed his mug back on the table. "My family owns a series of small businesses. I help manage those. I also lease out some of my land to hobby farmers. They run some cattle and sheep on the acres at the back of my property."

Aunt Maya's eyebrows lifted. "Land?"

"Nate owns eighty-three acres right across from Bells Beach, Aunty. You can see the ocean from nearly every window. It's beautiful. You should come see it some time." I glanced at Nate to make sure I wasn't overstepping by inviting her. He seemed unfazed.

"And what about that brother of yours? The one who married Alesha? Does he do the same as you?"

"There are five of us in total. We all help in some capacity."

"Your family's business portfolio must be extensive if it can keep five brothers busy. Exactly what are these holdings?"

"Aunt Maya," I hissed, finding her prying rude while also knowing that the more questions she asked, the less answers she'd get, which would cause a problem.

Nate sat back and wiped a hand over his face. "Let's see, there's a storage facility, a laundromat, two bars, a caravan park, a surf shop, my two youngest brothers run a landscaping business—oh, and there are a handful of real estate holdings on top of that."

"Your family has fingers in a lot of pies," Aunt Maya responded, while I wondered if any of what he said was true. Either way, my aunt seemed appeased that he was independently wealthy enough not to be after the five-hundred-grand inheritance I had placed in a term investment as my early retirement plan.

That meant she could move on to other things. "Explain something else to me, then, Nathaniel. What possessed you and your brother to elope with two women you only just met?"

An uncontrollable grin spread across Nate's features as he draped an arm over the back of my chair. "Love at first sight," he stated without flinching. "I saw Holland and couldn't imagine the rest of my life without her."

When his eyes landed on me, I couldn't help myself. I leaned over and kissed him.

"Good answer," Aunt Maya said when I finally released him. She was leaning with her elbows on the table, her chin in her hand. "OK, you win. I like him."

"DOES your family seriously own all of those business-es?" I asked Nate on the long drive back to his property—a place I was going to have to get used to calling my home.

"Sure does. It's how we legitimise our earnings."

"I see. So, you use all those businesses to launder the profits of your illegal activities."

He touched his nose and winked.

I sat back in my seat and thought on it for a moment. "These businesses, do they turn a profit in their own right?"

Nate looked ahead, his focus on the road as he shrugged a shoulder. "I suppose. Jasmine looks after all the books, we do all the grunt work—picking up takings and paperwork, fixing things that are broken… you know, normal shit you'd need to do when you have a portfolio to manage. What's your point?"

"OK. It's just that there are so many of them, and there's obviously a lot of money to go around if you're able to afford the property we're living on—"

"I have my own investments. The others aren't as well off as I am," he interrupted.

"OK, but that only presses my point more. Why are you still robbing people? You, in particular, have so much already. Why do you need more?"

He glanced at me, and I could tell by his expression that he legitimately didn't know the answer to that question. "It's just what we do," he said eventually.

"At what point do you think you'll decide you have enough?"

He licked his lips and shook his head. "I don't know. When everyone in the family is as wealthy as I am, I suppose."

"They're all adults, Nate. You aren't responsible for them."

Speeding up to merge onto the freeway, Nate stayed quiet for a while. "They're family, duchess. Of course I'm responsible for them."

THE SLIM, tallish woman I'd always known as my best friend came hurtling out the front door and practically threw herself at me when we arrived at the Cartwright family home. Nate told me on the way that we'd been invited to dinner so they could discuss the business and, more importantly, make amends after what went down in the Cook Islands.

"I've missed you so much," Alesha whispered, hugging me so tight that I almost couldn't breathe.

Tears sprang to my eyes as I hugged her back. I'd been so focused on my own feelings and Nate that I hadn't thought enough about her and how her new relationship was going. Was Sam treating her well? Did they still feel as strongly for each other as they did in the beginning? Was Jasmine being good to her? What about the other brothers? I did hope she was living somewhere with Sam on her own and wasn't here cooking and cleaning for them all every night. She did have a tendency to try and please....

"I've missed you too," I returned, pulling back so I could look into her eyes. "How have you been?" It was the one question I felt safe asking while all the family was around. I would know how truthful her answer was by the look in her eyes. The rest would have to wait for a more private time.

She pressed her lips together, wrapping her hands around my forearms as she nodded. "I'm OK."

My heart sank—she wasn't happy. I could see the sadness in her big brown eyes and the slight quivering of her lip. My instinct to protect her overwhelmed me, and I drew her into my arms.

I didn't know what else to say, so I just held on tight, only releasing her when Jasmine's voice cut into our moment, reminding Alesha that there was something in the kitchen that needed her attention.

"I'm glad you both came," she said, looking between Nate and me. "I'd hate for our family to fall out of contact."

"Then maybe my family will refrain from touching what's mine," Nate said coolly, stooping slightly to kiss his mother on the forehead.

"Of course." Jasmine smiled. "I do hope you've forgiven me, Holland. There was a lot of pressure on us as all that day. I'd never intentionally do anything to harm you." Her saccharine voice made me sick to my stomach. She'd threatened me with that voice, threatened my life and those of everyone I loved. She'd have to forgive me if I didn't believe her.

"What's for dinner?" I asked, redirecting the conversation instead. "It's been a long day and I'm starved."

"Alesha has made potato au gratin, Toby has some lamb on the rotisserie, the twins are on salads, and Sam is on drinks. I'm doing dessert. We have everything covered." She held out her arm to welcome us inside. "Come. It's time we celebrate properly. It's not every day a woman with five sons gets to entertain two daughters."

As food and drinks were passed around the outdoor table, it was easy to relax into the festive atmosphere. Kristian and Abbot were like two halves of the same person, talking interchangeably about whatever topic caught their interest in the moment. They even laughed at the same time, syncing to the same beat. It was funny to watch.

Despite Alesha's demeanour when we'd arrived, she did seem highly content sitting next to Sam. When the food was finished and the conversation continued to flow, he draped his arm over the back of her chair, gently caressing the bare skin on her arm. She relaxed into him. The only times she seemed uncomfortable were when Jasmine addressed her, or if she had to interact with Toby —who was once again fairly silent for the most part. I noticed it was rare that he looked my way, spending most of his time focused on his beer bottle instead while the Boston terrier, Rogue, sat at his feet and he slipped her scraps under the table.

Then he caught me watching him. He raised a single

finger to his lips, glanced at Jasmine, and then smiled at me. I looked away, the interaction feeling odd. The last time we spoke, he'd told me he thought I was trouble and looked as though he wanted to kill me. Now he was smiling at me?

Perhaps he was drunk.

"Will you ladies excuse us for a while?" Jasmine asked during a lull in the conversation. "My sons and I have some business we need to discuss."

Standing obediently, Alesha started clearing the plates, so I stood and did the same. Nate grabbed my wrist and shook his head.

"I should help," I whispered.

"You aren't a servant," he reminded me.

"Neither is she." I glanced towards Alesha, whose arms were laden with plates and cutlery.

Releasing his breath, Nate nodded, then stood to help clear.

"The girls can get that, darling," Jasmine said with a shocked laugh.

"It'll be faster if we all pitch in. Once all this is clean, we'll talk business. I didn't bring my wife here so she could clean our mess."

"I think I just came a little," I whispered in his ear as we walked towards the kitchen together.

He pinched me on the arse and I let out a little yelp. Everyone else stood and grumbled a little, but they ultimately helped to clear the table, tidy the kitchen, and put everything back where it belonged.

Once everything was pristine again, Nate grabbed Stollis from the fridge, handing me two before telling me to go relax with my friend.

Alesha and I retired to the living room at the front of the house, putting a decent amount of distance between us and the rest of the Cartwright family.

"Are you OK?" Alesha asked immediately in a hushed tone. "I've been worried sick about you since the wedding. He hasn't hurt you, has he?" She grabbed my arms and inspected every part of me she could see with a keen eye.

"I'm fine," I assured her, laughing slightly out of confusion. "Why would you worry about me? I'm the one worried about you."

"Me? No, I'm great! I love it here. I mean, it gets a bit much sometimes having so many people around, and I admit to being a little homesick and bored hanging around the house all the time. But Sam is amazing whenever we're together, and I can pretty much do whatever I want the rest of the time. Kristian is teaching me to surf. Jasmine is teaching me to cook. I'm pretty much perfect."

"So, you're living here? Not at Sam's?"

"Sam's?"

"Nate said they all had their own places."

"Nate and Toby are the only ones living on their own. But Toby is here a lot."

"And you're happy living with them all?"

"I like the noise and the company."

"Wow. So I imagined all the discomfort out there?"

"Discomfort?"

"Yeah, between you and Jasmine, and Toby."

"Toby?" She scrunched her face as if the idea of being uncomfortable around him was insane. "He's a pussycat."

"Are you sure about that?" I eyed her carefully, and she nodded emphatically.

"I've just been worried sick about you. After our

wedding, Nate went crazy on Kris and Abbot. Kris had a split lip, and Abbot could barely see out of one eye for a whole week. And I saw him yelling at Jasmine." Her eyes went wide. "Lord, Holl, I was so scared. I thought he was going to hit her."

"Did he?"

"No, but he threatened to, held his hand up like he was going to backhand her the same way she did to you. And I thought, 'God help Holland if that's the kind of temper that man has.'"

"He doesn't have a temper, Leesh. He was angry because Jasmine hit me and the twins covered for her. I really don't think he would hit his own mother."

"So you're OK?"

"More than OK. I'm ridiculously happy. I'm in love with him." It felt silly sitting there admitting that, but at the same time it was wonderful because Alesha was the only other person on the planet who understood exactly who it was I married and how it all came about.

"You do? That's such a relief. We got real lucky with these guys, Holl. I reckon someone was watching over us."

I nodded. "My parents, perhaps."

"Or maybe God. Or my mum if she's up there. Lord knows I've prayed enough for a man to whisk me away from my crappy life."

"I want the fairy tale," I quoted in my best Julia Roberts voice.

Alesha smiled at the *Pretty Woman* reference. "And as far as men go, it seems we got exactly that."

"Yes. But what about the rest of it? Their... business activities?" I nodded towards the back of the house where the family meeting was underway.

Alesha shrugged and sighed. "I try not to think about it. The less we know the better, right? That's how mob guys protect their wives."

I smiled. "You watch far too many movies."

She shrugged. "Up until now, they've been better than my life."

"You said you're a little homesick. Have you gone to visit your dad?"

She shook her head, lowering her eyes slightly. "He won't take my calls. We went to visit when we got back and he lost it. He's angry with me for getting married without him, and especially because I didn't get married in a church to a good Catholic boy."

"I'm sorry, Leesh."

"Ugh." She shrugged. "He was never going to like anyone I brought home. I always expected something like this to happen."

"He'll come around," I said, patting her leg.

"We'll see," she said with a nonchalant shrug of the shoulder. Then she adjusted on the couch, tucking her knees beneath her as she looked at me and grinned. "Now tell me about Nate. I want to know *everything* about him."

I smiled at the mischievous glint in her eye as I was taken back to a simpler time where we shared everything. That seemed so long ago after this whirlwind of events.

"How about you tell me all about Sam. Start with the moment you locked eyes, and don't leave out a thing."

CHAPTER TWENTY-TWO
A LOVEABLE ROGUE

LIFE SEEMED FAIRLY normal for the next couple of weeks. The commute from Torquay to the city was a bit long, but having Nate with me made it a hell of a lot more bearable. Still, almost four hours of travel every day was wearing on us.

"You know, if you put some furniture back into my apartment, we could stay there during the week and spend weekends at your place," I suggested when I noticed him yawning uncontrollably Monday morning. He'd had a busy weekend doing 'business' things with his brothers that meant I'd stayed at the family house to keep Alesha company while they were gone—although, I also thought that Nate didn't like the idea of leaving me in the Bells Beach house alone because of how secluded it was. Maybe he was still afraid I'd run away.

While the men were out 'working', Jasmine procured our help to prepare a grand feast for their return. She had said with great authority that her boys would be starving when they got back, and she'd been right. They shoved food in so fast that I'd barely cleared a quarter of my plate before they'd started on seconds. After that, Nate had gone caveman on me and dragged me upstairs—I say dragged, but I went rather willingly—to have his way with me. We hadn't gone home that night, falling asleep exhausted in the family home instead. I had to wonder if it was the adrenaline rush that kept Nate going back to the family line of work when he clearly had enough of his own. He'd been an absolute animal that night.

"It's *our* place," he corrected, referring to the Bells Beach house. "There is no mine and yours anymore. It's all ours."

"Fine, *our* place," I said. "But by that same thinking, *we* have a perfectly good apartment only fifteen minutes from my work. Do you think staying there could be an option? I love living by the beach, but the commute is killing me, babe. And by the looks of things, it's killing you too."

He glanced at me and took in a slow breath. At first I didn't think he was going to go for it, but then I held my hands together and batted my eyelids, making whimpering puppy noises that made him laugh. "OK, duchess. I'll get the boys to move your shit back into the apartment."

"*Our* shit," I corrected.

He chuckled and agreed. "We'll stay there until the end of the school year, but I want you to look at transferring schools so we're not in the city for long."

"What's wrong with the city?"

"I *work* in the city."

"So?" I started, and then it hit me—you don't steal where you live. It compromised the job. "Oh." I sat with my arms folded across my middle, silently staring out the window. "I really like the school I'm at, Nate. It isn't as easy to get a good position as you think."

Reaching across the car, he took my hand and squeezed. "There are plenty of good schools farther down. Marriage is compromise."

I snatched my hand back. "Then quit *your* fucking job," I snapped.

We drove the rest of the way in silence. Just because I was aware of what Nate did for a living didn't mean I was OK with it. The fact that he was expecting me to change my entire career trajectory so he could keep travelling through the city, robbing people without being identified while out picking up groceries really pissed me off. So far, my life had been the only one to make compromises. His was going on, uninterrupted and unencumbered.

I spent the entire day pissed off about it and was ready to give him a piece of my mind when the wind was knocked out of my sails the moment Toby pulled up outside the school.

"Where's Nate?" I asked, peering through the window of his black BMW sedan.

"Hello, Holland. How was your day?" he asked in return, gesturing for me to get inside.

Since I wasn't in the mood for a kidnapping, I stayed on the outside.

"Where's Nate?" I insisted.

"He's busy. He asked me to pick you up."

"Busy? Doing what?"

"Just get in the car. You're attracting the attention of the locals." He looked over my shoulder to the group of students craning their necks.

"That's not your husband, Miss," one stated, crossing her arms.

"Not that it's any of your business, Jessica, but this is my brother-in-law, Toby."

She and her friends leaned closer to get a better look and Toby grumbled, rolling his eyes.

"Want a copy of my license and registration too?" he asked as they gathered around.

"No, but I don't see a ring. Can you be my stepdaddy?" Jessica asked.

"All right." I held up my hands and gave them my most severe-looking teacher face. "That's enough. He didn't come here to be the butt of your lewd comments, girls." When they moved back, I opened the car door and slipped in, deciding it was safe enough since I had a whole gaggle of witnesses to attest to my last known where-abouts. It was unlikely that Toby would take me shopping for concrete boots and then sightseeing at the edge of a really high cliff.

"See ya, Miss. See ya, Daddy!" The girls blew kisses and giggled uproariously as Toby planted his foot and sped off, his cheeks bright red.

"That's the calibre of girls you're teaching these days?" He shook his head.

"They get raised by YouTube and social media. It's a different generation than what we grew up with."

He shook his head again and drove on in silence.

"So, what has Nate so busy?"

"Well, it seems whatever the—what does he call you? Princess?"

"Duchess."

"That's right. Whatever the duchess wants, the duchess

gets. We all had to drop what we were doing today to move furniture for you."

That so wasn't what I was expecting to come out of his mouth. "We're going to my apartment?" I couldn't help but smile. Some husbands bought their wives flowers, others bought jewellery. Mine, he returned the things he stole. It made my heart soar.

"*And* you're happy about it. Of course you are." He turned down a familiar street and I immediately relaxed—which, in Toby's presence, was a big thing for me. He always made me feel on edge, but today, he seemed… OK. "We strain our muscles all day so you get to sit on your plush couch in your love nest while the rest of us get to drive all the way back to Torquay and listen to the other loved-up couple go at it like rabbits all night." He rolled his eyes. "It's enough to drive a man to drink."

"Careful, Toby, you're sounding jealous."

"Maybe I am." He glanced at me as he indicated to turn into my parking garage. "I *did* see you first."

My heart jumped into my throat. What an odd thing to say. I thought he hated me.

"Why don't you stay at your place, then?" I asked, clearing my throat, trying to steer the conversation to more comfortable grounding.

"It's not really mine at the moment. I'm renting it out for a while to make some extra cash."

"Extra cash?"

"We aren't all rolling in it like Nate. I have legitimate goals, and I need legitimate money to make those goals happen."

He pulled into a guest parking spot and I took a moment to regard him, his tone suggested more than just jealousy over Nate's bank account. "Why is Nate having more money a problem for you?"

"It's not. It's just that Nate plays his own game outside the family. A game I don't agree with."

"What game? I don't understand. Are you talking about his investments?"

He laughed at that. "Yeah, his *investments*. That's exactly what I'm talking about."

"What do you mean? Is there something I'm not aware of that I should be? What investments does he have?"

"That's something you'll have to take up with him. But if you ask me, it's probably better if you don't know."

Better if I don't know? Those words resonated deepest. Toby was a thief, just like Nate was a thief. But if Nate was into something that Toby didn't agree with, then what the hell was it? What could be worse in another criminal's eyes? Guns? Black-market organs? It was something I was going to take up with my husband. I barely coped with the idea of him stealing, Lord knew what I'd do if it was something worse.

When we got out of the car, I was more confused than ever. I'd been angry all day about our argument this morning, and now I was questioning exactly how loose my husband's morals were.

"Come on, Holland," Toby urged when I didn't move right away. "He's waiting."

"Do you like your job, Toby?" I asked as he followed me up to the apartment. I kept running our conversation through my head and wanted to know what he meant by 'legitimate dreams'.

"If I answer truthfully, will it stay between us?"

"Of course." I was a firm believer that a person's

secrets weren't to be shared with anyone except the people they chose to share them with.

He stopped on the staircase, and I turned to face him. With our height difference, we were basically eye to eye. "I hate it. Always have. Always will."

"Have you ever tried to be something else?"

"Jasmine won't allow it. Let's go." He gestured for me to keep moving. I obliged, but I had more questions.

"Toby," I started, but he cut me off before I could say anymore.

"Your husband's waiting for you, Holland." He was obviously done talking.

When we got upstairs, Toby pushed the front door open to reveal an apartment full of furniture and a champagne-wielding husband.

"Welcome home, duchess," Nate said. Despite my troubled mind, I melted. He looked like he was fresh from the shower, wearing the jeans I loved because they hugged his arse just right, along with a soft cotton T-shirt in dark grey. Other than that, he had a sparkle in his eye and nothing on his feet. He looked like a wet dream.

The stress of the day slid from my body and I fell into his arms, deciding that my questions didn't need to be an angry confrontation. I didn't want to attack him and sound ungrateful when he'd just given me back a massive piece of my life. I didn't realise how much I'd missed it until I walked through the door.

"I'm sorry for biting your head off this morning," I said, resting my head against his chest.

"Don't even mention it." He kissed the top of my head, then handed me champagne. Taking it, I turned around to offer some to Toby, but he was gone.

"Where did he go?" I looked back to Nate.

"Toby? He left once he walked you to the door."

"He's a strange man," I noted, taking a seat on my couch—my original couch, not the replacement one. I'd forgotten how comfy it was—and let out a sigh. It was good to be home.

"How so?" Nate asked, coming to sit beside me. I wasn't going to say he was a pussycat like Alesha thought, I wasn't there yet. But he hadn't been as cold or cruel today. Weird.

"He was talking about living in the same house as everyone else because he was renting out his own place for extra cash. Made a comment about not being as well off as you, then said something about you playing your own game?"

Nate released an amused burst of air and slid his arm around my shoulders. "He's just pissed about his own life choices."

"It sounded a lot like he didn't agree with the way you've invested your money." I touched lightly on the subject to gauge his reaction.

"He was given the same opportunities that I was. He just chose not to take them. But there's a lot of history there. Toby's always hated risks. Which is why he tends to be the driver and lookout. I trust him more than anyone in my life though."

"More than me?"

He chuckled, then kissed the side of my head. "It's a different kind of trust. You, I trust with my heart. Toby, I trust with my life. He's always had my back. It's why he was the one who went and got you today—you're a part of that life."

Sipping at my champagne, I thought about his words and wondered if that meant that he *didn't* trust his other brothers, and what about his mother? Did he trust her? With a sigh, I rested my head against Nate's shoulder. My brain had begun to ache with the complexities of his family dynamic. I'd probably never understand it, but I was going to keep trying, question by question, puzzle piece by puzzle piece until I had the full picture.

With a sigh, I took in my full apartment. It felt good to be back home. "Thank you for doing this. I've missed this place."

"Me too. Goliath and I have a *lot* of fond memories within these walls," he said, looking around and nodding.

Smiling at his response, I looked up and sucked gently against his throat. "Want to make some more?"

"Let me check with Goliath first," he joked, looking inside his pants. "Yeah, he's up for it."

I giggled, watching the bulge in his pants grow. "Quite literally."

When I saw the glint in Nate's eye, I knew he only had mischief on his mind. "He said he wouldn't mind filling you out like an application."

I laughed at the euphemism, loving that he was such a loveable rogue. "You sure he doesn't want to park his car in my garage?"

He took my glass and set it on the coffee table before guiding me so I was straddling his lap. "Well, he *is* partial to a game of hide the sausage."

Laughing, I leaned down and pressed my lips to his. "I love you, Nate," I whispered as his hands roamed over my body.

"I love you too, duchess," he replied without a

second's hesitation. It was the first time he'd said it outright. My heart danced about in my chest. He loved me.

I kissed him deeper. Despite everything I wished I could ignore, everything I still didn't know, I was completely smitten by this man.

But alongside love in a marriage is honesty. There was a lot I didn't know, and probably a hell of a lot I didn't *want* to know. Could love teach me to turn a blind eye and accept what he was? Or would his profession—his other life—become a cancer that slowly ate away at our relationship?

CHAPTER TWENTY-THREE
TEACH ME

"DO YOU STILL PICKPOCKET?" I asked one night when I was lying on Nate's chest. We'd made love and were having that post-coital talk that women loved and men wished would end so they could just go to sleep. He'd been playing with my ring and I wondered if he could remove it without me feeling it, the way he'd removed my earring the night he proposed.

"Rarely. We did it a lot as teenagers, but we only do it out of necessity these days."

"When is it a necessity?"

"It's easier to get in when you have keys."

"I see. So you've quit robbing lonely women and are pickpocketing keys to let yourselves into someone's house?"

"You know we quit that scam. You are the last woman I ever went home with. On or off the job." I grinned and blushed in response. I couldn't even try to explain how happy that made me. "Our marks of late have been of both sexes and at work when we hit them."

Half of me wished he wasn't telling me. The other half was eager to know more. "And how do you choose your marks?"

"People on the inside."

"Like, in prison?"

"No. We have people in a couple of insurance and security companies. They give us information, and we pay them for their time and their silence."

"Aren't you worried these people will talk?"

He shook his head. "It's not in their best interest to talk."

"I see." I imagined they'd been threatened the same way Alesha and I had in the beginning. Do or die. "So you get your information and then what? You just steal their keys and go inside their house?"

"If we were junkies, sure." He smirked and tucked an arm behind his head.

"Obviously I'm wrong." I ran my fingers through the light smattering of hair on his chest. "OK then, expert thief, explain it to me."

"The more you know, the more you're stuck with me."

"I'm already stuck with you, remember?" I flashed my ring at him and he chuckled.

"Recon. We get the name of a mark, and then we watch them for a while, work out their movements, their habits. Then we formulate a plan based on that information and the items we're planning to take. We don't act until we have every detail down pat."

"Is that what you did with me?"

"No." He laughed while he said it. "It's what we were doing with *Alesha*. Then Goliath messed up that plan and I followed him home with you, so we had to wing it. You see where that gets us." He tapped his wedding ring against mine.

"Happily married?" I batted my lashes at him.

He kissed me. "Best bad decision I ever made." His comment gave me butterflies.

"So, is that why you took everything? Because you didn't have a plan of what to take?"

He nodded. "There's normally more finesse to a job. Although, the second time, I was just messing with you. I was a little pissed that you kicked me out after our moment in your kitchen."

I thought back to said moment, remembering how he'd clenched his jaw when I'd told him we could never be.

"That's when you slipped something in my drink."

"Not my proudest moment." That was right before he'd made the toast, *"To the man who steals your heart."* In that moment, I never guessed it would be him.

"Show me how you do it."

His brow knitted. "Slip people drugs?"

"Pickpocket. I want to learn."

A smile curved his mouth. "All right. Get dressed and I'll show you."

When we were both wearing clothes, Nate placed items in both our pockets: phone, wallet, envelopes, jewellery. Then he explained what I had to do.

"It's basically the art of misdirection," he said, standing across from me in the living room. "Working in a pair is most effective, but with practice, you can do it on your own and your mark will have no clue until it's too late. First, I'll teach you a quick smash and grab. This is best done in a crowd because then it's less obvious."

"I'm guessing by the title that you're going to bump into me and take something."

He smiled. "Exactly. But there's a technique. One, you have to know where the item is, and two, you need to lift it so they can't feel it. Ready?"

"Go for it."

We walked into each other and he bumped me like a rude pedestrian. When we were at opposite ends of the room, we faced each other again.

"Without checking, what do you think I took?"

I thought back to the way he'd knocked me and the things he'd slid into my front and back pockets. I decided he'd stolen from my back pocket, that had contained a mobile phone. "You took my phone," I replied with confidence.

He lifted his brow. "Your phone. You sure that's the right answer?"

I thought again. "Well I was, but not anymore."

He held up his left hand, my necklace dangling from his middle finger. Immediately my hand flew up to my neck.

"How in the world?"

"A ridiculous amount of practice." He smiled. "Pockets are easier. Why don't you try me?"

We performed the pass again, except that time I knocked into him and attempted to take his wallet from his back pocket. It got caught and I got busted.

"Again," he said, moving back to our starting positions. "But this time, make sure you lift at the same time as the crash." I tried several times, attempting each of his four pockets, but each time I either fumbled or he felt it.

"This is *really* hard."

"It's not meant to be easy. There's an art to everything."

"So I'm beginning to see."

After many attempts and pointers on positioning and handwork, I got hold of something and grinned triumphantly as I stood across from him.

"My wallet?" he asked.

My grin broadened and I shook my head, holding up his phone. Pride overwhelmed his features moments before he crossed the room and lifted me in his arms, crashing his lips against mine. "I knew you had it in you, duchess."

"Now you'll have to check your pockets every time I'm around you."

Thinking that was funny, he kissed my nose, then carried me back to bed and made sure I felt *every* touch.

Over the coming weeks, he became my practise dummy. I'd decided that I wanted to master the art of emptying his pockets, and almost every hug was an opportunity to hone my skills. You'd think it would piss a man off to have his wallet, keys and phone lifted at random times throughout the day, but every time I called Nate back and showed him what I had, he was nothing less than impressed, even offering to teach me more.

As I grew more competent, each successful grab brought me closer to understanding why Nate did what he did. It felt good, plain and simple. And it was a fun game. Well, until I came home one day, sick to my stomach over something I'd done.

"Don't teach me anymore," I whispered once we were enclosed in the privacy of our own apartment and he'd asked what was wrong.

Nate narrowed one eye. "What happened?"

Reaching into my bag, I closed my eyes and retrieved what I took, holding out my shaky hand. It was a Mont Blanc pen. I'd stolen it. "I didn't even think. I just saw this woman use it and slip it in her purse. Then I walked past and took it. What have I become?" Harried, I let the pen drop to the floor.

Immediately, Nate wrapped me in his arms. "Duchess," he whispered, pressing kisses against my head. "It's OK."

"No," I cried. "It's not. Just don't teach me anymore. Don't tell me anymore either. I don't want to know. I'm not equipped to carry the guilt."

"OK," he whispered, his lips in my hair. "OK."

"DO you mind if we stay in the city this weekend too? I have a wedding I'm booked to sing at. It's the last one for the year. I haven't even had a chance to book anything else since meeting you, so this is kind of a one-time thing."

Nate and I sat across from each other at the breakfast table eating muesli, yogurt and fresh fruit. I was also sucking down a very strong coffee. I hadn't been sleeping particularly well lately.

"I've got some work this weekend." He gave me a wary look, as if he expected me to explode. As far as I knew, he hadn't been out on a job in weeks. As requested, he'd been keeping his illegal activities away from me, and I had refrained from asking.

I swallowed my food and cleared my throat. "I see."

"I was kind of hoping you'd stay at the house with Jasmine and Alesha."

"Just us three all weekend?" I actually laughed. "Considering your mother barely tolerates me, and Alesha has become her doppelgänger twin, I'd rather not." It had been nearly four months since our weddings. In that time, my best friend had completely ceased to be the person she once was. It pained me when she sided with Jasmine over me. And worse than that, I felt lonely without having a girlfriend to talk to. I missed her ridiculously. It was like she'd moved from being under her father's thumb, to being under Sam's. As if she didn't know how to function without a firm boundary governing her behaviour. It saddened me and annoyed me at the same time. "I think I'll just stay here on my own, thank you very much."

He pulled his lip back a little, wincing. "That's not gonna happen, duchess."

I put my spoon back into my bowl. "Excuse me?"

"You're not staying here by yourself."

"Why not? Just leave me a car and I'll get myself to the wedding and back. It's not like I haven't driven myself places before. I did just fine taking care of myself for the thirty-two years before you came along to chauffeur me everywhere. Unless...." His eyes met mine, his jaw set tight. *Oh.* "Unless I'm not *allowed* to be unsupervised for extended periods of time."

He didn't say anything, just dug his spoon into his bowl and shoved a mouthful of cereal past his lips.

"Oh my God. That's it, isn't it? You don't trust me not to run or go tell the cops everything I know. I'm still a fucking prisoner, aren't I?" His eyes were dark and hooded as he stared back at me. "How was I too stupid not to see this before now?" I pushed my bowl to the side, suddenly not hungry.

Nate dropped his spoon into his bowl with a clatter and wiped his mouth. "It's for your own safety. You're not a prisoner, Holland. You have your own phone, and you go to work and out shopping all the time. However, I do need to know where you are and who you're with at all times."

"So, this is *The Truman Show*? I have the illusion of freedom, but I'm constantly being watched and monitored, is that it?"

"I give you everything you want and then some. But there are also limitations that come with a life like ours. We didn't get where we are without being careful. This life is new to you, and whether you like it or not, I'm going to take precautions to keep you and everyone else safe." I could tell he was choosing his words carefully.

"Because you think I'll run, or because you think I'll spill my guts to the police."

"Because the world isn't a very safe place. I should know, duchess. I'm one of the bad guys you were warned about as a little girl."

"I thought you didn't feel like a bad guy."

He looked at me pointedly, and I dropped my gaze as tears burned at the back of my eyes. He was right; he was one of the bad guys. I couldn't ignore that fact. It was easy to forget it—just like it was easy to look past the activities of the characters in *Fast and the Furious* and *Ocean's Eleven*. They were all criminals, but they were charismatic and gorgeous, and the viewer sat there rooting for them to get away with their crimes. I was sitting in a live-action version of one of those movies, where I was the one married to Paul Walker or Brad Pitt.

My husband is a bad guy.

"I'm not spending my weekend with them," I said in defiance when I'd gathered some of my composure.

"This isn't a negotiation, Holland."

I stood so fast my chair fell backwards. "Fuck you, Nate. *Fuck*. You."

———

"TROUBLE IN PARADISE?" Toby's face greeted me at the end of work again.

"So when my husband doesn't want to deal with me, he sends a glorified babysitter instead?"

He laughed. "I prefer to call it a security detail, but whatever floats your boat. I'm here to drive you out to Torquay."

I slid into the car without hesitating that time. Over the months, Toby and I had come into an easy acquaintance. We weren't friends by any stretch of the word, but we tolerated each other, and I didn't feel like he wanted to kill me anymore.

With a sigh, I folded my arms across my chest. "I take it he's left already?"

Toby nodded. "Took Sam, Abbot and Kris around lunchtime today. They'll be back Sunday."

"What are they doing, robbing a whole estate?"

Toby grinned. "Cleaning houses isn't all we do. Plenty of stuff in this world to steal, princess."

"It's duchess."

"Whatever."

"Are you pissed you aren't going with them?"

He shrugged, using one hand to turn the wheel. He looked very cool, calm and collected in his button-down shirt and charcoal slacks. His clothes fitted his muscular frame well, and his wayfarers topped off the look. If I had met him away from the family and outside the strain of our situation, I would've found him extremely beautiful—he did, after all, look very similar to Nate. Just...*harder*.

"You know I don't mind staying behind. Jobs don't...," he paused, searching for the word or phrase. "Get me off like they do the others." I thought back to how voracious Nate's sex drive was after returning from the only job I knew he'd done. If I hadn't known the reason behind it, I'd have sworn he was on drugs.

"I know you hate the work. But don't you get excited by a *good haul*?" I asked, an undertone of mocking in my words, lingo I pulled from my limited knowledge of their world, mostly gleaned from TV and movies.

"Nah, it lost its lustre a long time ago for me. Although, I doubt it ever had it. I'm pushing forty, so it's all just a means to an end now."

"What's your end?"

He looked over and met my eyes, holding them a little longer than he should've while driving. "Between you and me?"

"I didn't tell last time."

He nodded once. "It's getting out."

My heart kicked up a beat. He was speaking the words I'd wanted to hear from Nate but that my husband seemed unwilling to say. He'd made out like exiting the family profession couldn't be done. "Is it possible to get out?"

He shrugged. "Anything is possible. You just have to want it enough. Plan it better than you plan a job."

I sat up a little straighter in my seat, angling my body so I was facing him more directly. "Well, what would you do? I mean, if you weren't working with your brothers anymore."

"My dream is to run a fishing boat. There are some

great game spots a little farther down the coast, and I could do whale-watching tours too. I'd need the capital to set it all up, but once it got going, I wouldn't need much myself as long as costs were covered. Just food and a little shack somewhere, enough to live on."

"You wouldn't miss the fancy cars?" I gestured around the cabin of the BMW we were sitting in.

"It's just a car."

"OK. So you save up the cash and you're ready to christen your boat, then what? How do you quit being your family without causing a whole bunch of shit?"

"That's the part I'm working on. How do I walk away when no one else has walked away before?"

"I suppose you could tell them over dinner? That was always when I delivered my most disappointing news to Aunt Maya growing up."

He chuckled and shook his head. "I don't know. I think this might be a little more complicated than 'Sorry, Aunty, I dented your car. '"

"It was actually the garage door, but I catch your drift."
He nodded.

"Do any of your brothers know about this?"

He glanced at me quickly. "Just you. I'm trusting you not to tell any of them."

Clasping my hands together in my lap, I wrung my fingers, then nodded. I wasn't going to tell, but why in the world would Toby trust *me*? I didn't even think he liked me that much. But every time we were alone, he shared a secret. Was this some kind of trap? Was he testing my loyalty? Loyalty to him? To the family? To Nate?

Something told me I needed to be very careful. Nate said he trusted Toby above all others. But my instincts told me that Toby was *not* the pussycat Alesha thought he was. He'd said that Nate had his own angle, but I was fairly sure he was also playing his own as well. Otherwise, why did he act one way when we were alone and another when we had an audience?

"I hope you realise your dreams one day, Toby," I said finally, keeping my focus on the scenery as it shot past my window.

"Who knows. It's nice to have dreams though, don't you think? We shouldn't always have to settle for the life thrust in front of us."

"I suppose not," I replied, taking in his words and analysing them in my mind. There was definitely an angle he was playing, I just didn't know what it was yet.

I WAS ALSO VERY wary of Jasmine. Ever since she'd apologised for the slap, she'd been sweet as pie, but I could feel the undercurrent of her distaste towards me in every interaction we had. I didn't know if it was me she didn't like, or the effect I had on Nate—he had, after all, threatened them all when he'd found out she hit me. That alone could be enough for her. It was hard to stay angry at family, and much easier to blame an outsider for any newfound problems. Either way, I wasn't sure I was interested in getting along with her at all. In my eyes, she was the reason for my problems. Because of the life she'd created for her sons, Nate would never walk away, and my best friend wasn't my best friend anymore. I didn't like how far her claws had dug into my life. Jasmine Cartwright was my greatest obstacle—my nemesis. I didn't know if we could ever get along.

"Perhaps you and I can spend the day together tomorrow," Jasmine suggested when we were tidying up after dinner that night. "Nate mentioned you're singing at a wedding on Sunday. Maybe we can find you a nice dress to wear? We can make a day of it, have lunch at this great bistro I know of, get massages and have facials at the day spa. It'll be great, just the two of us."

I looked behind me because I really wasn't sure if she was talking to me. But seeing that we were alone, I had to take a moment to think about what she said. "Uh… sure?" *What the hell is going on?*

Jasmine laughed. "Don't look so frightened, Holland. I don't bite. And I think it's high time that you and I got to know each other. Don't you agree?"

"Uh… sure?"

Again, she laughed. "Great. We'll leave right after breakfast. Eight OK with you?"

"Sure," I replied again, my surprise at her olive branch outing messing with my vocabulary.

When I'd gone to bed that night, I'd thought about calling or texting Nate to tell him about her offer. I wanted to know if it was her idea or his, or if he thought this was a normal, or even a *wise* thing to do. But when I'd held my phone up to bring up his number, I decided against it. He hadn't called me all day. He hadn't even taken my own desire to stay in the apartment this weekend into consideration. He'd just steamrolled all over the top of my plans, done what he wanted, and forced me to do what he wanted too. No, I did not want to speak to my husband. I was still pissed at him.

Switching my phone to silent, I set it on the bedside table, then rolled over and attempted to go to sleep, something that wasn't easy to do when you'd grown accustomed to drifting off naked and in the arms of a giant man listening to the sea.

AFTER SPENDING the morning browsing stores and making small talk, Jasmine and I finished our day of bonding with spa treatments. It had been odd trying on dresses and receiving compliments. I was still trying to understand her motives, so it was impossible to relax around her.

"What made you choose the profession you're in?" I asked her when we were alone in the spa room with mud drying on our skin. They'd put cucumbers on our eyes too, but I'd removed mine to keep an eye on Jasmine, just in case this whole day was an excuse to get me alone so she could smother me with one of the plush towels. Where Nate's family was concerned, I had terrible trust issues. I may have been in love with her son, but my Stockholm Syndrome had never kicked in enough to make me feel an empathy towards my captors. *Maybe that's what happened with Alesha?*

"You really want that sad and sorry tale?" Jasmine laughed, pulling my attention back as she removed the cucumber from her eyes.

"I do, actually. I'm trying to understand this life. I'm trying to understand *you.*"

"I'm honestly not that complicated, sweetheart, but OK," she said, rolling to her side and propping herself up on an elbow. "I'll play this game. The short and simple version is like this: I grew up mostly on the streets. My mother was a heroin addict and would turn tricks whenever she couldn't pay for a hit—which was more often than not. Stealing was how I survived for the most part, so I got real good at it real fast. Growing up with her for a mother taught me two things." She held up her fingers and counted them off. "Drugs are a waste of a life, and sex can get you anything you want. And I'm not talking prostitution. I'm talking control, manipulation. I saw how those dealers used their power to make her do whatever they wanted her to do. It wasn't long before I realised that I had power too. I was young, I was beautiful, and there is a certain type of man out there who will do anything to have that. At first I used them for survival, but then I did it just because I could. And I found myself living a pretty comfortable existence. All that changed when I set my sights on a man called Derek Cartwright. He *looked* like money, you know? Plus, he was *beautiful*. I thought, if I could just land that guy, he could make all of my dreams come true. And in a way, he did. It turned out he was an even bigger thief than I was. He ran with a group—the family, they called it—who pulled big enough jobs so *everyone* lived well. They took me in, taught me everything I know. And the rest, as they say, is history." There was a wistfulness in her eyes as she pressed her lips together.

"Cartwright. You married him?"

She nodded. "I did. All five boys have the same father."

"Where is he now?"

"Prison," she stated simply, rolling so she was again flat on her back. "Tried to do a job he wasn't ready for and got caught with the rest of them."

"I thought Cartwrights didn't do time."

She laughed at that. A great big mocking laugh that told me she thought I was incredibly naïve. "Is that what Nate told you? Oh, honey. We do time. Nate did time. Got caught stealing cars when he was fourteen. Did six months. Sam, he wasn't so lucky. He was an adult when he got caught. An alarm tripped when he was stealing the overnight safe from a post office. Stupid boy was trying to do a job on his own." She shook her head. "He did eighteen months in medium security."

"What about the others?"

"Clean as a whistle. Nate and Toby took over planning. No one does a job without the others' involvement. Family sticks together."

"And what about you? Have you ever done time?"

She shook her head. "I was questioned over the robbery that got the rest of them. But they couldn't make anything stick."

"It must've been a big robbery if they're all still in there."

She smiled, but it wasn't happy. "Two security guards died. Derek took the fall and is serving two life sentences. The rest got out years ago."

"Where are they now?"

She shrugged. "They're around. Some went straight, some retired, others went their own way or got caught again." *Some went straight, some retired.* It seemed getting out was simple for some....

"Did you consider getting out yourself?"

"I had children, bills, a lifestyle. I didn't have the luxury of a career change."

"So you just kept stealing and passed your skillset on to your sons?"

She smiled. "You say that like it's a bad thing, Holland, but look at my sons. They're happy, healthy, well provided for. They're entrepreneurs, and they will never, ever put the coin in another man's purse. No, my boys live free. They live hard. And they take what they want."

But to what end? When will it be enough?

"Sounds like you've lived a rather interesting life."

"I have. And there isn't a single person in this world who's going to take that life—or my boys—away from me."

Her light eyes held mine, and suddenly her motives for the day out became clear. She was here to remind me that *she* was the matriarch of the family.

Well, that kind of talk might've worked in her world, but she was forgetting something important....

"They're not boys anymore, Jasmine. They're men. I think it will serve you well to remember that."

Placing my cucumbers back over my eyes, I laid back on the bench, hoping to God that her loyalty towards Nate would trump any desire to harm me. Thankfully, her loyalty won.

CHAPTER TWENTY-SIX
DON'T KEEP YOUR HUSBAND WAITING

WEDDINGS ARE FUNNY THINGS. They're supposed to be all about romance and love, but in reality they're filled with tension and worry. So much planning goes into the day and all eyes are on two people. When I stood on the stage, singing Adele's "Make You Feel My Love" as the happy couple turned around the floor for their first dance, all eyes were indeed on them. All except one set.

Toby's.

Instead of dropping me off at the reception hall and agreeing to come back when the event was over, he'd insisted on staying, stating he was there as my security. Now that I was singing, he was standing at the bar, drinking what looked like a neat Scotch and watching me intently.

There was something predatory about the way he watched me, something a little too intimate in his eyes. I'd thought our conversations in the car the day before had been a way to trip me up and test my loyalty, but what if it was something else? What if... what if he *wanted me?*

The idea made all the hair on the back of my neck stand on end, and not in a good way. *Did* he want me? The way he was watching me on stage certainly felt like it. It was eerily similar to the way Nate had been watching me that first night at the karaoke bar.

Was that what all the glares had been about? Was he angry that I'd chosen Nate? Was he angry that Nate had swooped in on me? *"I did see you first."* Was he jealous of Nate *because* of me? Nate said he trusted him most, but was that a mistake? Was I in danger being alone with him?

I had been angry with Nate for not giving me freedom, but now I wished he was right there, glued to my side to make sure nothing happened to me.

"I trust him with my life." It was why Nate sent him to look after me. *"You're part of that life."*

Perhaps Nate needed to rethink that.

"Why teach when you have a set of lungs like *that*?" Toby said, shaking his head in amazement when I walked to the bar to get a bottle of water during the speeches. The alcohol had obviously relaxed his normally guarded demeanour.

"Unfortunately, these lungs don't pay the bills," I replied, enjoying the cool liquid on my overused throat. I was seriously out of practise and should have spent a lot more time warming up before getting on stage. I was going to be croaky the next day.

"What bills? You're a Cartwright now. You don't even need to work. We take care of our own." His eyes moved down the length of my dress, hovering in places he shouldn't. There was a slight sheen to his gaze, telling me he'd sunk a few more of those Scotches than a man responsible for driving should.

"I guess that's true. Although, I do really love my job —both jobs." I seemed to always be defending my choice to work for a living to these people. "I don't want to quit and be completely dependent on you all."

"You mean like Alesha?"

"Alesha seems really happy with her role. I'm not trying to put that down, I'm just saying what makes me happy. I like some independence, and honestly this whole 24/7 detail I have on me is starting to wear a little thin." I glared at him pointedly and stepped away, making a beeline for the ladies'. It was one place I knew I'd get a little privacy and distance from his gaze.

He followed me anyway. "I'm just following orders, Holland. I would personally trust you to come and go as you please, but you're not mine to trust, you're Nate's. And he wants you under guard."

I stopped just before I reached the door and turned to face him. "And I should be thankful that he doesn't keep me under lock and key?"

He shrugged. "I suppose."

"And if I was yours, you'd let me go?"

His eyes dropped to my lips and his brow knitted. My stomach knotted in response. I was playing a dangerous game. "Yes," he said finally.

"Then give me your keys and trust me to get back to the house on my own."

"How am I supposed to get back?"

"Uber?"

He looked at me for a long moment, then sighed. "I'm under orders."

Leaning against the wall, I shook my head. Months of having my movements limited, my morals twisted, and my life turned upside down had finally gotten to me. I was sick of it. Sick of voicing my frustrations and having them stamped down. I just wanted them to *let me go*. I didn't even want to run; I just wanted a little independence. Based on what Toby had told me about his stifled dreams, he should've been the one person to understand. Instead, he was stifling me along with the rest of them. "And you just follow those orders instead of having the balls to man up and do what's right. That's why you'll never get out, Toby, despite your dreams. You don't have any get-up-and-go. You were born to do what you're told, born to follow everyone else." I snapped, poking him in the chest while I used my other hand to steal his keys. I was going to do this the Cartwright way—by taking what I wanted.

He looked hurt, but in that moment, I didn't care. I was tired of being told what I could and couldn't do. I'd had ample opportunity to escape or discreetly call the police, and not once had I even attempted to cause trouble. I loved my husband; I wasn't going to hurt him by sending him or his family members to jail. I needed a little credit for that.

"Just get out of my way." Holding the keys behind my back, I placed my other hand on his chest to push past him to get to the bathroom, but I didn't get far. He wrapped his hand around my wrist and pulled me back towards him, his lips crashing against mine in an intense kiss that I didn't for a moment reciprocate.

Instead, I shoved against his chest, and the moment he released me, I slapped him. "No! I love Nate," I hissed, registering the shocked look on his face while at the same time feeling confused because he was moving away from me rather rapidly. Then he was on the floor.

"Keep your fucking hands off my wife," came the roar.

"Nate," I gasped, covering my mouth in surprise. He was the last person I expected to see at this wedding.

"What's going on?" a male guest demanded as Nate picked up his brother by the scruff of his neck.

"Stay the fuck out of this," Nate growled, dragging Toby towards the exit like a rag doll.

Freaking out, I raced behind them, pausing for a moment to address the shocked wedding party. "I'm so sorry. I'll refund your money. I... I'm sorry. Please don't call the police. We'll go."

Then I ran through the door and into the parking lot just in time to hear Nate roar and punch Toby in the jaw. "No!" I yelled, running to stop them but getting held fast by a set of arms going around my waist and lifting me kicking off the ground. "Let go!"

"Best to let brothers fight these things out," Sam said as he set me back on the ground. I snatched myself away from him. "He's not going to do too much damage," he added, just as Nate let Toby get to his feet before pummelling him to the ground once again.

"Oh God, I feel sick. I can't look." I turned away.

"You should. That man's fighting for you."

"I don't want this."

"Ah." He shrugged it off. "This was always going to happen. Tobes has had a boner for you since he saw you while doing recon on Leesh."

"Toby was watching me?"

"He was watching your friend."

"That *friend* is your wife," I added before he could go on.

"And she's a fantastic one. I worship her tight little—"

"Please stop," I said quickly, holding up my hand to

shield my eyes from the words about to come from his mouth.

He grinned. "I was going to say arse, but yeah, that's tight too."

"Oh my God." I placed my fingers in my ears and closed my eyes. Everywhere I turned, there was either a fight going on or a man talking TMI about my friend.

Sam laughed. "Anyway, during that time, it seemed that maybe you'd be the better mark, but Toby forbade it. Then Nate went for you anyway. Toby has been furious ever since."

"He thinks Nate cut his grass."

"Yeah, but he didn't. None of us knew Toby had a thing for you. He keeps all that shit to himself."

So, he didn't want me dead. He just wanted... me. I didn't know what thought was more unsettling. These men had known us before we'd known them. They'd assessed our worth and viewed us as a business transaction, until feelings got in the way—until *I* got in the way. Now two brothers who would die to protect each other were fighting over me. I hated that, but at the same time, it was kinda hot. I wasn't used to any man clamouring after me, but now two hot-as-hell brothers were going at it and I'd be lying if it didn't inflate my ego a little. Did that make me a bad person?

"You had no right!" Toby yelled.

"She is my wife. *Mine*," Nate spat back. "I trusted you to take care of her."

"You did it to be spiteful and you know it."

"No, brother, I don't know it. You never said. I had no fucking clue."

"Why do you think I didn't want her as the mark? I fucking wanted her for myself!"

"How was I to know that?"

"It was implied!"

Nate stepped back, hands on his hips as his head shifted side to side. "I saw her. I wanted her. I took her. Now I love her. She loves me. I can't change that. It's something you need to accept."

I stood beside Sam, my hand pressed against my chest as I listened to the exchange. I was angry with Toby for kissing me, but I felt awful that he'd been made to stand by and watch while Nate's and my relationship blossomed. That must've been hard on him.

"You always win, don't you?" Toby spat. "I wonder if she'll still be devoted to you if she finds out the truth."

I spun around to face Sam. "What truth?"

"He's talking shit."

I turned back to find Nate holding the front of Toby's shirt, speaking so close and low that I couldn't make out what was being said. "He's not talking shit. What is Nate hiding?"

"There's a lot you don't know, Holland. It's better that way, trust me."

Letting out my breath, I looked up at him incredulously. "How can I trust any of you when you don't trust me?"

"Because you're alive. Because you have two men over there willing to fight over who would better make you happy."

"None of this makes me happy." I gestured towards the fighting men. "I either want to know everything or I want out. I don't want to be kept in some glorified version of a gilded cage, allowed out but only on a leash. This is bull-shit." I threw Toby's keys at him and he caught them without flinching. I obviously wouldn't be needing them anymore.

Sam shook his head and laughed before he draped his arm over my shoulders. "There is no getting out, Holland. This is it. Like it or... well, I don't need to explain what happens when people try to walk—or steal a car and drive —away from this life."

"Your mother's old crew walked away. She told me herself."

"How naïve are you? They didn't just *walk* away. They're all either dead, disappeared or in prison. You don't get a retirement cake and walk away when you know shit that can get people put away."

"But you're *family*. Surely if one of you wants out, the others would understand."

"What's to understand? Families don't quit on each other."

"*Duchess!*" Nate roared. "We're leaving." He started walking, leaving a bloodied Toby sitting on the ground, shoulders slumped in defeat. My heart went out to him. Knowing it was me who'd caused the fight made me feel sick to the stomach.

Sam gave me a light nudge. "Don't keep your husband waiting."

I followed Nate to his ute and got in, glancing back as Sam went to help Toby up.

"Don't look at him," Nate commanded.

I clipped my seatbelt without saying a word. There was so much tension in the cabin that I was afraid to make a sound. Then again, he didn't say another word either, simply drove us back to the apartment, and fucked me until I was begging him to let me come.

When we were finally done, he pressed his forehead against mine, his chest heaving before he said, "You are mine, duchess. *Mine*. Don't ever forget it."

CHAPTER TWENTY-SEVEN
THE BEAST YOU ARE

IT HAD BEEN ALMOST a month since the fight. Nate had gone to great lengths to keep me separate from his family, but mostly from Toby. He'd even taken on a bigger role in the day-to-day running of their businesses so he could take a step back from the 'jobs' that took him away from me. For the first time in his life, he didn't trust the members of his family, and I was the reason behind it. It made me feel like the Yoko Ono of the group.

"I don't want you to fall out with them over me. Despite their faults, family is hard to come by. I should know."

"You're the one I'm devoted to, duchess."

It didn't matter what I said or did—he wanted to be upset with them. In a way, I was glad not to have to worry about him going out and risking his freedom to steal shit none of them needed. But there was this underlying disquiet about him, a restlessness that simmered just below the surface of his skin, causing him to pace the floors at night instead of coming to bed.

Above all else, he seemed angry. All the time.

He fucked me angry. He spoke to me in clipped tones more often than not. Every movement was aggressive, designed to keep me quiet and compliant. It was something I'd never been before, but it was how I was behaving now. His anger scared me. I'd hoped that if I gave him time to calm down, he'd return to that effervescent man I'd fallen head over heels for in the beginning, but as the days moved on, I could feel that man slipping further away from me.

I approached him one night while staying at the Bells Beach property as he sat at his desk going through a mountain of paperwork. His quiet anger had gotten too much for me, and I knew if we didn't face what was happening, we were going to lose everything that had been good between us.

"I think we need to talk about what happened."

"There's nothing to talk about. Go read or something."

"I don't want to read. I want to talk to my husband. I want to spend time with him and laugh again. I don't know who this angry man is in front of me."

"I'm the same man. I'm just too busy for games right now."

"You've been too busy ever since your fight with Toby. Why won't you talk to me about it?"

"Because there's nothing to say. He touched my wife, and he paid for it."

"Are you angry with me too? Do you feel like I provoked him somehow?"

Finally, he stopped what he was doing and faced me. "Did you?"

I frowned, the fact that he felt the need to ask that

question hurting more than I'd expected. "No. I did nothing."

"Then what made him feel as though he had a right to touch you—*kiss* you?"

"I don't know. Maybe he did it because I insinuated he was weak."

"Insinuated how?"

"I was angry with you for leaving me in his care instead of trusting me on my own. I tried to get him to hand over the keys to his car and give me some space. When he refused, I stole them and told him he'd never have what he wanted in life because he didn't have the balls to go after it. That's when he decided to kiss me. I guess he decided to *take* what he wanted instead. That's the Cartwright way, right?"

He quietly regarded me before speaking. "Do you have feelings for him?"

"Of course not. I didn't kiss him *back*. And I slapped him for his efforts. Don't I get a little credit for that?"

He looked at me for a long moment, seeming to weigh words and actions against each other. Silence stretched out and caused static in the air. I could barely breathe through the tension in my chest. Then his eyes flashed and his expression softened, moments before he released his breath, took my hand and pulled me towards him. "I've been awful to you?" he whispered.

"Yes."

"You think I'm being awful to him?"

"I think you're cutting off your nose to spite your face. You're punishing your whole family because you're angry with Toby. You beat the crap out of him, so I think he got the message already."

"Don't be alone with him."

"I won't."

"And tell me if you ever are."

"I will." He pulled me to him and kissed me softly. The tenderness behind it caused my heart to sigh and tears to fill my eyes. "There he is," I whispered against his mouth. "There's the gentle giant I love."

His fingers speared into my hair as he pressed his forehead to mine. "I'm sorry, duchess. I'm trying to figure all this shit out. I don't want to lose you. And above all, I don't want you to get hurt. I don't know who to trust anymore."

"Trust *me*."

His mouth sealed over mine as his hands slid down to my waist. Then he sat me on the desk and we made a slow, gentle love that was so sweet, I cried at the end.

"No tears, duchess." He kissed my cheeks. "I'll always take care of you. I'm sorry I've been such an arse. I love you."

"I love you too."

Needing to finish some work, he assured me that he'd join me in bed shortly, but after reading for an hour, my eyes grew heavy and I fell asleep alone.

The whirring sound of a machine woke me sometime later, his side of the bed still empty. Squinting at the time on my phone, it was after four in the morning. *What the hell is he doing?*

I shuffled out to the kitchen, half expecting to find him at the blender making a smoothie. But it was clear and still dark. The whir sounded again.

Confused, I followed the sound, noting the light streaming under the door in the library. When I pushed the door open, I found him standing there, holding on to the completed ladder while testing that it would slide along the tracks.

"Oh my God." I gasped, my hand going to my mouth. "You finished it."

A grin pulled up one side of his sexy mouth, and by the shine in his eyes, I could see I had my Nate back. Lord, I'd missed his happy gaze.

"Thought it was time I followed through on a promise."

I rushed to him and threw my arms around his neck, kissing all over his face. "I love it. I love it. I love it! Thank you!" I said between kisses.

Chuckling, he wrapped his arms around my waist, then twisted until my arse was against the ladder rungs. "Want to give it a try?" he asked.

"Do I?" I slid my butt back and hooked my feet down lower, holding on while Nate slid the ladder from side to side.

"How's that?"

"It's perfect. I love it. I feel like a Disney princess."

"I'm sorry I've been such a beast."

I reached up and touched his face, running my nails over the scruff on his cheeks. "I wonder if Beast and Belle ever used the ladder in their library for something more fun than reading?"

He grinned but played along. "What could possibly be more fun than reading?"

I opened my legs wide, our hips perfectly aligned. "It's just the right height, don't you think?"

Sliding his hands over my smooth skin, his chest

rumbled as his pants developed a noticeable bump. "I didn't hear you beg."

Undoing the top button of his pants, I slid my hand inside and held Goliath tightly. *"Please."* He closed his eyes as my hand moved over his shaft, his cock hardening as I whispered in his ear. "Please, Nate. Fuck me like the *beast* you are."

That was all it took.

His eyes flashed open and then his mouth was on mine, devouring me while his hands shot to my hips, tearing the seams of my underwear. At the same time, I pushed at his pants, freeing his cock and adjusting my position so I was ready to receive him. With a swift push, he was in. I gasped at the speed of his intrusion, clinging to his large arms as his hips thrust back and forth, *bang, bang, bang*. A beautiful violence that had me calling out, overwhelmed by the force but loving it at the same time.

"Holy fuck," I yelled, lifting my arms above my head and gripping the shelf of the bookcase behind me. I held on for dear life, each thrust tormenting my body and my mind as we hurtled towards orgasm.

"I'm gonna come," he growled, his mouth moving to my neck as I arched back, gasping for breath.

Bang. Bang. Bang.

"Nate!"

Bang. Bang.

"Oh God."

Crack.

"Oh *God!*"

The moment we exploded, the ladder gave way too, sending us slamming into the bookshelf with a loud *whack*.

Books tumbled down around us, and then the shelves dropped, sending us sliding to the floor where Nate braced himself above me, taking the brunt of debris against his back.

"Shit. Are you OK?" he asked when it seemed the avalanche of books had ceased. When one more fell and hit against the back of his head, I couldn't help myself, bursting into a fit of giggles.

"I'm fine," I forced through my laughter.

"You think this is funny?" He tried to sound stern, but I could hear the amusement in his tone coupled with that sparkle in his eyes.

Another book fell, hitting him in the back and I lost it, nodding because I couldn't answer.

"Me getting hit by books is funny to you?"

By that point, I was rolling on the floor. "Yes!" Tears streamed from my eyes as I clutched my stomach, unable to stop.

"I spent all night building that ladder, you know."

I pressed my lips together, trying my best to control the bouncing of my shoulders. "I know." *Giggle.* "And it was wonderful." *Snort.* "While it lasted." *Hic.*

A smile took over his lips. "I guess home improvements aren't really my forte."

Holding my laughter in my throat, I shook my head. "No. But you're amazing at so many other things. Like fucking, for example."

Holding himself above me, he looked at the mess in the room and then down at me. He shook his head, a burst of laughter escaping. "Fuck, I love you, duchess. You make everything right, you know that?"

Smiling up at him, I placed my hand against his chest. "Thank you for protecting me from the books."

Dropping a lingering kiss on my lips, he whispered, "All I want is to protect you."

I didn't doubt the truth of that for a second.

ONCE NATE'S anger towards his family had cooled to a simmer, we headed out to Torquay, once again trying to make amends. It seemed to be the theme where I was concerned. Alesha fit into the family like a missing piece of a puzzle, and I was the burr in their britches, causing nothing but discomfort whenever I was around. Perhaps that was my fault for not trying hard enough. Perhaps it was theirs for not being genuine enough. Either way, I knew there was no way I could ever truly be comfortable around them. They'd threatened my life, for fuck's sake. The best I could do for them was be tolerant for the sake of my relationship with Nate.

"Welcome, welcome!" Jasmine smiled, meeting us at the door and ushering us into the air-conditioned cool. Nate and I exchanged glances; that kind of greeting was over the top even for her.

"I've made cocktails," she gushed. "Alesha said you like margaritas, Holland."

I didn't even get to respond before Alesha appeared

and placed a drink in my hand, Sam by her side handing a beer to Nate.

"Brother," he said with a formal nod. It seemed there was more going on than I knew about. Sam turned to Alesha. "Why don't you take Holland to sit outside while the boys have a chat to Nate?"

Alesha placed a hand on my arm and smiled. "Sure. Come on, Holland."

Nate gave my hand a squeeze and my arse a pat before I headed off, relegated to the WAG seating while the men did their thing.

"I've missed you," Alesha said, nudging me with her arm when we took a seat by the pool.

"Really?" I asked. "You wouldn't have known since you never call or text, and when we're all together, you're Jasmine two-point-oh. I don't even know who you are anymore."

Her doe eyes flashed. "That's not fair. I'm just trying to make the best of things. You see where fighting against all this gets you."

I closed my eyes against her truth. "At least I'm still me."

"Maybe," she said with a shrug, then looked away. "I'm going to see if Jasmine needs some help. Will you be fine out here on your own?"

"Sure."

She couldn't get away from me fast enough. I missed my best friend.

Dinner was, to put it in a word, strained. Everyone was so busy trying to act normal that they were overly nice, which just made things more uncomfortable. Toby spoke to no one but the dog, and Jasmine played Betty Homemaker, waiting on everyone hand and foot with Alesha joining in. The twins were oblivious as always, and Sam just seemed to think it was all funny. Nate seethed for the most part, glaring at Toby across the table and even growling like an animal at one point.

"Behave," I said out the corner of my mouth as I squeezed his thigh.

His solution was to suck down a few too many beers. In a way, I was relieved, because it meant I could get out of there faster and go home. But when it came time to load him into the car, I realised it wasn't going to be the easiest thing I've ever done.

"Why don't you just stay here?" Jasmine offered when I asked Abbot and Kristian to help get him into the ute. "You won't be able to get him out of the car on your own, and the room is already made up. It's no problem."

I didn't think Nate would be happy staying there when things were so tense, but I also knew that Jasmine was right. He was too big and too drunk for me to handle on my own.

"OK," I said, reluctance in my voice.

Once we got Nate settled in bed, I went to the kitchen to fetch him some water and painkillers for when he woke up.

I ran into Toby.

Alone.

Nervous after our last encounter, I looked past him to see if anyone else was close by.

"I'm not here to corner you," he assured me. "I just came for water."

Nodding briefly, I took my items and moved to leave the room, then stopped and turned to face him. "I'm sorry if I somehow gave you the wrong impression." He shouldn't have touched me regardless, but I did feel some guilt over the situation.

Shutting off the tap, he held his water partway to his lips and shook his head. "You didn't. I'm the one who owes you an apology. I drank when I shouldn't, and I behaved poorly. I shouldn't have put you in that situation, and I shouldn't have wronged Nate the way I did. This is all on me."

"I... I didn't know any of that. The stuff about how you felt towards me."

"How were you to know?" he asked, taking a mouthful of water. "It's not like I told anyone."

"OK. But... I just want to make things really clear between us—I love Nate. There'll never be anyone else for me. He owns my heart."

"I understand," he replied quietly.

"OK." *This is awkward.* "Well, I'm glad we cleared that up. Have a good night, Toby. Sleep well." I turned to leave.

"Holland."

I paused. "Yes?"

"Did you tell him?"

"Tell him what?"

"About my plans."

I shook my head. "I don't betray confidences."

He knitted his brow. "Thank you."

I gave him a small smile. I didn't hate Toby. He made me uncomfortable, but I didn't hate him. Out of all of them, he was the only one who was truly honest with me.

"And Holland?"

"Yes?"

"Ask him to tell you about his investment. Before...." He paused to clear his throat. "You need to know what he's into."

It seemed so important to him, so I nodded and promised I would.

When I returned to the room, it was to the tune of Nate snoring his head off and smelling like a brewery. I placed the water and pills on the bedside table, then slipped into bed beside him, gently running my fingers through his hair as I studied his passed-out form.

"What are you hiding in that head of yours?" I asked. "Toby seems to think it's important. Will you even tell me when I ask?"

His only response was a snorting grunt before he rolled over and flung his arm around my middle, pulling me close.

"I hope it isn't too bad," I whispered. "I love you too much to hate you too."

CHAPTER TWENTY-NINE
CASH OR CHEQUE

"MORNING." I smiled when I opened my eyes and found
Nate awake beside me. "How's your head?"

"I'm afraid that if I move, my brain is going to
explode." His voice sounded sandpapery.

"Luckily you have a wife who came prepared for this
exact moment." I leaned over him, my chest pressing
against his as I fetched the pills and held them to his lips.
"Ibuprofen," I explained. He took them, and the water. I
liked that his eyes seemed happy. I'd really missed their
sparkle.

"I tell you, duchess, I'm starting to feel better already."
He grinned as he looked down at my breasts pressed into
his chest.

"I see your hangover doesn't extend to Goliath or your
sex drive."

"They say an orgasm is a great cure for a headache."

"Oh yeah? Who are *they*?"

He chuckled and shook his head. "I have no fucking

clue," he said, grabbing his head quickly before he winced. "Ow. No moving."

"I think it's best if you hand me the reins this morning," I suggested, sliding on top of him so his length rested between my legs. "Don't want people thinking I'm hurting you."

"It'd be worth it." He smirked, and I teased him a little further by thrusting my hips back and forth, alternately wincing in pain and then moaning in pleasure.

"Argh. Ohhh. Argh. Ohhh."

He laughed and placed his hands on my thighs, squeezing gently. "Now they're gonna think *I'm* hurting *you*."

I leaned down and pressed my mouth to his, kissing softly. "You'd never hurt me," I said with the utmost confidence. I understood that in the centre of my bones. He was a man devoted to my protection. It was part of what made me love him so dearly.

I moved against him slowly, my breathing changing along with his as my hands rested on his firm pecs. The movement was enough to take me all the way, his firm shaft gliding perfectly along my sex.

"Duchess." He gritted his teeth, hands moving to pull my hair.

Sitting back, I took him inside me just as my climax hit, dragging him along for the literal ride until he came too.

"How's your head now?" I asked, a little out of breath when we were finished.

He grinned. "What headache?"

With a laugh, I slid off him and went to clean up. He was still lying in bed when I returned from the shower.

"How about you get in there to wash that beer stench off while I grab us some coffee and breakfast?"

With a slight groan, he forced himself to sit up. "We should probably go home first."

Pulling on my clothes from the day before, I sat next to him on the bed. "Actually, I think I should probably tell you something first."

Drawing his brow in tight, he sat up against his pillows. "Why do I get the feeling I'm not going to like this?"

"Because you probably won't. I spoke to Toby last night. After you passed out. He apologised for what he did."

"Good," Nate grunted. "Still should've kept the fuck away from you."

"He didn't seek me out. We were just in the kitchen at the same time." I watched the side of his jaw tighten and tic.

"Did he touch you at all?"

"No. He kept his distance the whole time. Like I said, he apologised. But… there's a few things I think we need to talk about."

"Like what?"

"Your investments, for one. Every time they get mentioned, your brothers get cagey and you deflect. I want to know what they are."

He nodded, his jaw tightening so much that I was worried he was going to crack a tooth. "You told me you didn't want to know anything about my work."

"I know that. But I'm asking now."

"What else?" He was deflecting again.

"The fact that you lied to me about prison. You did time as a juvenile. Sam did time too."

"I said Cartwrights *don't* do time, not that they never have."

"You also didn't tell me that your father is currently doing time."

"That's because I don't think of the man. He was never good to us." His eyes narrowed from what I thought was a bad memory, causing my heart to skip a beat. I slid my hand over his in comfort.

"I'm sorry."

"Don't be. What else?"

I frowned, knowing this one was the real kicker for me. "Is it true that even if we wanted to, we'd never be able to get out?"

He looked at me for a long while, then reached up and ran his thumb lightly along my jaw. "Why don't you go get that breakfast? I'll get cleaned up and we can talk properly when we get back home." Leaning forward, he pressed his lips to my forehead.

"Promise?"

"Promise." He smiled, then patted his hand against my thigh. I got up and headed for the kitchen, pausing in the doorway to watch that rock-hard arse of his as he sauntered into the bathroom.

"Food, duchess."

I laughed. "I'm going, I'm going."

Jasmine and Alesha were busy making waffles together when I made it to the kitchen, and I paused in the entryway to watch their interactions before they knew I was there. They had the radio on and were dancing about while one cut up fruit and the other whisked batter in a bowl. Sam sat across the bench and kept pinching fruit before it made it in the bowl.

Alesha swatted at his hand playfully, but he took the fruit anyway. "If you take all the blueberries, there won't be any for anyone else." He laughed and took another one.

It was the perfect happy family scene, and it struck me that Nate and I were the outliers. We were perfectly content in our own world, but whenever we merged with this one, problems arose. Was I the problem? Was Nate? Or was it us as a couple? I decided that it was probably because of me. I'd made it abundantly clear from the get-go that I was against their lifestyle choices, whereas Alesha had been much more accepting. She was fitting in, and I wasn't. And because I was refusing to fit in, to let go of the notion that they should all quit their thieving ways and run their businesses like fine upstanding citizens, I was causing a rift between Nate and everyone else.

I am causing the tension.

Maybe it was a bad idea to ask Nate about his investments. Maybe it was wrong for me to keep pushing for him to get out of the family business. Maybe, just maybe, I should be trying to fix the tension my presence was causing. Maybe I needed to relax my moral compass. After all, I'd fallen in love with Nate with my whole heart. I could either accept him for the man he was—family and all—or I could keep pushing for a change he didn't want and most likely ruin what we had for good. And I didn't want to ruin us.

Seeing this happy scene playing out in front of me was the clarity I needed. I was going to have to swallow my pride and try.

"Morning," I said as cheery as I could. "Something smells amazing."

Jasmine looked up and smiled. "Hope you brought your appetite. How's that husband of yours this morning?"

"A little hungover," I said with a laugh. "He's taking a shower."

"Well take a seat. These will be ready in a few minutes." She poured batter into two waffle irons that had been heating on the bench top, the sizzle and smell instantly filling the air. "Sam, go get your brothers," she said as she picked up an egg flip and watched over her creations. "We're going to have a family breakfast this morning."

Once we were alone, I asked if there was anything I could do. Being told there wasn't, I took a breath and decided to extend an olive branch of my own. "Jasmine, I want to say that I'm sorry about all the trouble I've caused," I said in a rush. Apologising wasn't easy, especially when both sides were at fault, but it was time for me to accept that my actions had caused their reactions. Jasmine was trying to protect her family, and she'd seen me as a threat. In turn, I'd demonised her, and I'd demonised Toby. Behind it all, they were just like most people, wanting to protect their way of life and their own happiness. It might not be a lifestyle I agreed with, but I could learn to see the truth in their hearts and focus on that in my interactions with them.

Turning to face me, Jasmine placed one hand on her hip and regarded me with an expression that was a mix between annoyance and understanding. It surprised me a little, but Jasmine was a hard woman, so I didn't know why I expected anything different.

"I appreciate your apology," she said after a breath, seeming to choose her words carefully. "I hope you can find a way to embrace us as your family instead of kicking out and creating waves."

Her words caused a tight sensation in my belly. I'd already realised that they viewed me as a problem, but having her point it out still made me feel bad.

"I can do that. I don't want to be the reason for tension. I just want Nate to be happy."

Handing the egg flip to Alesha, Jasmine moved to stand in front of me, her hands on the edge of the bench. "Then you need to make a decision. Are you in or are you out?"

"What do you mean?" I glanced over at Alesha, who was pretending not to listen while listening very intently. Her expression gave me no indication as to what was going on. The question had me confused.

They keep saying there's no way out....

"I'm giving you a one-time offer, Holland. If you're unhappy here, you can pack your things and leave. But you'll need to leave for good and never speak to anyone about our family. We won't exist to you."

I gulped. "I don't understand."

Jasmine actually laughed as if I was stupid. "I'm offering you your life back. But you'd have to never contact my son again."

Frowning, I shook my head. It was tempting—the lure of freedom was something I'd been wanting in the months I'd been involved with the Cartwrights—but I was in love. The idea of leaving Nate... well, that not only hurt my stomach, it hurt my heart too. *How can Jasmine be so callous toward her son? He loves me.*

"I don't want to leave Nate," I responded. My mind was at war with my heart as the words left my lips, but there it was, the truth, I was the kind of girl who was willing to stay with a man even though he was a criminal.

Love makes us do insane things.

She smiled. "Then you stay, and you give us something to prove you're in."

"I've already given you two cars and most of my possessions."

"We took those, sweetheart. And you got most of your stuff back."

"True."

"What I want from you is a job."

"A job? I don't even know how I'd find one."

"You work at a fancy school. Surely you have some sort of information on someone or something that could prove fruitful. You could be our inside man."

I thought for a moment, my eyes meeting Alesha's. She nodded, urging me to give up something, but I honestly drew a blank. I felt too sick at the idea to even think straight.

"I…." I shook my head.

"What about that fundraiser they do every year?" Alesha suggested. *What? Shut up, Alesha!* I shot her a look that said as much.

Jasmine's eyes lit up. "Fundraiser?"

I cleared my throat and blinked a few times before I could speak. "Er, yes. It's like a, um… festival, I suppose. They put on a fair, lots of games and stalls. There's a silent auction, and the drama students put on a play. This year it's *A Streetcar Named Desire*."

"And they collect a lot of cash from this event?"

With my mouth turned down, I nodded. "Last year they raised over a hundred thousand."

I swear I saw her pupils change to dollar signs. "All cash?"

"Some cheques, but mostly cash, yes."

Jasmine stood up and smiled. "Well that does sound like a nice payday. Do you know where the money gets taken at the end of the day?"

I nodded. "The principal's office. It gets put in a safe, then taken to the bank on Monday."

"Well aren't you just full of wonderful surprises. We can float this with the boys over breakfast. Welcome to the family, Holland." She leaned over and kissed me on the side of the head. The action filled me with dread and panic as I looked at Alesha, my eyes filled with horror. *What has happened to you?* I honestly didn't know her anymore.

What the hell had I been thinking, extending an olive branch towards this woman? What the hell had I been wanting? I wasn't OK with this. Remembering the horrid feeling I'd had after stealing that Mont Blanc pen was enough to sour my stomach and make me mentally kick myself for going against my own instincts. How was I going to feel knowing they'd stolen money given in charity, and that I had helped them do it?

I'm going to be sick.

"WHAT? No. Absolutely not. She doesn't need to prove herself."

My husband was my hero. Nate knew what I needed better than I did. And sensing that I'd gotten myself into this mess during a moment of weakness, he put his foot solidly on the ground and said I wasn't to be their inside man.

I'd barely touched my breakfast, instead feeling awful at the idea of helping set up a robbery at my place of employment. Sure, it would be a robbery where no one was physically hurt, and the school did have insurance against break-ins, but would that policy cover the loss of that much cash? That cash was used every year to fund programs like drama, music and art. We were a private school, and the tuition costs were high, but the allocated funding for the arts wasn't always the best.

"We don't need your permission," Sam pointed out around a mouthful of waffles. His appetite wasn't affected at all by the thought of devastating a school full of young girls. "We know enough to plan it ourselves." He gave me a wink as if thanking me.

"No," Nate insisted. "Can't we just let one member of this fucking family live a life that doesn't revolve around the next score?" I literally swooned a little at his side.

Jasmine waited a moment before responding. "She's either a Cartwright or she isn't. We don't allow freeloaders."

"The fact that she works means she's making her own money," Nate returned.

"How does that benefit us?" Jasmine asked.

Toby cut in, adding his own thoughts to the situation at hand. "Maybe since Holland is the one who gave us the job, she should be the one who decides if it goes ahead."

All eyes landed on me.

"I—" I started, gulping because I knew that my answer, whether it was a yes or no, was going to cause a shit-show.

Nate stared at me, his eyes disbelieving. "You don't want to be like *us,* duchess," he reminded me. "You're better than we are. You're *good.* Stay good."

"Ain't no room for good people round our table, brother," Abbot put in.

Nate stood up immediately. "Fuck this. We're leaving. Holland, go get your things."

I was quick to comply, happy to get away from the uncomfortable conversation. I heard him yell at them all, threatening to rain hell down on them if they dared touch this score. Even I was scared of what he'd do.

"What possessed you to tell them that shit?" Nate demanded once we were in the car. "Now they'll never let it go."

"But you told them not to do it."

"No such thing as an honest thief, duchess."

"But you're honest."

He shook his head. "I'm not. The only thing that's good and honest in my life is you. Now that's going to be fucked up when you're forced to lie to the cops about your involvement."

"Why would they interview me?"

"They'll interview *everyone* who knew about the money. What *possessed* you to mention it?" He slapped the steering wheel.

"I was asked to come up with a job. And when I couldn't think of anything, Alesha mentioned the fundraiser. Then everything snowballed."

"So you went out to get coffee, and they just slipped asking you to come up with a job into the conversation?"

"It wasn't quite like that."

"Then how was it? Explain this to me, Holland, because I can't wrap my head around it."

I considered not telling him how it came about, but I was never very good at lying and he knew that. I could keep a secret like the best of them, but lying? I was crap. "I was told to choose if I wanted in or out."

He glanced at me. "Who did that?"

"Your mother."

"She told you that you could get out if you wanted?"

"Yes."

"Then why didn't you *take* it? Why didn't you grab my car keys and run?"

"Because of you, you idiot! I love you, you know that! How can I walk away now?" The fact that he so easily told me to leave made tears flood my eyes. I turned my head away.

"Oh, duchess," he said softly, pulling over to the side of the road and wrapping me in his arms.

"Why don't you want me to stay?" I sobbed.

"Of course I want you to stay," he soothed. "I want you all the time. I love you more than anything in this world. But I see what this life is doing to you. You're too good for it. If she's given you an out, fucking *take it.* Run. Go back to what you knew and forget about our shit. Forget about *me.*"

"How could I possibly forget about *you*? I can't just switch off my feelings and go back to being the woman I was before. I'd be heartbroken. I won't go unless you come with me."

"I can't. They'll hunt me down."

"Not Toby. He wants out too." *Shit, I'm not supposed to repeat that.* Seemed my ability to keep secrets was also compromised in that moment.

He brushed his fingers through my hair, he didn't seem surprised to hear that. "It's not that simple."

"It is, Nate! We pack a bag and we run. So fast and so far that no one can catch us. We can leave everything. I have a little money invested and we could use that to get settled. We don't need anything from this life. I can't believe that your mother or your brothers would actually kill you if you try to leave."

He pressed his lips together, still running his fingers through my hair. "I want you to go, duchess. This is the best choice for you."

I flinched away from his touch. "Don't you think *I* should

be the one to decide what's best for me? Hell, you dragged me into this life with your marriage plan and now you're sending me on my way? Am I not enough for you anymore? Are you already bored? Was everything between us bullshit?"

"Jesus, duchess, no! In an ideal world, I'd be a regular guy, and we'd meet in a regular way and have a regular life together. But I'm not regular. Being with me is a risk to you. It was selfish of me to go after you, and even worse for me to keep you. And now this opportunity for you to be free is here, and I want you to take it." *He wants me to take the opportunity to* leave *him? He doesn't want me to choose to be with him? What?* I knew Nate was a good liar. And I had to wonder how many lies he'd been spinning to keep me, that maybe he couldn't wait to be rid of me? Was that it? Or was I still paranoid and a little raw? I'd lost Alesha, the brothers didn't want me around, Toby could barely look at me, and now I'd further ostracised Jasmine. *Fuck, I hate this.* But... I don't want to leave Nate. My life is him.

"I don't want to go," I said. "I don't care who you are or what you do. I love you, and I *want* to be with you."

He looked at me for a long moment, his eyes wide. I could see his mind churning with the stress of the situation. Then he took a breath and put the ute into gear. "I want to be with you too. But there's something you need to see."

We drove for nearly an hour, turning down an unmarked road that wound through thick bush and was bumpy as hell.

"Where are we going?" I asked, my hand pressed against the roof of the car to stop from hitting my head while on the uneven road.

He flattened his lips into a grave line. "You'll see. We're almost there."

AN EARTHY SMELL assailed my nostrils as I looked out at a sea of red. "Are they what I think they are?" I asked, my voice small and tight as I stood at the mouth of the gully that was filled with flowers.

"Poppies." Nate nodded, hands on his hips as he stood beside me.

"Poppies," I repeated. I couldn't believe it. "So this... this is your investment." My voice squeaked on that last word as my head reeled. I was struggling to stay upright and conscious.

Does this mean my husband is a drug lord?

"This is my investment," he whispered.

"And it's for drugs, right? Not the little black seeds on bread rolls?"

"That's right."

I sat on the ground, unable to stay up any longer. "This is what Toby kept referring to?"

Nate nodded.

"Do the rest of them know about this?"

"Only Toby and Jasmine. We were approached at the same time. A big-time dealer needed someone to build the crop and supply them. I'm the only one who was greedy enough to do it. They didn't want any part of it, but they hold it over my head. I help with their business, and they keep quiet over mine while letting me launder my profit through the family businesses."

"Why are you showing me this? Why now?"

"Because you asked. You think my family is bad. They steal and they'll kill to protect their way of life. But I'm worse. I'll do anything for the love of money."

"I don't believe that," I whispered. "Explain this away, Nate. Tell me this isn't a field of drugs. Tell me why this is needed for the economy. Do something, say anything that will make this OK."

"I can't do that, duchess. I'm a monster who cares more about money than people. You're looking at the proof." His voice was so soft that his words had to be a lie. This couldn't be real.

I shook my head. "I can't believe this," I whispered, shifting to kneel so I could stand, Nate reached down to try and help me but I shoved him away. "Don't." I looked again at the flowers. "Just... don't touch me."

I took a few steps away, shaking my head as I tried to register the full extent of the day. My brain wanted to explode. "Drugs, Nate? *Drugs?* All this time? We talked about this. I told you I'd hate you if you were a drug dealer. And you are. *You fucking are.*" I kept walking backwards, shaking, too shocked to cry but knowing there was only one option left for me.

I couldn't be a part of this.

I couldn't stay with him.

Not anymore.

I had to *run.*

Had to *Leave.*

Go.

I held up the keys I'd stolen from his pocket when he'd moved to help me up. "I love you, Nate. But I can't do this. Not drugs." He closed his eyes for a moment and nodded once. "Goodbye, Nate."

A set of tortured blue eyes met mine, but he didn't speak or do anything to stop me when I got into the driver side of the car. Didn't move an inch as I turned the key and the engine roared to life. And when I drove away, his form becoming smaller and smaller as I increased the distance between us, he remained statue-still. He didn't try to stop me.

I burst into tears as I turned off the dirt road and planted my foot, going where, I had no clue. I just kept driving until the petrol ran out and I found myself in a town I didn't recognise, somewhere on the New South Wales coast. *He didn't stop me.*

CHAPTER THIRTY-ONE
ME OVER YOU

EVER SINCE I watched *Pinocchio* as I child, I knew a conscience was an important thing. Every time that little puppet went against the advice of Jiminy Cricket, he got himself in trouble. Heck, he'd almost been turned into a donkey! Those were some pretty severe consequences, and all that kid wanted to do was have fun with his friends. What would be the consequence if he decided that supplying the drug trade with an essential ingredient to make heroin was a good idea? I couldn't imagine the consequences would be good, and those Disney people had really crazy imaginations. I couldn't even reason it away as being 'just flowers'. Because they weren't just flowers. They were drugs.

After Nate's ute broke down from a lack of fuel, I walked until I made it to a little town called Narooma. There wasn't much there, which was just as well because it was the perfect place to sit and think. To be honest, I spent that entire first week wallowing in my sorrows, drinking wine from a cask and watching free-to-air television.

Microwave meals had become my staple. It didn't really matter what they tasted like because I wasn't really tasting anything; I only ate to assuage the ache in my stomach.

I'd holed up in a place called the Coastal Comfort Motel. It was nice enough and didn't cost me a fortune considering I had no idea when I'd work up the energy to decide what to do next. The ocean was close by, and at night I would sit outside and stare out at the water, thinking about my time with Nate and how much I missed being around him—his smell, his laugh… I even missed his bad morning breath.

I missed Nate.

So.

Much.

But my husband was a thief. I accepted that much about him. I'd even deigned to live with it if it meant we could be together, but learning that my husband was also involved in the drug trade? How could I be OK with that? How could I live in that house knowing it was purchased with the proceeds from the misery of other people's desperate addiction? I'd witnessed that addiction first-hand with Alesha's mother. It tore families apart and turned good, normal people into the worst version of themselves.

There had to be a line somewhere. I couldn't cross that far. I had to go.

But I missed him. My heart ached each time it beat without him. My lungs burned, trying to breathe the air he wasn't breathing too. There were moments when I didn't want to keep going when I knew I wouldn't have the chance to look into his eyes or touch his skin again. I was never going to be the same. I'd had true love, and now it was gone.

Why did my soulmate have to be a bad man?

Perhaps Alesha's God could tell me that. He was supposed to be a lover of tests, after all. But what was the point of this test? What was the reason behind completing my heart and then breaking it apart again? I couldn't understand.

Two days into the second week, I was staring at the ceiling, trying to work out if the flaking of paint near the light fitting was due to a collection of moisture or age. It was fascinating stuff, not to be outdone by the hour I'd spent trying to count how many bugs had met their doom after venturing into the light fitting. The count? Thirty-two, and an indistinctive blob of them I couldn't decipher any individuality from. But there I was, contemplating the moisture-versus-time debate when there was a knock on my door.

There was only one person who ever knocked on my door: the daughter of the owners, who came around to vacuum and ask if I wanted any clean linens. I didn't even want her to vacuum, but I got up to let her in nonetheless.

"How the fuck?" I muttered when I opened the door to find Toby on the other side.

"Credit card," he replied simply, stepping into the room without being invited.

"Of course that's something you'd do." Closing the door, I followed him in and took a seat on the vinyl chair that went with the tiny dining table provided with my room. "I'd offer you something, but I have nothing but an empty cask of wine." I waved my hand around nonchalantly.

"It's fine. I don't need anything."

"Then what are you doing here? Please tell me you're

not planning on swooping in now that Nate and I are….” I swallowed hard, unable to say the words 'broken up' before tears hit my eyes.

"No, Holland," he said gently. "That's not who I am."

"Then what is this? Are you running away too?"

"I wish. I actually came to pick up Nate's ute and give you these." He pulled a set of keys out of his pocket and placed them on the table in front of me.

"Are these…? Are they *my* keys?"

"Your car is parked outside. You can return to your apartment—all your stuff is there—and there won't be any consequence. Nate's seen to it."

"He's seen to it," I repeated, poking my finger through the ring in the centre of the keys. I didn't think I even wanted to guess what that meant. "So you knew, didn't you? About the… flowers?"

He nodded. "Nate's been playing his own game for years. We chose not to be a part of it because the risk is far greater when you get involved with those kinds of people, but Nate's always dreamed big and wanted more. He was like that even as kids."

"But to what end? It's not like he can quit if he gets bored. Seems he'll be stuck growing those things until he either dies or gets caught. And what happens if the harvest is bad, or if the weather goes to shit and that gully floods? What happens if there's a *fire*?"

Toby chuckled. "You sure do ask a lot of questions. But I'm sorry. I don't have the answers to any of them. I stay out of the poppy business as best I can. I doubt Nate would tell me even if I asked."

"That's what I expected, I suppose. Nate's need to protect is far greater than his need to share."

"Yes." Toby folded his hands in front of him. I looked away and tried not to cry. "He's hurting too," he whispered finally.

"Good," I replied, my tears falling at last. It sounded spiteful, but it wasn't. I simply felt that if a couple who loved as hard as Nate and I didn't hurt when it ended, it wouldn't be fair. I wiped at my face and sniffed. "What are you going to do now?"

"Get some petrol for the ute you abandoned, then drive it back home."

"Not right now," I explained. "For your future. Are you going to stay, or are you going to chase your dreams?"

He pressed his lips together and shrugged. "I don't know, Holland. I've spent my lifetime taking orders. Maybe I don't know how to be my own boss." I stared a moment into his kind and weary eyes. I could see the struggle in them.

"I'm sorry, Toby," I said, placing my hand over his. "That day at the wedding, I shouldn't have insulted you the way I did."

"It was all true. You're a far braver woman than I am a man. You took off when you were given the chance. Me, I just keep staying."

"It wasn't brave, Toby. I ran scared. It would've been brave to stay, to love purely despite the danger. At the end of the day, I chose myself over Nate."

"I don't think he sees it that way."

"That's because he told me to run. He chose me over himself."

"I TOLD you those good-looking ones weren't to be trusted," Aunt Maya said as I walked through the grocery aisle with her. I couldn't face going back to the apartment when my relationship with Nate was basically all over it, so I went to stay with her instead. "They sweep you off your feet and then break your heart, and you're never quite the same again." She paused at the end of the pet food aisle. "What do you think about getting a cat? I wouldn't mind having a little friend to come home to at the end of work. I like that one." She pointed to a can with a fluffy white cat on it.

"Why not get a cat each?" I said, figuring that I may as well get started on my lonely life cliché. I certainly wasn't planning on ever finding another man.

"Now there's an idea. We could call them Tweedledee and Tweedledum. Or Hop and Scotch. Oh, I know, Chess and Shire so that together they're Cheshire cats. How clever." She beamed and dropped two cans of food for our non-existent pets into the trolley.

"Sure, Aunty. Those are fine names." My voice was void of emotion.

"I don't think you're taking this very seriously."

"Sure I am. Two cats. Tweedledum and Tweedledee."

"No, Chess and Shire. Although, now that I'm saying it again, I'm not sure I like those. Should we stick with the *Alice in Wonderland* references or go with something else?"

"I don't mind, Aunty."

She stopped pushing the trolley and looked at me sternly, studying me for so long that I almost started to cry. It felt like she was reading my emotions. She knew me so well that she probably could.

"Why don't you call him?" she said after a while. "Surely the two of you can work this out?"

"We can't." I shook my head.

"Did he cheat on you?"

"No. He'd never."

"Then what is so unforgivable that you can't work it out? I wish you'd tell me."

"We just can't work, OK?"

"All right," she said, adding a few more cans of cat food to the trolley. "But when we get the cats, I don't want you calling it something ridiculous like Fluffy or Mittens just because you're too depressed to be creative."

"We can call them Blanche and Stella."

She smiled. "I like that. We'll make sure we get sisters and keep them away from any tomcats named Stan."

"Perfect."

I PICKED a stray cat hair off my sleeve as I gestured for my students to gather around me. With only one week left until the Christmas break, it was finally time for the end-of-year performance. This was the final stage of the fundraising fair that had been taking place on the school grounds all day. I was trying to focus on the girls, but I did have a little voice in the back of my mind wondering if they were going to do it—were Nate and his brothers going to steal the proceeds for their own pockets?

I didn't know if I could forgive them if they did. Not that it mattered—I was already out. I hadn't had contact with any of them in over two months. That included Alesha. She was one of them now. I'd lost my love and my best friend to the Cartwright way of life. Doing the right thing had never felt so bad.

"Ladies, if I can have your attention please," I said as we stood behind the curtain ready for our performance of *A Streetcar Named Desire*. It would be the one and only show, and after the work the girls had put in on not only learning their lines, but also on the props and costumes, I knew the whole thing would go off without a hitch.

They crowded around me, their various character guises donned and ready to show the audience.

"I just want to take a moment to tell you all how unbelievably proud I am. You've worked so diligently on transforming yourselves into your characters and supporting each other in your roles. I honestly couldn't be prouder. So when you go out there tonight, I want you to take that knowledge with you, and know that at the end of it, I'm taking you all out for pizza to celebrate what I know will be a fantastic show."

Their excitement and nerves bubbled with the positive

comments. There wasn't a Debbie Downer in the whole bunch. These girls were ready.

"OK, places everyone, and don't forget to break a leg. Metaphorically, of course." I smiled and moved to the side of the stage while they all scattered and got ready. We had our music students at the side of the stage, ready to provide the soundtrack, and the auditorium was packed with family, friends and faculty.

I gave the thumbs up to our head of music, and she readied her students to play. We were using a simplified version of the score that accompanied the 1951 film, and soon the drama of that classic main theme filled the auditorium as the lights dimmed. I held my breath and clasped my hands beneath my chin, taking it all in.

Besides Blanche's pearls getting hooked on the back of a chair and scattering about the stage, the performance was perfect, the music fantastic, and the audience appreciative. For the first time in the months since I'd run away from my life with Nate, I had a genuine smile on my face. I felt like me again.

"Thank you all so much for coming," I said as I took the microphone at the end of the performance. "The students worked incredibly hard to make this performance the work of art that it was. I'd like you all to give a big hand to our stars. Emily MacNamara as Blanche DuBois! Rachael Emerson as Stella Kowalski!" I went through our actors one by one, handing them all a small bouquet of flowers as they took their bow to an uproarious applause. At the very end, they presented me with a bunch of flowers I hadn't known I was getting, and I shed more than a couple of tears from the gesture as I hugged them all for being so thoughtful. Then I pulled the music director onto the stage and made the school orchestra and stage crew all stand up and take a bow as well.

"And let's not forget our sound and lighting crew in the back of the room."

It was when the spotlight turned their way that I saw him. Up the back of the auditorium, smiling and clapping along with everyone else. *Nate.*

He looked... proud of me.

My heart caught in my throat, and if I hadn't been crying already, I would've started. He was there. And oh God, he was even more beautiful than my memory was giving him credit for. I wanted to call out to him, to run through the audience and fling my arms around his neck. But what would be the point? He was still doing what he was doing, and I was still against it.

When it was all over, I stepped back with everyone else before the curtain closed. We held hands and bowed, and I kept my eyes locked on Nate's until the heavy fabric of the curtain cut us off from each other. My heart sank at the separation, hitting the bottom of my belly with a thud. He wasn't there to watch and be proud of me. He wasn't silently supporting me. He was there to steal the takings. I felt sickness and longing all in one moment, and I wished I could go home and curl up on the sofa with my cat. But I had girls I'd promised pizza to.

"Who's ready to go out and celebrate?" I asked, putting on a fake smile and steeling myself for the inevitable phone call the following day, telling me that the money was gone.

CHAPTER THIRTY-THREE
I KNOW IT

STRUGGLING to find the motivation to get ready for work, I was still in my dressing gown when a knock sounded on the door at seven the next morning. Aunt Maya was waving about a laser pointer that projected tiny green paws on the wall, and our kittens, Stella and Blanche, were jumping all over it.

"Get that, will you, sweetheart?" Aunt Maya said, not even budging from where she chuckled at the cats.

Setting down the kettle I was in the middle of filling, I tightened the sash around my waist and headed for the front door. The moment I saw the shadows through the stained-glass panels I knew it was the police. *Oh no.*

"One moment," I called out, pausing at the hall stand and studying my expression in the mirror. I practised my shocked face for the moment they told me the money was gone. I tried one with wide eyes and an open mouth and decided that looked too contrived. Then I went with wide eyes only, which seemed to work a lot better. I practised a few more times, making sure I was ready to perform on cue. Then I whispered a couple of responses.

"That's horrible. Who would do such a thing? We needed that money to upgrade the sound system in the auditorium." God, I really was a terrible actor.

"We're looking for a Mrs Holland Cartwright," the police called out, knocking again.

"I'm coming." Gulping, I met my eyes in the mirror and took a breath. "Showtime," I whispered.

"Mrs Cartwright?" The officer took his hat off and held it against his chest when I opened the door.

"Yes," I responded, a little off balance by the action coupled with a very sombre-looking expression on the female officer's face who accompanied him. It was terrible that the money was taken from the school, but surely they didn't feel *that* horrible about delivering the news. And how did they know already? No one would even be in the office until eight. "Has something happened?"

The male officer gulped and looked at the female officer, who stepped forwards. "Is it possible to come inside, Mrs Cartwright? Somewhere we can sit, perhaps?"

"Sit? Why?" *What's going on? This isn't what I was expecting.*

I moved to let them inside, gesturing for them to sit in the lounge.

"Who was it?" Aunt Maya called out.

"It's the police, Aunty."

She arrived in less than a beat of my rapid heart. "Has something happened?"

"We were hoping we could sit down."

"Who died?" she blurted. "You don't ask to sit like this

unless it's bad." Her eyes were wide. She'd been through this before, the night my parents died. *Oh God.*

"If we could please just sit down," the female officer responded.

Both Aunt Maya and I sat with straight backs as we stared at the officers. I didn't even want to think about what they were about to say to me. Who could they possibly be coming to tell me about? The only family I had was in the house right beside me.

There was only one other person who would earn me an official visit.

Nate.

No. no. no. no. no. no.

My entire body trembled as I grabbed Aunt Maya's hand and squeezed. Tears fell silently. I quit breathing.

"We're sorry to report, Mrs Cartwright, but your husband has been in an accident."

My breath burned in my lungs and escaped in a pained gasp. I clapped my hand over my mouth and shook my head. *No.*

"What happened?" Aunt Maya asked, wrapping her arm around my shoulders as I held her hand for dear life.

"A bushfire broke out along the coast yesterday afternoon. It got out of control very fast, and it seems that his car got caught in its path with Mr Cartwright inside. We're so very sorry, ma'am."

Oh God. Nate. My beautiful Nate.

Wait. What did they say?

"Yesterday afternoon?" I asked, struggling to see through my tears.

"Yes, ma'am."

"And he... he died?"

The male officer nodded. "I'm sorry."

"But…." I frowned and shook my head. "Are they sure it was him?"

"The coroner confirmed it a short while ago. We came to inform you as soon as possible."

"But I—" I stopped myself from saying any more. *What's going on? I saw Nate last night with my own eyes. He was there, I know it.*

"We're so very sorry, Mrs Cartwright."

After going over a few formal details, we walked the officers to the door and watched them go, standing silently until they drove away.

"I'm so sorry, pet," Aunt Maya said, rubbing her hand up and down my back.

Pushing the front door shut, I shook my head. "He's not dead."

She gave me this pitiful look that told me she thought I was in denial.

"You don't get it. I saw him. Last night at the performance."

Her look didn't really change much.

"Did you speak to him?" she asked.

"No. I saw him in the back of the audience. He was smiling and clapping with everyone else. I *saw* him."

"Oh, honey," she said, gently stroking the side of my face. "When your mother died, I swore I saw her sitting beside me on the couch. But it wasn't her, it was just a random dream I had while waiting for them to come back from dinner."

"This wasn't a dream, Aunty. I was awake, standing on stage." *Why doesn't she believe me?*

"Some people think it's their way of saying goodbye to

the people who are most important to them—their way of letting you know they're OK."

"No." I pulled away from her. "No. I saw him. He isn't dead. They're *wrong*."

"Where are you going, Holland?"

"I'm going to check for myself." I grabbed my bag and keys, then shoved my feet into a pair of shoes. I was going to drive out to Torquay and demand answers. This wasn't happening. *I saw him.*

"Maybe you should get dressed first."

I looked down at the robe I was still wearing. Feeling too panicked, I shook my head. "I don't have time," I ground out, marching for the door. "He's not gone! I'd feel it if he were gone. I'd feel it right here." I jammed my finger into my chest, then threw the door open.

I saw Aunt Maya's expression change, but I didn't register what it meant until I slammed into a massive wall of muscle in my haste to leave.

Two big beautiful hands caught me. "Duchess."

"Oh thank God."

CHAPTER THIRTY-FOUR
PINCH ME

MY BONES DISINTEGRATED and refused to hold me upright anymore. Tears streamed down my face and I clawed at his shirt, babbling incoherently, "They said. They said you were.... I knew it wasn't true. I saw you. Last night. I knew they were wrong."

"God, I missed you." He smiled that smile that warmed my heart, and then his mouth came down on mine, kissing the life back inside me. I wrapped my arms around his neck and held tight, wanting to crawl inside him and curl up into a little ball as long as it meant we wouldn't have to part again.

The moment he released me, I pulled my hand back and slapped his face.

"Holy fuck," he muttered, his hand covering the blooming on his cheek.

"That's for scaring the life out of me," I yelled, and then I fell against his chest, crying into it, so incredibly relieved that he was standing in front of me alive and well.

I was barely coping living without him when I knew he was only a couple of hours away.

His arms wrapped around me like a comfortable dream. "I'm sorry, duchess," he whispered. "It was the only way I could do it."

"Do what?" I pulled back so I could see his face.

With gentle fingers, he brushed the tears from my cheeks. "Get out."

My heart jumped into my throat. "Out? As in *out* out? For good?"

He nodded. "But we have to go, duchess. We have to start again. That's what you wanted, right?"

It was exactly what I wanted. But I'd never expected it, never dreamed he'd actually make it happen. I stood there with my mouth open, unsure of how to respond.

"You do still want this, right? You still want me?" The fear in his eyes almost broke my heart.

"Of course," I answered quickly. "But *go*? Now?"

"Right now. Grab anything you can as fast as you can. Can you do that for me?"

"Wait. We're leaving? You're giving up your entire life *for me*?" I couldn't wrap my head around it. He'd made it sound impossible to escape.

He placed his hands on either side of my face and kissed me before looking deep into my eyes. "No, duchess, I gave up my life the day I let you walk away. Doing this, it's giving me my life back. It's giving me *you*. As long as you still want me." His eyes grew serious as he studied my expression.

Mine were wide as saucers. I couldn't believe it. Nate had faked his death and given up *everything* just so he could be with me. If that wasn't a declaration of love in the highest order, then I didn't know what was.

"I want you," I gasped, my eyes brimming with tears.

"My God, girl! Go get your things!" Aunt Maya interrupted. "You can ask questions later. Can't you see the man is in a hurry?"

"Yes, but…." I looked back to Nate. "Are you sure about this?"

"It's already done. The only thing I want in this world is you. The rest of it." He lifted his hand. "It's up in smoke."

"OK." I grinned, excited butterflies flapping in my stomach.

"OK?" he asked, looking at me closely.

"Yes, I'll run away with you." I stood there smiling like an idiot, stunned at what he'd done so we could be together.

He chuckled. My God, I missed that chuckle. "Then get your stuff, duchess."

"Oh!" I snapped out of the trance and spun around to do exactly that. At the same time, Aunt Maya came rushing down the stairs with a duffel bag in her arms.

"I grabbed everything I could from your drawers, and anything else that would fit in the bag. I also got you this," she gasped, out of breath from racing around. She held out a rolled-up wad of cash. "It's only five grand, but I want you to have it. Go. Live. Be happy."

I took what she was offering, caught up in the moment before the thought hit me. "But what about you, Aunty?"

She shooed me away. "What about me? I've already lived my life. And it's been a wonderful one. Now go live yours. I'm fine here. I have my cats. I have friends. I'll be fine. Just please don't ever tell me why you had to make everyone think you were dead, young man. I'm too old to be like one of those *Orange is the New Black* girls. I want to tell them honestly that I had no clue what you were into, but I'm assuming it has something to do with my niece's robbery?"

Nate opened his mouth, then closed it and smiled at her, shaking his head. "Best you don't know," he replied with a wink.

"He's a thief like Pierce Brosnan in *The Thomas Crown Affair*, isn't he?" she said with a whimsy in her voice I'd never heard before.

"How did you figure that one out?" I asked, stunned that she'd never said anything if she did. My aunt wasn't one for tiptoeing.

"Because when you introduced him, I noticed that he looks a little like Hugh Jackman in your police sketch."

"You never said."

She ran her hand down the side of my face, tears in her eyes as she smiled. "That's because you were so happy, and I could tell you loved him."

I hugged her tight. "I'm going to miss you."

"I'll be glad to see the back of you," she joked, wiping at her eyes as she smiled and blew kisses, then waved us both out the door. "I love you, caterpillar."

I could barely see her through my happy tears, but I blew kisses back. "I love you too."

"Ready?" Nate said as he threw my duffel in the back of the car.

Nodding, I climbed into the passenger seat and turned to get my last glimpse of Aunt Maya as we drove away.

"Will I ever get to see her again?" I asked once we were on the road and I couldn't see her anymore.

"I don't know, duchess. Maybe someday when all this has settled down." He rested his hand on my thigh, giving it a light squeeze. "Regret leaving with me yet?" In response, I wrapped myself around his arm and pressed my face against his warm skin.

"I could never regret you, Nate. I've missed you so much."

"I missed you too, duchess. So fucking much." My entire body hummed with joy.

"And what about Goliath? Did he miss me?"

Nate chuckled. "You have no idea," he responded, leaning over to kiss the side of my head. "I'll show you how much he missed you when we get to where we're going."

"And where is that?"

"A little town at the very bottom of the country. It's called Portland, and Nathan Duke and his wife just bought property down there."

"Nathan Duke? That's your new name?" My smile grew wider.

"Of course. Every duchess needs her duke." I loved it.

"I still can't believe you're doing this for me," I mused, biting at my lip in amazement as I looked out the window at the passing scenery. He was everything I wanted, and all that I needed.

"I'm not doing it for you, duchess. I'm selfishly doing it for myself because I can't stand living another moment without you."

"What would you have done if I said I didn't want to come?"

"That wasn't an option. I'd have gone caveman on you and slung you over my shoulder. You belong to me. You're my wife."

"Actually, I'm a widow, it seems."

"No, you're my wife." He pulled out an envelope from the centre console and handed it to me. Inside, there was new identification for the both of us—Mr and Mrs Nathan and Hannah Duke.

"How did you manage to do all this?" I asked, astounded at the quality of the fake IDs as I sifted through them.

"I paid a lot of people a lot of money."

"And what happens to everything you had before? Your house, my apartment?"

"*Our* house. It's all being taken care of. Toby is helping out. We'll be sitting pretty, the way a duke and his duchess should."

"And when we get to Portland, we'll work like normal people do? No more stealing, no more growing poppies or any other sort of drug farm?"

"Straight as an arrow. I was thinking maybe a bookshop would be nice."

My eyes lit up. "Will it have a ladder that moves? Except this time, I think we should refrain from any sort of hard fucking on it. And maybe get an actual builder on it."

"It can have anything you want—a coffee shop, a section for classic DVDs. We could even have a mini theatre—show old movies, put on plays. You'd be in your element."

"That does sound like a dream," I gushed, my heart so full and hopeful that I feared I was about to wake up from said dream.

"Sure does. My dream is to spend my life with you. Everything else is a cherry."

"And kids. Will we have kids in this dream?"

He glanced at me and smiled, devastating me with how handsome he was. "Is that something you want now?"

"Yes," I replied. "I'd love to have little Nates and Hollands, I mean Hannahs with you. There's nothing standing in our way anymore."

"Then we'll get started on that right away."

I squealed with happiness. "Pinch me, quick!"

"What?" He laughed.

"*Pinch* me." When he wouldn't, I did it myself. "Ow." I blinked a few times and looked around.

"What the hell was that for?"

"I had to make sure this was real."

"Oh, it's real, duchess. But in about ten hours' time, you might be questioning your reality while I rock your fucking world."

"Promise?" I laughed.

"Goliath has *really* missed you."

"And I've missed him. But I missed you more."

"Me too," he said, just as we turned to merge onto the highway that would pave the road to our new life. A life where we could have everything we ever dreamed and then some.

I turned around, watching Melbourne recede in the rear window.

"Goodbye, my old life," I whispered. Then I took my husband's hand and kissed his knuckles. "Hello, my world."

As I settled into my seat, ready for the long drive to our new home, I couldn't wipe the smile from my face.

Some people would call me foolish for giving Nate a second chance after the way we met and the way we left things, but the man owned my heart, just as I owned his. And now that he'd given up a huge part of his life to start fresh with me, I didn't feel foolish at all. I felt willing to do the same. Nate told me months ago that he didn't understand what love was. Now he did. Truly loving someone meant moments of sacrifice. Moments of allowing the other to grow and flourish, rather than holding ties over them. My husband loved me, loved me enough to let me go, loved me enough to relinquish the ties that had bound us. He'd given me the fairy tale by setting us free. I felt hopeful for our future but most of all, I felt unconditionally loved.

THE END

Want more of Nate and Holland? Find out what the hell Alesha was thinking in her and Sam's story, *Fools Rush In*.
books2read.com/u/mqpLN1

for more info on Lilliana's books visit
www.lillianaanderson.com

For information on upcoming releases visit

www.lillianaanderson.com/preorders

ABOUT THE AUTHOR

Bestselling Author of the Beautiful Series, Drawn and 47 Things, Lilliana has always loved to read and write, considering it the best form of escapism that the world has to offer.

Australian born and bred, she writes New Adult Romance revolving around her authentically Aussie characters with all the quirks you'd expect from those born Down Under.

Lilliana feels that the world should see Australia for more than just it's outback and tries to show characters in a city and suburban setting.

When she isn't writing, she wears the hat of 'wife and mother' to her husband and five children.

Before Lilliana turned to writing, she worked in a variety of industries and studied humanities and communications before transferring to commerce/law at university.

Originally from Sydney's Western suburbs, she currently lives a fairly quiet life in suburban Melbourne.

For more information on Lilliana and her work:
www.lillianaanderson.com
info@lillianaanderson.com

facebook.com/LillianaAndersonAuthor

twitter.com/confidante_lili

instagram.com/lilliana_anderson

ACKNOWLEDGMENTS

AS ALWAYS, there are people to be thanked! Many sets of eyes go in to the creation of each of my books and I am very grateful to every person who takes time out of their lives to help me.

To **Marion Archer, Tammie Lee, Cyndi Hart-Duplessis, Marissa Burns** and **Mary Sart,** thank you so much for beta reading and giving me excellent feedback to work with. I can't tell you how much I appreciate your sage advice. To my editors at **Hot Tree Editing**, I thank you all for your keen editing eyes and funny comments. **Helena Cullen** and **Margaret Neal,** thank you for helping to proof the final copy—hopefully we got them all!

To my team of sharers, you're all so wonderful. I don't ask you to do what you do, but you see something I post and share it far and wide. I'm eternally grateful. Thank you all so much. I love you all!

To every blogger and reviewer who has an ARC or has signed up to post about my book – I thank you too. You are the first step to announcing my work to the world. No author can do this without you xoxox

Also, a big thank you to my husband for putting up with my bitching and moaning and his unending support and encouragement.

Thank you to my kids for being so patient while I stare at a computer screen and finish typing out a thought. I love that you all come and sit with me while I work just to spend a bit of extra time with mummy!

And of course – thank you to all of my readers. You are the most important of all. Without you, I would be writing to the crickets.

Mwah! xoxox